Published by Three Muses Ink.
www.3musesink.com
Haunting Weir is a work of fiction. Names, characters, places, and incidents either are the product of the author's imagination or are used fictitiously, and any resemblance to actual persons, living or dead, business establishments, events or locales is entirely coincidental. The publisher does not have any control over and does not assume any responsibility for author or third-party websites or their content.

Kari L. Ronning and A.M. Gagnon
Haunting Weir
Haunted Weir Workings Book 1

Haunting Weir©2016 Kari Ronning & A.M. Gagnon
Cover art, images, art, and graphics are by Kari Ronning©2016, Kari Ronning.
Edited by Daniel Wilson (MrProofReading) https://www.fiverr.com/mrproofreading

For rights information please email: manager@3musesink.com
ISBN 10: 0-9882989-6-1
ISBN 13: 978-0-9882989-6-5
Library of Congress Control Number: 2016956237

This series was written in response to very tangible demons, both real and inside, that I thought would swallow me. My response to that time of trauma and trial was to create something from all that dark energy. This book is dedicated to that: the magic and majesty of writing, storytelling and the true power it gives us when we create, read and experience something that can come from nothing but a few written words.

– Kari L. Ronning

Haunting Weir

By

Kari L. Ronning

A.M. Gagnon

Artwork by

Kari L. Ronning

The Haunted Weir Workings

Book One

Table of Contents

Prologue
Weirimen

A barrier exists between your soul and pure evil. A hint of evil exists in all people, just as even the cleanest water has imperfections. Like a lake, your own inner dam keeps the majority of evil out of your soul's waterways. Bad thoughts still happen, dark intentions, crimes against each other, but there is this device in all people known as a Haunting Weir. The Weir protects from Primary Evil, a force altogether different from everyday bad thoughts, petty ugliness and random acts of unpleasantness.

Primary evil has a face. Its voice perforates your dreams. It hums to you when you are at your lowest, comforts you with ideas of self-harm, violence against those you hate or covet, and incites the most depraved unthinkable plans, ideas, and maladies that should not otherwise exist in the world. Primary evil has a grin.

It takes the forms of demons, devils, and creatures of nightmare: things born of nothing but hate, darkness and the secretion of neglect, starvation, and hopelessness. The manifestations are vast and varied, in as many forms as any malignant cancer, born of darkness in both people and random swirling energy in a universe not fully understood. They can be dealt with as a doctor would a parasite.

When something breaches a Haunting Weir, it causes sickness, possession, unexplained harrowing acts and the Weirimen are sought out. Pillars against the darkness, they are trained as surgeons of the soul, able to root out and remove the evil that has attached itself to the light of someone's existence. Both hunters and healers, these gifted few serve those afflicted by darkness rarely even understood. Inside everyone exists a Haunting Weir but only the Weirimen can reseal it once evil has broken through its barrier.

Chapter One
The Haunting Weir

Anticipation is always thick, like the flavor of dark wine. It stays on your tongue, in your breath until you cannot swallow without tasting all that is infused into its meaning. The weight of anticipation is always directly proportionate to the amount of time invested in the thing being anticipated and Art Storygrove had devoted six intense years to this very moment. The weight was almost palatable.

Waiting outside the great old doors of the observation hall, he knew this would be the test of every moment of those six years of training. Not many were even able to apply to become a Weirimen but Art had been taken in by a great one. As one of the few acts of kindness he could remember in his short, bleak life, it had been a very profound victory when he started to show a talent for the rare occupation his guardian was so apt at performing. Knowledge of the dark trade had always been a part of his life.

Most would not even want to venture into such a profession as dangerous and unpredictable as it was. Needing to be something of a warrior, exorcist, and demonologist, but also born with rare gifts and the ability to rescue one's self from the darkest, most pervasive forces of evil was a mix seemingly against all odds. Yet, there Art stood, before the doors of the observation hall of the Seminary of Weirimen, where his last and final test would take place, and he would finally be declared one of their ranks.

The single most important thing a Weiriman had to understand was a Haunting Weir. Everyone and everything thing had one. This inner barrier, inside the soul, kept true evil out of a natural pure life force. It was the primary task of a Weiriman to exorcise evil from within someone should that wall be breeched and then close the Weir. In natural succession with this responsibility, a Weiriman had to control their own Weir. The final exam would test the strength of this very ability. Of the things he had learned, all the trials he had faced and evil he had been exposed through classes and in the training field, the opening of his own Weir was the most basic of abilities. Allowing evil inside to do both physical and spiritual combat with was a foundational ability in a Weiriman's arsenal, but it was also the most dangerous.

If Art could not cleanse his own soul of whatever demonic force invaded him, he would become fully possessed. The evil would burrow inside him, seek to devour, torment, and ultimately annihilate him, claiming his soul and adding to its own power. That was not the worst of it, however. Though the danger was real, a powerful demon could do him permanent damage should he be unable to turn it back and close his Weir, though the likelihood of that occurring was minimal. His instructors and professor would be present and intervene should it appear Art was losing the battle. The real tragic conclusion of failure would mean Art would never be a Weiriman. The final was a once in a lifetime trial. Fail this test and the trainee would be turned away from the guild, unlicensed and forbidden to practice. Everything would be lost, and Art knew nothing else to do with his life; there was nothing he wanted more than to be a Weiriman.

The doors were opening and his breath caught sharply. Lifting his head, Art tried to pull his shoulders back, feeling stronger and more confident. He had worked hard to build a strong frame, though he felt little more than average in height and weight. His weapon of choice did not require the great bulk of muscle some of his fellow students had acquired by swinging a great axe or long broadsword. His muscle tone was, however, still good. He felt confident that if he could exorcise the demon from inside him and it took to a physical form as it always did, he would be ready to face it.

Tracing the cold metal of the long knives fastened to each hip and at his waist, the sheathed lethal presence brought him a measure of comfort as his name was called. The leather of his tall boots whispered a slight creak as the click of his heels echoed in the dark chamber. It was not an unfamiliar room, but it seemed entirely alien with only low candlelight casting a yellow haze onto the panel of professors who would act as his judge, jury, and possibly, professional executioners.

"Art Storygrove," an elegant woman with silver-white hair and eyes so blue they almost glowed in the dim lighting announced his name tonelessly. "You stand before the Guild now to face your final trial. Should you succeed, you will become one of the few to bear the title Weiriman. You know your fate should you fail."

Art tried to swallow the lump in his throat. Having worked with Professor Cindervail often, he knew the coldness of her words perfectly conveyed the severity of the situation. He steadied himself.

The doors of the observation Hall closed behind him with a great bang of their heaviness. There would be no spectators but the judgment panel, Art had no one who would come to such an event; no family, no friends. The only person that had ever cared for Art had passed away recently. The life of a Weiriman was dangerous and though Art could not get the details of how she had passed and on what assignment, as the Guild was very secretive, he knew his guardian, Evendale, had perished doing what he was hoping to one day die doing as well. He would accomplish this for her. He would make her proud, pay back her kindness to him, and he would become a great Weiriman.

Confidence renewed, Art squared himself. Running a hand through his long dark blond bangs, he announced, "I am ready, Grandmaster."

There was nothing but silent acknowledgment as the judges seemed to sink even further into their huge, tall-backed chairs, with the light in the room dimming to almost nothing. Eyes straining, Art widened them and drew a deep, controlled breath. Many did not understand the Haunting Weir. How could there exist a barrier inside one's mind, deep within their soul that could keep evil out? And if something like that existed, how could it be controlled?

Classes had taught Art all about the doors in and out of the mind. Those born with the ability to work the mysteries of a psychic mind were able to do things others could not. Some could perform acts of telepathy, telekinesis, mind reading and other skills not so easily categorized. Art had many of these, and he knew he would likely need all of them in this final test. The cleansing of one's own Weir was a far more dangerous and difficult trial than exorcising another's. Having the evil within meant it was far closer, far stronger and could easily trick, mislead and confuse a Weiriman. But working with evil all the time and running the risk of being possessed themselves, Weirimen had to have the skills to both protect and heal themselves. This was necessary.

The Haunting Weir was not physical, though a part of the mind did control it. A Weir existed in the space between the soul and the body. But Art knew this place and his training had brought him there many times: the mind's eye. He could feel it now, and he closed his eyes as he entered his own inner mind. He had often wondered what each person's psychic space looked like. He imagined they would all be different based on the person.

Art's psychic space always started out with an old archway, stone aged and slightly crumbling. Around it hung the richest red velvet curtains like something seen at the grand theaters. Beyond the arch it was even stranger, like an old chapel, carved out by time. Huge half walls rising into the black of his mind, draped in crawling ivy and other thick foliage. The lighting was always dim and misty, as if eons had passed with no breeze, no rain, only a haunting cloud of shadow. It made him shiver. Why did his own mind look like this? Should he have a dilapidated half castle, like an abandoned temple of a time long past lurking inside him?

The place never made him feel welcome. It was always eerie, as if eyes were on him, as if his whole mind had gathered to observe his entrance. Art tried to put that aside for now, knowing he had a task to accomplish. While some novices were skilled with their mind's eye, Art tried to avoid it. The lack of connection he felt to the creepy place kept him from both practicing there as well as sharing his discomfort with his instructors. He worried it would hold him back from becoming a Weiriman but, he was sure he was not the first person not to like their own inner mind.

Walking through the archway, he was now in the broken temple. A strange river ran through it, flowing through the floor's tiles as if the world had just cracked and the water bubbled up to run through it. His eyes followed the water, but it disappeared into the black edges of the space, reminding him once again he was not in a real place but inside his own mind; even though it felt like he was standing there and everything was real. Not wanting to dally, he ignored most of the details of the place he had explored during exercises, going straight to the door at the back of the broken chapel.

It looked like a door. Wide, old, metal tooled at its edges and reaching across its whole plane to make designs Art did not recognize. But he knew this was not a door. This was his Haunting Weir. This kept his mind safe from everything evil that wanted to get in to make a home inside his mind, eventually consuming his soul. Moving the Weir aside would invite something in. Art squared his jaw, amber rimmed green eyes on the center where he was taught to place both hands and push with all his force. This would jar the thing and if the right strength of mind was applied, the Weir would move aside as if it were floating. Should he grow skilled enough, one day he would be able to command the movement of this Weir with his thoughts alone.

Art did as he was taught, placing both hands on the wood he started to push. Even through the leather gloves he wore, he could feel the strange texture of the door as if the wood was ancient, tired and battered. Frowning, but trying to push back the horrible feeling coiling up inside his stomach, he felt the Weir suddenly give way and its heavy weight changed, lifting free and moving away. Art leaned back, lifted off the thing as it floated into a gathering darkness behind it. He was starting to feel more like he was in a dream now.

He was told he might have to wait a while, that something would have to smell the life's air wafting from his open Weir. It would come crawling in and he would have to battle whatever it did to his mind. Yet, that was not what happened to him. The Weir had just disappeared from Art's sight when something was suddenly in his face. It had rushed him so fast the scream that issued from him was swallowed up by his fall backward onto the broken floor of the ever-darkening temple.

Wild with confusion, Art snapped his head up, trying to scramble to his feet. But as he did so a huge, massive form loomed over him in black clouds. Eyes huge, Art watched as the thing wrestled with its own form, spinning and wrapping the blackness about itself until it took the shape of a tall, slender thing, more bone than flesh. Its skin a shinning onyx, long arms and finger-like claws extending to impressive length. Darkness moved around it like a cloak. But Art's eyes were not on the strangeness of its smoky form. He was staring at the massive horns, almost too heavy for its head crowning its gaunt face, a maw full of teeth, a skeletal fused face and empty black eyes that bore into him despite the lack of actual eyeballs.

This was unlike anything Art had learned about or encountered. Demons, with many horrible forms, typically had to be called out and forced to be seen. This thing was in Art's face. It was grinning at him, an expression somehow clearly discerned through its grotesque, ebony colored skull. Fearsome as its form was, that was not truly the thing that set it apart. Demons could be felt; their presence to a Weiriman was like hearing a voice or touching with something cold. Art had done it many times. But the feeling coming off this thing was oppressive, malevolent, and so overwhelming that Art felt all the breath sucked out of him.

"Well," the thing's voice spilled over his skin like cold, wet slime, "this is unexpected. *You* are unexpected indeed."

Art knew he had to fight back, but the thing was on top of him so fast he felt his whole body turn cold. A cry caught in his throat and his eyes rolled into the back of his head. The thing was devouring him, he was dying and it was so powerful, so ancient, so evil there was nothing the young novice could do to stop it from consuming his whole soul. He had failed.

Chapter Two
Soul Lantern

Art was suddenly breathing hard as if air had been forced through him like water through a narrow tube. Sitting straight up, he hacked and wheezed, tasting blood and smelling a foul odor similar to scorched flesh. Eyes blurry and mind pounding, his attention went to the woman sitting near him. Professor Cindervail stared, expressionless, though if Art had to guess she might be worried.

"This is the infirmary?" The white walls, a light stone, were instantly recognizable. Most of the Weirimen Seminary, where the novices lived and trained, was made of heavy dark stone. "What happened?"

His head ached but it was second only to the pain of his entire body. Trying not to wince even when he breathed, another man came to stand over Art.

"What indeed! It's an abomination! He should be expelled from the program and confined. He can't be allowed to exist like this!"

Professor Minevur had never liked Art. He first thought it stemmed from his bad blood with Art's guardian, Evendale. After being in the program for a year Art learned the man was just a sour, angry person. They were not destined to get along. However, what he was saying now was over the top, even for Minevur.

"Confined?! Allowed to exist? What?!" Art stumbled over his words when yet another instructor stood from her chair.

"You cannot have him condemned! We do not even know how that thing got in there. We still don't know what this all means."

"Yes, we do," the short man blasted back, pointing his finger at Art. Art secretly believed Minevur hated him because Art was just taller, and the little man always had to look up at him, even when he was scolded, which was often. "We know he's possessed with a demon none of us can exorcise. That alone should qualify him for imprisonment, or even death."

"Death?! Wait! I'm not possessed! What are you talking about?! What happened?" Art's head was spinning. They were talking about him; Minevur was pointing at him and Professor Shimthil was clearly upset, but Cindervail had said nothing yet. Art's eyes went back to her, desperately hoping she would clarify.

"You saw that thing! No one has ever seen anything like that! We're lucky we were not all consumed! He kept this a secret from us! He should be brought to the active Guild Grandmasters for judgment. But I know they will condemn him. It's too dangerous to be let loose on the world."

"Stop! I don't understand," Art barked. Minevur, who had been acting like the young man was still unconscious, turned his wide face at him.

"You don't get a say here! You kept it secret that you have an abnormal Weir. Yours does not connect to the outside world, it's like a closed pocket in your mind. Instead of keeping demons from the world-in-between and the beyond the Veil out, you had one imprisoned inside you! What were you hoping for? That it would get out and kill us all?! Are you working with the demon to destroy the Weirimen?! Are you a blackened? You made a pact with this thing?"

"What the hell are you talking about!?" Art snarled, completely confused and starting to become overwhelmed by his aching body.

"Enough," Cindervail's calm voice silenced the pair. "Art, look at me."

Frowning, Art obeyed. He knew Cindervail had the ability to look into someone and know if they were lying.

"When you opened your Weir, we discovered what Minevur said. Your Weir is not a dam holding the evils of the nether out. Your Weir is like a floodgate; you actually have two. They imprison the evil between. Inside you was something called a Pith demon."

Art knew the term Pith demon: very rare, very evil. So rare there was only one record of a Pith demon ever recorded in Weiriman history. It had killed several members of the early Guild and records on the incident and the thing were incomplete and somewhat confusing. How it was defeated and what its true name might have been were unknown.

Art wanted to ask how his Weir could be different, and if they were certain it was this rare kind of demon, but Cindervail went on.

"It appears this thing has been sealed inside your Weir. When you opened it you released this evil. Had it not been for the whole judgment panel's presence and participation you would have been consumed."

"Vestor is still in surgery." Minevur's lip was curled, his anger barely contained.

Cindervail ignored him saying, "We had to force the thing back inside your Weirs when we were unable to exorcise it."

"The whole Judgment panel was unable to exorcise this thing?!" Art was in disbelief.

These were some of the most powerful Weirimen in the entire Guild. The fact that they could not bring the thing down together, meant a level of evil and power Art had never heard of or even read of.

"We had to seal it back inside you."

"But not completely," Minevur added gruffly.

"What do you mean?" Art's brows were pressed down so hard on his forehead he was causing himself even more discomfort than his throbbing head already was.

"We were unable to completely close your Weir," Professor Shimtil said quietly, wringing her wrists, the marks of the battle showing in long cuts bandaged on her fingers and forearms. He now noticed all three professors were banged, bruised, or injured in some way. The battle that must have taken place had to have been terrifying to cause these hardened veterans of this dangerous profession so much injury.

"The demon was too powerful," Cindervail explained. "The force of its power keeps your Weirs just slightly open. In time the thing will break free."

"Break free?" Art asked the question but his mind was colliding with the horrible answer.

"Yes, and consume you," Minevur's voice was cold. "And in doing so it will become even more powerful, because you know what happens when a demon consumes the soul of a powerful psychic."

"Its strength will double at least," Shimtil murmured, fearfully.

"We can't allow an evil like that into the world!" Minevur blustered. "He has to be imprisoned until we can figure out a way to destroy the thing, or he has to be put down and the demon with him."

"Put me down?!" Art started but Cindervail was speaking again.

"It is true we do not know how to deal with this demon, Art. However, I have no intention of confining you or putting you down."

"WHAT?!" Minevur exploded.

Cindervail continued to ignore him, "You will be given the chance to save yourself. Pith demons have two references in our archives. First, you must travel to one who was there when a Pith demon was battled."

"Someone is still alive who was there?" Shimtil looked baffled. "It was so long ago, no one could possibly still be around."

"There is one. He's touched by many different bloodlines, mostly Fey, and has an unusually long life span."

"The Weaver," Minevur mumbled, still visually angry at Cindervail's decision.

"That weird old man who lives near the Woods of Reaching?"

"Yes," Cindervail explained. "You will go to him and perhaps he can tell you more about this Pith demon. There is no use in taking the steps we normally would to research this demon. No book here has this thing's name, nor are we powerful enough to stop it. Your only hope is the Weaver."

Art was starting to understand the severity of what was happening to him. "But how did this thing get inside me? Why is my Weir different?"

"We don't have these answers, Art. But, allow me to ask you just to satisfy all, did you know this thing was within you?"

The color of Cindervail's eyes always showed her ability to see the truth in others. It was common when Weirimen used their special skills that their eyes changed or glowed. As her gaze bore into him, they shown silver gray, like moonlight bouncing off frosted windowpanes. Art could sense her using her mind, looking into his, and if he wanted he could try to block her. But he did not need to try or to lie, for the truth was he did not know about the demon. Answering, he simply told everyone in the room that Art was just as much in the dark as the rest of them. He had no idea why he was different or where this malevolent thing had come from.

"Now," Cindervail's eyes returned to normal and she rose, "come with me. The second thing mentioned in the account of the Pith demon is in the Wine Vault."

"The Wine Vault?!" Minevur screwed his wide face up, alarmed but Cindervail paid him no mind. Painfully, Art rose and followed her, leaving the other two professors behind, Minevur burning holes into his back with his gaze.

Art had never been to the Vault. As far as he knew, no novice ever had. It was off limits, forbidden, and said to be dangerous. Even getting to it seemed like an unnatural act. Cindervail led him to the back of the Seminary's compound, through a dense crop of trees that felt more like a wall than a line of them. The archway to get to there was too low for anyone to walk under without having to duck deeply. After navigating the path, they came to a strange building Art always thought was some kind of crypt. The door on the front had no handles and it was commonly thought that it did not open.

The ground came up around it, as if the Vault had been built partially into the small hill it was nestled against. Pillars of stones and carved statues of fallen Weirimen still doing battle with demons adorned the sides, giving its deeply gothic look an even eerier tone. Some novices had speculated that it was an actual mausoleum and the bones of the most prestigious Weirimen were buried inside. Art never believed that though, because Evendale was not buried there, and she had been one of the best that had ever lived.

It stood tall over the pair as Art, still nursing a pounding head and sore body, watched as Cindervail placed her hand on the front panel. The slab, a carved shield inscribed with the motto of the Weirimen: "Life within to dam the darkness throughout," rumbled when somehow Cindervail pushed the thing open without much effort.

"Only those with the greatest control of their Haunting Weir can open this," she explained as she took a lamp from the hook just inside and it burst into light with a tap. "The only light that will function in the Vault is a soul lantern, and you know, only one with an unpolluted soul can use such a tool."

Art nodded, Weirimen often used such devices. It kept the possessed or those being controlled or haunted by demons from using their weapons or getting into their most important places, such as the Library of Demonic Antiquity, used to research the Weirimen's cases.

Inside was small, but hosted a pointed ceiling. It smelled old and dusty; the only light from the soul lantern. Cindervail guided him to a hidden door and pushing the heavy stone aside, started down a steep set of spiraling stairs that descended into more darkness.

"The Wine Vault, is where we keep the most dangerous artifacts collected over the years of Weirimen battles and cases. Cursed items, weapons, books and even imprisoned demons are housed here."

Art was surprised. Never had he expected that such things were so close to the Seminary and all stored together.

"I know." Cindervail smiled, having a little more than a touch of mind reading ability. "But in the Vault they are quite safe. Severe precautions are taken to maintain the Vault and its safety. There is some evil you cannot destroy and so it has to be locked away. So, they are still in the world but kept out of it. My colleagues did not want me to bring you here," she continued as they moved down stairs, passing strange alcoves and openings in the walls that lead to hallways and other places in the Vault.

Finally, they stopped at an archway, deep in the earth. Cindervail led them through and off the stairs though Art noted the stairs did descend even deeper. The hallway was primitive, hewn from the earth and rock with just enough room to walk through. Art felt mildly claustrophobic at the close walls, the stale air, and the deep darkness that swallowed up anything that the lantern did not illuminate.

They passed weird cages built into the walls, windowed holes and other strange displays that Cindervail did not give them enough time to inspect. Uncertain about what else to do, Art followed her silently until they came to a tiny cell in the wall. Quickly, Cindervail drew a key out of her pocket and put it into the lock. The metal glowed when it clicked in the locking mechanism and the wall rumbled to life. Art watched, eyes wide, as the wall changed first into a briar patch of twisted metal, then peeled back as if organic and living, like leaves. It opened to the pair and Cindervail reached inside to pull out a strange lantern.

"This will be your one true weapon against all the evil you will face in your search to rid yourself of this rooted demon."

Chapter Three
Umbra Sweets

"You are really leaving?"

Art was brought out of his thoughts by the voice of Senny Greiventine, formally a fellow novice. She had passed her Haunting Weir test and was now officially a Weiriman. By now, the whole graduating group of no more than ten people, knew Art did not pass his test due to "grievous complications". Though it was rumored that once his "affliction" was cleared up he could try again, Professor Minevur had made it clear he would be protesting Art's re-entry into the Weirimen Guild.

Art could barely contain his rage. He felt his whole life had come up against a wall. Everything he had worked so hard for had been snatched away by this mysterious demon. How could he have a demon inside him? Why was his Weir some kind of prison? How could they not have known? He felt a certain amount of unwanted anger towards his instructors and the Guild. Should not the foremost elite group of demonologists and exorcists have known he was carrying a demon so malevolent, so vast in power, that not even the best group of Weirimen could banish it from Art? The only thing they knew was to kill him and send the demon back to hell? He bit his lip hard at the bleak options.

Perhaps, if he knew more about his family, his parents, something about his past more than just that night he was found by Evendale, alone. He had no memories and she did not seem to care. She raised him as her own, without questions and Art never felt right to ask. She always seemed like she did not know. But, perhaps she did. Maybe she knew more about him than she had let on and was unable to tell him before she was suddenly killed. He hated the idea that she might have been able to prevent the horrible situation he was in.

"Art?" Senny asked again. Much smaller than him, she leaned in to look up to his face.

"Oh, I'm sorry," he mumbled through full lips and clenched teeth. "Yeah, I have to leave."

Looking at him with large eyes, he could see pity there and it made him feel all the more angry. He had been top of his class, so promising, so ready to jump into his life and now this. The very thought of it burned a hole in his stomach.

"Is it true?" Her voice was gentle but he loathed that she had asked the question.

"Which part?"

She looked uncomfortable but Art did not care. If she wanted the answer she would have to clarify.

"You didn't graduate?" He had harbored a slight hope she would not actually say it. "And they say you have a demon trapped inside you."

"It's true," he reluctantly answered. "I'm going to see someone called the Weaver. All they gave me was this lantern." He held up the small wrought iron lantern, deep bronze, nearly black, with long a glass housing. It emitted no light, but when Art placed it on the stone wall, by which they stood, its handle sprouted a mounting from which the lantern hung. The handle could change from hanging to standing, metal bending as if the thing were alive.

"Wow." Senny blinked, watching the metal fully settling in the ornate beautiful shape of a hanging lantern. "Is it a soul lantern?"

"Cindervail says it's more than that," Art explained. "Of course, it will aid me against the evil I will now be attracting, since my Weir is not fully closed. But, I don't know how to use it as anything special. She said instinctively, I'll know when the time comes."

"So, you really are leaving."

"I have to." Art nodded, quietly, running a gloved hand through his long dark blond hair, and over the shaved parts under the lengths. "If I can't cure myself before the demon breaks out and consumes me, the Guild will hunt me down to put me down."

The statement was grave and there was little for Senny to say. She knew at the very least, Professor Minevur and his supporters would carry out the threat. A demon the Guild could not exorcise could not be unleashed onto the world. Making matters worse, the type of demon was very rare, so it was near impossible to know how to make the demon tell its name. Without the name, it could not be deported back to its own hell.

"I'm sorry, Art," was all Senny said before several of the other graduates called her and she had to leave him waiting at the front gate alone.

"Yeah," he mumbled, "me too."

"Self-pity will do you no good, Storygrove." Cindervail was suddenly at his side. "You will need great inner strength to see you through this journey." Art frowned but did heed her words. "Here," she held out a book and a rolled up map of old soft hide. "This will show you the way to the Weaver, at least the last known location of the man. I hope he is still there. It is a treacherous road, so you must be careful. Our world is not a safe one, even for someone who would have become a Weiriman."

Art tried not to wince at the reminder that his dreams were likely gone. The reality of it was, he had to forget about becoming what he desperately knew he could be and concentrate on staying alive now.

"Is there anything else I should know about this man?"

"He is a strange one. He lives just beyond the Woods of Reaching. Do not go into those woods if you can help it. Most who travel that route do not come out and those who have are half mad. We have even lost Weirimen to the woods. Go to the town nearby and stay on the east road. Little is known about the Weaver, other than he helped found the Weirimen, but he had a falling out with the Guild and left long, long before my time."

"Is he even going to allow me audience?" Art frowned. "I may not be a Weiriman yet, but I certainly have the look, manner and abilities of one. If he's part fey, as you say, I might even smell like one to him."

Cindervail smiled just a little, something her face did not often do. It was clear his memory and intelligence would serve him well. Had it been any other novice, she would have condemned them and spared them the fleeting hope and the painful, dangerous attempt Art was about to undertake. "If you come through this you will be an even greater Weiriman, Art Storygrove. Evil will be drawn to you and the night will only bring further danger. Life and light is your only refuge. Remember all that has been taught you and believe in your own heart. It will see you through the darkness. Farewell."

She did not allow Art any words of goodbye or thank you. She only turned sharply, her long brown jacket, billowing in the evening air as she disappeared into the growing fog gathering around the seminary.

The place had been Art's home for many years, especially after Evendale died. He rarely returned to the small cottage she left him. It only made him feel even more alone now. He let his eyes linger on the large stone buildings for only a moment longer before snatching up the lantern once more. It morphed and changed in his hand until it formed a handle. His own soul would light it when it was needed. Art wondered how long he could sustain such a thing. If he felt any darker than he did now, would the lantern too abandon him to the darkness?

Art took the train out of the city. It was the fastest way to Riftenshire, the first place Cindervail told him he needed to go. He would not find the Weaver there, but there was a very special place he had to visit prior to his quest. The Bohurst Shadow Confectionary was the best among its rivals and competitors. Though a Shadow Confectionary could be found in nearly all the large towns and cities, the Bohurst brand was owned by one of the oldest and most talented families of Shadow Confectioners. In a world filled with demons, evil, and darkness there was more than one way to combat dark forces and the making and consumption of Umbra Sweets, as they were called was one way. These could help protect against possession, minor demons, negativity caused by evil, and other things seeking to feed on people.

Art did not have what Weirimen referred to as a nuisance haunting, where certain kinds of these Umbra Sweets could dispel hauntings and minor creatures of the night. His problem was far more severe than most things treated by Umbra Sweets but Cindervail said certain candies, specifically from the Bohurst Shadow Confectionary, might aid him in dispelling some of the evil that would be attracted to him. She also thought they might have something a little stronger to help him fight the demon that would soon be trying to claw its way out of his cracked open Weir.

Trying not to dwell on the thought that there was a Pith demon within him, perhaps watching him now, maybe even listening to his inner thoughts, Art tried to turn his attention to the train car. It was lavish, beautifully adorned as all the gilded first class cars were. Weirimen were handsomely paid by either the afflicted or the towns and institutions that hired them. A prized and most needed skill against the darkness, they could afford to make at least part of their long journeys in some comfort when traveling by train, stagecoach, or flying ship. The train ride to Riftenshire might be the only part of Art's trip that was comfortable. The region in which the Weaver was said to live was a landscape of horror, dark forests, treacherous paths, and lost towns: the Wyld. When the evil first spread through the world, some places became like cesspools of dark energy unable to be reclaimed by people, given over to the demons. Not knowing when he would be able to sleep again, Art tried to lay out on the couch provided in the roomy train car; thankfully it was a private place. Dressed as a Weiriman on Cindervail's orders, he did not truly want to be approached. He only had a temporary license and felt uncomfortable explaining his reasons. Weirimen were almost always in pairs. He already knew he seemed odd.

He did not think he would actually be able to sleep, his chest tight, his mind racing but before long he was lost in misty, dark dreams of the terrifying figure that had emerged out of his Weir. The voice melted over him like cold fog, deep, familiar, and horrific. When it spoke to him he would not listen, trying to run through darkness without footing until he was waking at the sound of the train whistle.

Shaking slightly, feeling dry-mouthed and sick, Art gathered himself up along with his pack and long knives. He waited until the rest of the train had disembarked before making his own exit. Pulling his hood up, he hoped to go unnoticed as he followed the crowd out of the train station.

The city was darkening, lanterns were being lit, and the business of the day was coming to a hurried close. Riftenshire was closer than most large cities to haunted ground and could be very dangerous at night. If he did not hurry, he would not make it to the Shadow Confectionary before they closed. Cindervail had told him to get the candies before the end of the first moon that night.

Using a compass with a special needle attracted to strong concentrations of demonic energy, Art was quickly pointed in the direction of the Bohurst business, just on the outskirts of the city. He was glad it was nearer the train station then he thought it would be. After a short walk through a darkly wooded area, he saw the shop aglow and the smell of confections lacing the night's growing chill. Quickening his pace, he went up to the door of the old but well kept building and knocked heavy. The sign already read closed and Art cursed softly, hoping the owner would open despite the night's growing dangers.

After a few nervous moments, a face appeared at the window of the shop. The man paused a moment but then noticed Art's manner of dress. The Weirimen did not have a uniform but the silver and red knives strapped to his thighs and belt were a clear indicator of his profession. It did not take him long to open the door, eyes slightly wide.

"Good evening," the man said cautiously. Art assumed he was a Bohurst, long bangs of brown hair and strange colored eyes. Shadow Confectioners usually had very distinctly colored eyes. "Can I help you, sir?"

"I apologize for the late hour. I only just arrived in town but I am in great need of your services," Art said gravely.

The man looked at him for a moment longer than most would have, his silvery purple eyes turning a brighter shade before his expression turned to alarm.

He knows! Art thought to himself as the man ushered him inside.

The place was large, all manner of shelves and displays lining the store and littering the sales floor. Sweet and delicious smelling, Art could hardly believe the things they sold were actually manufactured from demonic energy, purified and treated to function as sort of an anti-venom to evil. It was a remarkable skill and discovery that aided people in protecting themselves from little evils that whispered and paved the way for greater evil to invade. Art had been to the confectionary in his town but the Bohurst place was something else entirely. It was far more beautiful and elaborate; each candy and confection in a jar, basket, or some other form of lovely display all labeled, explaining their use and function.

"Being a Weiriman, I know you must know that your Haunting Weir is not fully closed," the man spoke quickly, his voice tinged with urgency knowing the true meaning of how much danger Art was in from possession as well as the evil he might draw to him.

"Yes," Art nodded. "That is why I am here. Professor Cindervail Grandmaster of the Weirimen Seminary sent me to your establishment because she said you would have product that would aid me in suppressing the 'scent' of my Weir to demons and perhaps something stronger."

"Something stronger?" The man frowned. "What truly ails you, sir?"

Not wanting to explain but knowing he had to, Art relayed a small part, emphasis on the demon within him.

The man's face paled. "A Pith demon...! That...that is a very serious problem... I..." he seemed at a loss for words, his face bending into a hard frown. "While I have nothing specific for such a powerful demon, I do have something that might give you more time while you hunt for your answers." He turned and headed towards the back, indicating Art should follow. When they reached a long orange curtain separating the showroom floor from back room, the man indicated Art should wait, though he continued to speak to him even as he disappeared behind the thing.

"This is very rare, I was only a boy when these were made but it has no expiration date so please do not worry about that. Though I think this will help you, please note that nothing I have will keep this thing at bay for good." Re-appearing he handed Art a small jar of little red spheres, looking like the most delicate cherry flavored candies. "Use these only when you cannot keep the thing in check yourself. They will function almost as soon as they dissolve in your mouth, but Sir, use them sparingly. This is not something I can make again quickly. It will take two years of work and rare ingredients for me to make half this batch again."

Art's amber rimmed green eyes turned serious. "I understand. Thank you."

"Also take these." He handed him a pack of twisted vine sweets. "I have written the dosage on the card inside. They will suppress your open Weir's scent and help with demons, but there will still be things that can smell you and sense you. I would advise staying away from haunted ground."

Art chuckled darkly. "I wish that were an option, good Sir, but my quest takes me to one of the darkest places."

"Then you will need skill, luck, and hope." The man tried to give him a smile but Art could not return it.

"Thank you." Art nodded as the pair moved towards the door. He fished in his pocket and pulled out his wallet. "What do I owe you?"

"Nothing," the Bohurst shook his head. "A Weiriman in such need, your coin is no good here." He gave Art a comforting smile.

"But the item is so rare." Art held up the red candy reading the label: Scarlet Extinction. "I must give you something."

"Your survival and service to our world against the darkness will be payment enough. Life against darkness, Weiriman." He held out his hand and Art shook it, grateful beyond words. The kindness was enough to at least shift, slightly, the burden he had so suddenly taken on alone.

Chapter Four
House on the Other Side

A night train was much harder to find and Art ended up riding in a small speed train with a group of Scarborough Knights heading out to help eradicate a nest of touched creatures sighted near the city. Animals could also be afflicted, possessed, or tainted by demons and their ilk. When it happened, they would sometimes become twisted, turning into touched creatures. These things were no longer an animal but a monster, destroying, killing, and maiming with no reason other than to hunt and kill. Sometimes, Weirimen would deal with these things but usually the task fell to Scarborough Knights, an elite fighting force consisting mainly of elves, but also did employ half-elves and mixed fey blood descendants. They had superior martial ability and faced these fearsome things with far more success than races of men.

Grateful they were mostly a quiet lot, taking to the bunks and sleeping compartments of the train, Art was left alone in a car to himself, Far different from the luxurious first class cabin had been, Art did not mind the modest couch provided. He was not sure he could sleep again after his last dream. He worried that the encounter had been more than just a vague nightmare. Perhaps it had been an actual interaction with the demon inside him. Frowning, he watched the reflection of his cabin in the dark window as the train raced through the night. Art munched on the chewy twist he had gotten from the Shadow Confectionary. He had yet to take one of the red candies, hoping it would not come to that.

Morning came slowly, and Art had spent a restless night between waking and disturbed sleeping, his dreams confusing and heavy. The Scarborough Knights were up early, most of them needing less sleep than a man, and they were in the breakfast car when Art arrived. Some of them eyed him, nodding respectfully if they made eye contact. Even among full blood elven Knights, who did not often care for the races of men, Weirimen were held in high regard. Art wondered if he would even be wearing the badge of one having earned it, rather than just the shadow of it, still a novice. He could see why Cindervail allowed him the temporary license, telling him he should behave as one. It gave him rights and eased some things that might be more awkward for him if he were just an ordinary citizen.

Sitting at a back table by himself, he had coffee and toast, watching a hazy pink sunrise peak through the growing woods around them. The Knights would be exiting soon but Art would be continuing to a smaller town and then he would have to arrange another way of getting out to the haunted ground and the Woods of Reaching. He might be traveling by foot soon. He doubted there would be many who would want to take him to such a dangerous place.

He picked up food in the next town as a train would not arrive for a few hours. He had been outfitted with the best traveling equipment the Guild had to offer and had special compartments on his pack that would preserve his food for extended periods, allowing him to take more supplies. The area near the haunted ground would be scarce of food or drinking water. The very land itself could be tainted, resulting in even demonic vegetation. It might be trying to eat him more than he would want to try and eat it. Animals could be hard to find and the ones that he would run into could be more toxic than edible.

Bearing all this in mind, Art supplemented his supplies as wisely as he could. The Seminary had taught survival skills, as well as all the book learning and combat training. Weirimen often had to travel to the strangest places in the world and face the worst conditions in order to deport a demon or exorcise a person or building. He never expected to be doing everything on his own the way he was though. Weirimen always had a partner or worked in teams. Art was resolved to the fact that he could do it on his own if he had to. He was not that popular with his classmates anyway. He was not sure why, perhaps too quiet? Or maybe he was too gifted. Things came to him easily in the Seminary. He was both talented and intelligent. Whatever the reason, he was on his own a lot. He just had to view this as no different from those instances.

As he was departing his last train and heading into the small town that was the last piece of civilization before the haunted area, an ugly thought did occur to him. Would Minevur be recruiting Weirimen from his graduating class to help hunt Art down should he loose the battle with the demon? Would former classmates be running him through with their silver infused weapons? Would he be watching Senny fill him full of crossbow arrows when the end came? The picture of his bloody death at the hands of his former colleagues filled him with a cloudy mood. It lingered still as he ate lunch and inquired to the café owner about the forest east of the Woods of Reaching.

"You don't want to go out there, love." The big round woman shook her head as she served him a meaty smelling soup and crusty bread. "That's real close to the Woods of Reaching. That place will swallow you up if you get too close. It eats people, you know. The trees will actually eat you whole!"

"I don't want to go to the Woods of Reaching," Art tried to clarify, wishing she would put his spoon down. The stew smelled so good, he wanted to start eating it. But when she started talking she forgot to put his spoon down and started waving it about like a baton, emphasizing her alarm at the very idea he would go anywhere near the cursed place. "I just need to go to the forest on the East side of the trail."

"Oh you don't want to go in there either, love! That place is not as bad but it is still real near haunted ground. Weird things live in that forest. I wouldn't be surprised if the taint has spread across the road from the Reaching to the Other Side."

Art decided to give up explaining. "What is it called?"

"What's what called, sweetie?" She started to put the spoon down but pulled it back when she spoke again and Art tried not to follow it with his eyes.

"The woods."

"The Woods of Reaching. I thought you knew that. You asked about 'em."

"No." Art shook this head thinking maybe he should just reach out and take the spoon from her. "The wood across the road from the Woods of Reaching."

"The Other Side."

"Yeah, the other side. What's it called?"

She laughed, "No, honey, we just call it the Other Side. It all used to be under one name many, many years ago. But since the woods became haunted, we call one side the Woods of Reaching and the other, the Other Side."

"Ah." Art nodded, watching as her hand brought the spoon down, nearing the table. "That's not on the map."

"Of course it ain't," she laughed loudly again, a booming laugh, abrupt, not feminine at all. "No one wants to go there, or hardly anyway. Guess they didn't update the map with places people shouldn't go."

She turned to head back towards the kitchen when Art reached out and nabbed the spoon from her. She blinked a couple of times startled but Art did not care. He was content to start eating.

"But you should heed what I say. You got no business going to the Reaching or the Other Side."

"Leave him alone, Mable," the cook from the back called. "Can't you see he's a Weiriman?"

She turned and took a long look at Art, then gave a slight snort. "Weiriman or not, you'll die if you go there, love." She did not say another word, but waddled her round form back to the bar.

Art said nothing, returning to his lunch. It would be pointless to tell her he did not want to go there either. He knew the dangers and with a powerful demon inside him, it might only make matters worse.

No cart, buggy, or guide would take Art out to the Other Side woods. No one wanted to even pass the Woods of Reaching. There were extreme rumors that the forest could enchant people and pull them inside. Others said the path that ran between the two sides was tainted and could lead you into the wrong woods before your senses were regained. Under the fear of the area, Art had no choice, and as the noon sun started its decline, he was walking out of town towards the haunted forest beyond, alone.

The woods still looked like a beautiful place. As the worn path changed from well walked to a country trail, Art was surprised by the natural beauty. Rich greens of the trees were tempered by ruddy reds of the lower brushes and trail's clay. Shining in the sun's light, the forest did not seem to live up to its fearsome reputation. The path between the two sides became much more apparent when Art actually stepped from the open path to the tree lined corridor of the woods.

The East side was warm, basking in the afternoon's rays. The Woods of Reaching to the West was dimmer somehow. Staring into the trees, Art noticed how his vision blurred the further he looked in. A heavy fog lingered just beyond the threshold of the wood, muting the colors until it seemed only black and brown, muddied by a bramble of trees much too dense to be natural.

As he stood, the sun warming his back and hood, he frowned. Something was coming out of the woods, a very low, slight whispering. He felt a tinge of cold in his hands and a bristling of his skin. He was well dressed, a long leather coat, vest, and hood worn by most Weirimen. Tall boots, well made gloves, and the leather face mask that covered just his nose, mouth and chin completed the signature look. There was little skin left exposed to the elements, so the deep cold creeping in now was wholly not natural.

Art flexed his hands open and closed, listening to the sound of the leather move. He was nervous and he did not want to be. It was common to hear whispering, noises, and voices from haunted places. Even people without gifts could at times hear the noises of the unnatural. Art had been hearing them most his life, the callings of demons, the weeping of tormented souls. There was something different now. The voices were clearer, almost lyrical. There was a seductive beauty in them that he had not heard before.

He worried this could be because of the demon within him. Was that creature making the sounds of evil more accepting to him? This might make him more vulnerable. If he could not see the difference between beauty and danger he really would be unfit to be a Weiriman. The evil would consume him before he knew he was in its embrace. Turning from the woods and the quiet singing of the monsters within, he took the path into the Other Side. Perhaps the Weaver would have answers and he would not have to face these growing questions.

There was little direction on his map to where the Weaver would be found. Cindervail told him to use the Weirimen's compass because the Weaver worked heavily with demonic energy. He had been a tinker and an inventor, responsible for many of the weapons, traps, and prisons the Weirimen used to the current day. His genius was credited with a great deal of the reason the races of the world could hold back the darkness that threatened to invade, one possession at a time.

Drawing the thing out, Art held it in his hand and watched the tiny delicate needle spin. It whirled and whirled until finally stopping in a clear direction. Art was thankful that it was away from the Woods of Reaching. His tall, thick boots aided him when he had to veer from the path and head into the dense woods, some of the ground muddy. Traveling nearly into twilight, Art saw the glow of a cottage. He hoped it was the home of the Weaver.

Coming up to the place, he was surprised there had been little effort to get there. Cindervail had indicated it would be far more difficult, fearing there would be traps, guards and other such things that she could hardly imagine. With the cottage in sight, covered in vines, a triangle of a building seeming to rise out of the forest, Art felt he should pause his trek forward. His instincts had always served him well in training, but there was something else now, something stronger, he could almost taste the metal of something wrong in the air.

Art scanned the forest around him, the little cottage beyond. It was dense, quiet and strangely still. Eyes squinting, he let his senses open, his gaze shifting from their amber rimmed green, to a bright gold. This ability was called the Demon Sight; it allowed those with the gift to see beyond the Veil of the world and into things unseen. All Weirimen had to have the ability.

Looking again, Art was amazed by the activity in the forest. There were all manner of incorporeal spirits, some benign and harmless, some hungry and viscously watching him. All were floating around a strange energy field that encased the cottage like a dome, clear and barely there, but radiating power.

"A spirit shield," Art murmured, wondering how he would cross such a thing, or perhaps it was only meant to keep the spirits, ghosts and demons out.

He took a step forward but yelped as he fell. The ground that looked to be there had been an illusion and he was tumbling down, arms scrambling back to catch the branches of the fallen tree he had been standing near. Grasping, gritting his teeth he clung on, trying to get a better grip to pull himself up. The tree was slippery, the branches bending and threatening to break under his weight.

Dropping a quick glance below, Art's heart leapt into his throat at the dark pit that greeted him. He had no idea how deep it was but it should not have been so opaque, so completely black. Something was keeping the light from entering it. Watching, still trying to pull himself up, Art saw the black pit move. Perhaps it was actually filled with dark water, or maybe oil. It rippled but seemed to have no physical substance. He had no idea what it was but he knew he did not want to fall into it.

"Hey!" A man's voice jerked Art's attention away from the strange blackness. "Who are you? What are you doing here?"

"Are you the Weaver?" Art's question tumbled out. "I'm here to see the Weaver! Please! Help me, I don't think I can pull myself up."

"Damned tree," the man grumbled. Art was unable to swivel his head well and he could see little of the man, save a long coat. He was standing on the cottage side of the pit. "I should have moved that thing away. I didn't mean for you to catch it like that."

"What?!" Art squeaked out. "I don't mean any harm! Please, I'm from the Weirimen Guild. I need to see the Weaver."

"I don't want to see anyone," the man almost spat, sounding even grumpier. "This pit is here to keep visitors away. You shouldn't be out here this close to dark fall anyway, unless you were meant to be hunting. Very dangerous. What are they teaching young people in that Seminary now? Oh well, your mistake. You wouldn't have lasted long as a Weiriman anyway with instincts like that. No good being in a wood near haunted ground this late in the evening, and alone. Not good. No one to pull you out, right?"

"You could pull me out!" Art pleaded.

"Nah," the man's tone was so light, as if Art falling into the pit meant little more than if he were going to have tea or coffee that night. "Why would I do a thing like that? I don't want visitors. I just want to be left to my studies. I didn't ask you to come out here."

"I had no choice!" Art barked, his arms tiring, his grip not improving. "I have to see the Weaver; my life depends on it!"

"Well, presently your life depends on you getting out of that pit, doesn't it?" The man broke out in dry, harsh laughter and he started back into the cottage.

"Wait!" Art yelled after him but the call fell on ignoring ears.

Cursing, struggling, and accomplishing nothing, Art knew he was failing. The grip was too awkward. Swinging his body up would snap the branch, breaking it before he could reach for another. He knew there was no way he could pull himself out without aid. Anger at the man meant little, as in the next second the branch gave out and with a cry, Art disappeared into the black, swirling pit.

Chapter Five
Weaving Pit

Pain had sparked Art's departure from consciousness and then reignited it as he woke in the pitch dark of the pit. The last thing he recalled was falling through what he thought would be water, but turned out to be a thick strange mist. He dropped a troubling distance and landed hard on the floor of the trap. How long had he been unconscious? For a moment, he could hardly move. Worried he was broken somewhere, he carefully checked his stiff body, rolling over onto his stomach to start to rise slowly.

He was just on his knees, about to pull his body into a kneel, when he drew his breath in and held it. His senses were whispering to him, his eyes going completely gold on instinct. Head pounding, eyes slightly watering, Art strained his Demon Sight to see through the deep ink of the pit's darkness.

His ability compensated a little for the lack of light. As his vision adjusted, he saw the outline of it. Emerging out of the bolted dark, sat a creature. Hunched and bent, the thing cocked its head at him, neck loose and strangely agile, like a bird. Larger than Art, it was tall, rail thin, a mane of ebony hair sprouting out of its head and floating around its shoulders in wispy thinness. Two crooked and mangled ears poked out of the black mop, twitching and moving. Yet, the majority of its appearance escaped Art's attention, for it was its face that had the man rising very, very slowly to his feet, breath still held.

No skin, no lips, nothing that resembled flesh covered the alabaster skull of its face. Not rounded like a person, its skull had a long angular snout, all sharp bone and huge teeth of some canine or feline beast. Predatory and sinister, it stared at him with two bulging sacks that made up its eyes, more white than yellow, pupilless. They scanned Art as his hand moved slowly, almost painfully to one of his long knives at his hip.

He was trying to get a grip on the hilt of his weapon, hoping against reason the thing might just go away, when it shuffled across the uneven ground. Moving on all fours with clawed hands and maybe feet too, the thing was fast as a cat. He tried to control his fear, eyes wide on the long sharp teeth, it scurried to one side, circling the man, its teeth gleaming in a hideous grin. There was intelligence in the sack eyes, not a mindless beast but something darker, something evil. It was so happy Art was here, as if it had just been waiting for someone to drop in. Art swallowed his trepidation and readied his grip on the blade.

It dove at him, faster than he expected, but his knife pulled free of its sheath and caught the thing in his mouth. The force of the creature's jump toppled Art over, and the pair rolled on the ground, slashing and clawing at one another. Art grappled with it, the strength amazing. All his training had prepared him for such a fight, but he still was white knuckled and cursing aloud as the thing cut him, tried to bit him, and threw him across the pit like a rag doll.

Free of it for a moment, Art was able to get his other knife out. Armed with two blades he was better equipped and turned back to the advancing monster, he readied himself. Slashing and cutting, Art finally managed to get his boot in the thing's neck and plunge the knife in. But this was no mere beast; this thing was a demon, in the flesh, something that could only be let into the world via a hell mouth or the eating of enough souls to give it physical form. Strong as it was, it was not the worst thing Art had seen. Gold eyes nearly glowing, in his Weirimen's voice, an altered deepened rasp of his usually rich tone he bellowed, "Tell me your name, demon!"

The thing howled in pain but did not yield. Art had yet to put enough of his own soul's weight on it to force the demon to give its name. Twisting the knife in the thing caused more pain but it would not kill it. A demon could not be killed by physical means alone. Art had to have the name.

"Your name!" he demanded again, his eyes still gold, the pressure of his soul flexing on the creature just as a muscle would, if Art's hand had been on the thing's neck. It was his will against the creature's, his own inner strength verses its evil.

He could feel the thing now, his soul close to the essence of what it was. It was made of nothing but hunger, malice, hate, and driving need to harm. Its thoughts were all dark, murderous and brought the taste of iron flooding over Art's tongue. He grit his teeth and plunged the second knife in, holding the creature down with the blades and the weight of his own body. He demanded the name again and pressed his psychic self to wring the information from the demon.

He could do it; he could feel the thing starting to yield. It was not a greater demon, not a devil whose will would take several sessions, more abilities, and perhaps spell crafts of enchanted natures to drive its name from it. Had it possessed a person, slinking around inside them like a bad dream or memory, Art could have slipped into the mind of the afflicted and battled the demon there for hints of its name, hints at to who it was in the demonic realm. With that information he could have gone to the Guild's library and searched for the demon from its clues. The Weirimen kept very detailed records of their demonic encounters and most evils could not be destroyed, they could only be deported back to the hells. Once strong enough, they would surface again back in the world and have to be expelled once more. Professor Minevur said all demons were repeat offenders against life. They would never stop trying to destroy and devour, it was the chaotic nature of evil.

"Your name!" Art screamed into the thing's face as much as he did its mind.

The psychic connection hurt it far more than the blades in its neck and chest and Art could feel it starting to yield. It was difficult to keep his mind focused, strong and taunt, like a muscle but he would not give. Should the thing slip from him and get free, wounded it would be even more dangerous.

He was beginning to tire physically. The creature was not a greater demon but it was strong, and it fought him inside and out. He had to get its name or he might lose this battle just to the size of the monster. Again he pushed, focusing himself so he felt like a scalpel peeling back the inner defenses of the fiend until he felt it, inhaled it, the name of the creature.

"Vishfahl!" He burned its meaning and all the power behind a demon's name into the thing.

He said it again and again commanding the thing back to hell. The wail that issued out of it was deafening and shook Art's whole body to the core. Its eyes rolled back into its head, the angular mouth parting in such an awful gape that it almost looked unhinged. A light burst from within, a dark red fire so deep it was garnet in color. Art withdrew himself and his blades, as its body grew so cold it was burning. It screamed and screamed as the body seem to disintegrate in flakes of smokey ash.

Breathing hard, Art stood. Trembling, his whole body hurting, his mind slightly spinning as he stared at the spot where the demon had disappeared.

"Deported back to whatever hell it came from." A voice melted out of the darkness.

Art spun around, knives up. A slight man, looking not much older than Art, but eyes far deeper, gazed at him with mild amusement.

"You!" Art snarled, recognizing both the voice and the long coat the man wore. "You let me fall down here!"

"I did," the man confirmed, crossing his arms and making no apology for his behavior. "But you did all right. What are you complaining about? You wanted to be a Weiriman, right? You volunteer for this kind of work, I assume."

Art pursed his lips shut, before sliding his knives back in their sheaths. He could not argue with the snide comment, but that did nothing to diminish his anger.

"Are you the Weaver?" Art cut a glance over the man's face, not thinking he looked old enough to be the person Cindervail had spoke of. She had mentioned he had unusually long life due to his mixed fey blood. That could mean he was immortal to age like a pure blood elf or had a more unpredictable lifeline. Fairy kin had all different spans of life, depending on their heritage. Whatever their length, it was almost always longer than man's.

"I have been called that." The man lifted his chin, revealing a surprisingly youthful face. He had a small beard goatee like Art's, but his skin seemed to glow with life, eyes large, a bright teal color. His hair was silver gray and did give him a slightly more dignified look than his young appearance commanded. "The newly budding Guild of Weirimen gave me that name."

"Do you have another name?" Art asked, just a little curious.

"Several," The man smiled, a quirk at the corner of his thin mouth. "Now come along, little Weiriman. You've earned the right to talk with me for now."

Art tried to stifle a sigh of exasperation and followed the man into the darkness of the pit. He hoped it would lead to a tunnel of some kind, something that would take them back to the surface, but to Art's surprise they just walked into the pitch black. When it became too dark to see, Art opened his mouth to protest, worried he might trip over something. But when he blinked again, he was suddenly standing outside the cottage, its pointed roof towering over him

Confused, Art snapped his head back and forth until he spied the Weaver fiddling with a plant near the big front door, also pointed like the cottage.

"What…what just happened?" Art frowned. "Was I inside someone's mind or something when I fought that demon?"

"No." the Weaver looked over his shoulder giving the young man a look like he had said something stupid. "You were in my front pit. Did you hit your head or something?"

"But how did we get up here?" Art pushed his brows together. He had heard of magical places, enchanted with the ability to bend time and space but he had never experienced one so seamless.

"Nothing is solid in my own little pocket of the world." The Weaver shrugged. "You really don't know anything about me, do you, boy?"

"I'm only a novice," Art admitted. "There was just a little talk of you at the Seminary, nothing specific."

"You short lived races," the Weaver laughed, putting his watering can down. "How quickly you forget things. I helped found the whole Guild of Weirimen. You would think they would know something about the founders."

"Well, we at least do know something of you," Art tried to offer, worried he had actually offended. The Weaver did not seem to care, opening the door and beckoning Art inside.

Following the man, Art stepped through the triangular frame and into the warm fuzzy light emanating from the house. The cottage did not look large, but inside it took Art's breath away. Seeming built entirely of trees, trunks and their branches, the place was a masterful use of the natural form. Everything from the walls, to the floors was tree. The spiral staircase they passed had a massive tree growing up its center, the branches built in with the stairs themselves. Counter tops, chairs, tables, and any other surface were a giant slab of beautiful wood.

"Your home is remarkable," Art marveled as he came to sit next to the huge hearth the Weaver lead him to.

The man removed his outer coat, revealing he was dressed in elaborate leathers of many colors, bits of it braided, woven and shaped. His silvery hair was cropped short but for the few long braids that hung down near his ears and over his shoulders.

"Pull your hood down, boy," the Weaver commanded. "You are making the fairy folk nervous."

"Fairy folk?" Art questioned his eyes drawn to the sudden flitting of light, dancing in the corners of the room's vaulted ceiling.

Art's mouth parted in awe as from the pillars of trees that framed the small room, delicate creatures peeked out at him. Some were glowing in many different hues of light, tiny lithe bodies backed by fluttering wings. Others were darker, dressed in furs, their wings like leaves of different seasons. All were beautiful and primal, made of elements and light, ranging widely in appearance and form, all with eyes wide and curious about the new visitor.

"Fairies!" Art gasped, "Actual fairies!"

"Well, of course." The Weaver perked an eyebrow. "What did you think I meant?"

"They are real?" Art continued, unable to hide his smile of wonder. "I've never seen one, let alone so many!"

"Of course they are real. Did you think I meant I had little painted statues of them and a hooded man would scare my amazing collection of figurines?"

Art ignored the man's sarcasm. He had known there were fairies in the world. Every now and again someone would sight one in the city. More often, the stories came from those who visited the elven settlements or the deep woods untouched by evil. He had never given their idea much thought. Consumed each day with study of the darkness and how to protect from it, Art forgot that with the darkness there was also light. Creatures of good still existed in the world, things untarnished and natural. As one stared down at him from inside a lantern, her large black eyes and blue hued skin shimmering in the light, Art felt a small moment of relief from his recent anxiety.

"These fairies would never do anyone harm." The Weaver's voice brought Art back from his thoughts. "But not all fey are good and kind. You remember that. Though it is true most are good, even kind and do not wish anyone any harm, they are in the same bloodline as demons. You trace the magic along the line. At one end you have natural fey, like these." He lifted a finger to the growing audience of tiny colorful observers. "But at the other end of magic's spectrum are the worst evil that you can imagine. They are all connected. Good and evil, light and dark, death and life. That's what a Weirimen does. They use their life force to battle the force of destruction and death a demon is the embodiment of."

"So there are fey out there that are closer to demons than they are to fairies?"

The Weaver confirmed. "I'm sure you've learned about some of them."

Art nodded. "I do remember a few, but mostly Weirimen deal with possession demons."

"Out here in the world, boy, you deal with whatever comes for your blood and by the smell of your open Weir, I would say you will be dealing with all manner of darkness before the Guild comes for you."

Chapter Six
Weir Wisp Memories

The Weaver's words felt even heavier than all the talk of hunting down Professor Minevur had threatened before Art left. This man seemed to know about things Art hardly felt comfortable questioning.

"Sir," Art started when the Weaver handed him a cup of oddly colored tea, "I've come for your help."

"Hm?" The man flashed him a look as if somehow he had forgotten Art was a guest and was suddenly surprised Art had an agenda. "You did? What is it?"

"My Haunting Weir," Art paused at the smell of the tea, an equally odd scent to match its color tickled his nose, "it is slightly open. I'm told I actually have two."

"A crack, yes." The Weaver nodded, not reacting as if this was a problem. The contrast to the serious words the he had just spoken before serving the tea had Art confused.

"I need to close it." Art said plainly.

"Indeed you do," the Weaver agreed, taking a sandwich from a stack of small sandwiches he had brought with the tea. "If you don't, you'll attract hordes of demons. Powerful, dangerous ones that will want to eat you, especially since you have all those psychic gifts. You'd be quite a feast, wouldn't you?" He chuckled a little, darkly, before popping a cookie into his mouth and nabbing another sandwich. "They would gain great power by eating a talented young man such as yourself. If you got a smart one, an old one that had been around for a long time, it would know to keep you alive, and feed off your life force for a while. It would torment you, drive you mad. The energy and negativity that would generate would make you all the more nourishing to it. It would be a horrible, slow, painful descent into madness and then finally death. But sometimes these things don't let you go even in death, and it will keep you inside it to watch it devour others, even seeming like you were participating. Your own personal hell."

All hope Art had been nursing until this moment fell flat, crushed and dribbled on, by the dark chuckling that bubbled out of the Weaver. Art seriously doubted this man would help him. He seemed far more amused by the idea of Art being condemned as a prisoner of a devil than he seemed concerned or interested in the details as to why Art might need help.

"That aside," Art said dryly, putting his untouched tea on the table. "I need your help to exorcise my Weir and close it."

"What would you need my help for?" the Weaver popped up aggressively as if the very thought of Art coming all this way to bother him for such a thing was completely absurd. "Close it yourself. It's what you people do, isn't it?"

Art shook his head, the long cut strands falling into his eyes a little, "I can't. No one in the Seminary could. My professor sent me to you. A very unusual thing happened to me during my final test to become a Weiriman."

"Unusual?" the Weaver suddenly seemed very interested. "I like unusual. Explain, boy."

The explanation still felt surreal as Art relayed all that he knew and all he had been told. The Weaver listened, half curled in his large easy chair, the back carved out of a huge tree trunk lined with pillows. He was still listening to Art describe the details of what the Guild had tried to do and their ultimate decision to leave it in Art's hands, even though he knew even less than they did. When he finished his tale, the Weaver stared at him a long moment and then broke out into laughter. Art was frowning, but waited saying nothing, hoping this was just another eccentric outburst. Then the Weaver tilted his body out of the chair and with an acrobat's grace he lifted himself to his feet and moved towards Art at alarming speed. Confused and surprised, Art could do little more than bump into the back of his own chair and slightly turn his face away as the Weaver pushed his face within inches of the Weiriman's.

He smelled of spice and herbs laced with a hint of something Art had only experienced while in the presence of a demon. The Weaver stared a long time, teal eyes large, the pupil widening so much that it almost overtook the color. Swallowing hard, Art tried not to move, having no idea what was happening, but desperately hoping it would lead to a good outcome. He had little else to go on and had to put at least his partial trust in the odd man.

"Ahhhh," the Weaver exclaimed deeply, his light voice dropping to a slight gravelled drag. "There he is, I sense him. It is indeed true, you are host and house to a Pith demon. Ancient, evil and very, very hungry. I can almost smell its desire to devour you and escape its fate. This won't keep you alive to feed on. This thing is already so strong. Eating you will free it entirely."

"Can you do anything about it? Can you exorcise it?" Art stammered, wishing the Weaver would back up, but the man did not move, using unseen abilities to feel around inside Art's psychic space.

"Don't know anything yet. I've just got a taste of his air," the Weaver snapped, rolling his eyes into the back of his head. "I'm going to need to do a more thorough examination. I need to pop inside your mind. Let's go now."

"Uh," Art stammered, really wanting to say no but knowing he could do nothing but agree.

"You don't have a choice, Weiriman. You either let me look or you go back to your useless colleagues and let them put you down. What's it going to be?"

The Weaver leaned back, crossing his arms over his chest, smiling just slightly, as the fairies around them whispered in their own language. They seemed to understand what was happening, fearful of the thing caged within Art.

"What do I have to do?" Art asked quietly, hating his situation but refusing to relent completely to self-pity yet.

"Come with me."

The house continued to amaze Art. They ascended another staircase in the back of the place made entirely of a long, stretching tree, bent and shaped to make both banister and stairs. His eyes fell on the large window looking out into the back of the Weaver's grounds. The sun was setting and it would be night soon. He had been lucky to be on a train the night before, and nothing had happened. Now he was in the woods, too near a haunted ground to know if this night would be eventless or not.

"Come on," the Weaver said gruffly as he opened a large heavy door at the top of the stairs, carved with a tree relief that extended the entire length of the hallway. "This room will be best for this."

Circular but small, Art craned his neck to the most pronounced thing in the room: a tall, narrow tree that snaked against a wall, its branches crawling along the skylight that took up almost the entire ceiling. In the center was a ring of sitting cushions and the Weaver motioned for Art to take to one opposite of him. Smelling more like the forest than the inside of the house, Art could not help but feel like they were actually outside. The large overhead window, showing the ever-growing evening, aided the feeling, and before long, he was experiencing a still chill. As he sat it started to feel even odder. Like the walls were thinning, the air turning foggy and slightly light.

"Don't let that bother you," the Weaver said sitting in a cross-legged position.

"What bother me?" Art frowned, wanting to pull his hood up, but remembering as he was still in the house and had been instructed to take it off. He thought it might upset the strange man.

"The feel of this room. It is more outside than in. It's actually set just inside the Veil."

Art was suddenly alarmed. "The Veil? Like the Veil, between the physical world and the realm between worlds?"

"There's just the one still, isn't there?"

He did not find the Weaver's humor or sarcasm amusing. Going beyond the threshold of the physical world could be very dangerous. The Veil was the intangible corridor realm that connected the plains of existence together: physical, the hells, and the other places Art knew little about. It was always said that one should not cross the Veil unless the situation was dire. It opened up psychics, made them more vulnerable. There, things that did not have form had much more power and physical things had much less. One could easily be possessed there and get dragged off to a place best left out of even the imagination. It was decisively unsafe for mortals with souls.

"I can't be in here! It's dangerous under normal circumstances but with my Weir slightly open I could be—"

"Could be what?" the Weaver leaned towards him, brimming with grinning. "Invaded? Possessed? My boy, if that happens whatever attacks you will have more than some little Weiriman to deal with. The demon inside you will completely consume anything that gets into your soul. The most you have to worry about is a demon killing your physical body and releasing that thing within you. You don't want that. Now, be still. We are about to begin."

Art was scowling heavily but obeyed, still not liking the idea of being within the Veil and hating the idea that the demon within him was so powerful no other demon beyond the Veil seemed to pose it much threat.

"Hey, are you listening to me?"

Art's attention snapped back to the Weaver whose silver eyebrows were pinched together tightly.

"I'm sorry, Sir."

"Right! Now, as I was saying, close your eyes. I need you to enter your mind as if you were going to your Weir. Once inside you will need to find the door to your mind and let me in."

"That's not my Haunting Weir?" Art asked confused. They had never done something like this in training.

The Weaver rolled his eyes, slapping his thighs irritably.

"They aren't teaching you babies anything in that Seminary anymore, are they? The Weir is for incorporeal creatures. If you want to share a dream or allow someone into your mind, you use your Mind's Door. Everyone has one, but a psychic's is easier to find. Now, do as I say before I get bored with you and kick you out of my house." He closed his eyes and took a deep breath, waiting for Art.

Art turned a lip up at that remark but had to ask, "Demons can't get in through this door?"

The Weaver opened his eyes slowly and smiled, looking dark, even creepy before saying saying, "Most not. But there are a few who can slip in. Some Weirimen who have faced these great tricksters never lived to tell the tale. Their souls are likely still in torment, play things for the evil that found them. You always have to be careful, Weiriman. This is a dark world you navigate, but after seeing the Pith demon within you, I'm sure you know what I mean. You did not stand a chance against him, did you? It frightened you beyond your wildest nightmares, didn't it? All that evil, all that power, all that intelligence honed in on the singular focused task of devouring your soul. I'm honestly very surprised you still want to be Weiriman at all. If you've seen a Pith demon, you've seen real primary evil."

Art stared hard at the Weaver, the bleak honestly of his haunting statement rippling over the man. He had not allowed himself to dwell very much on the actual demon itself. The experience had been harrowing, almost too much for him to process. In the light of day it felt like an unreal nightmare. But when the Weaver spoke, a feeling inked back into him like needle on flesh. It carried a weight greater than anything Art had known.

"I really had not given the thing too much thought," he said honestly. "But you are right, it is the purest form of evil I've ever encountered or even learned about. That's why I want it out of me."

The Weaver chuckled. "I bet you would like to know who put it in you too."

Art blinked fast, he had not even considered that it had been put inside him. "What do you mean by that?!"

Again, the Weaver was laughing. "Boy, this thing didn't just grow within you. It was put inside your double Weir. I've rarely seen one with two Weirs. So functional a prison: one keeping it out and another keeping it in. I won't know more until we go see it. But if my instincts are right someone put this thing inside you. You're its jail, but not if your Weir is cracked open, it will get out. There is no stopping it, unless you figure out how it was imprisoned in the first place. Now, do as I say. Let's go see your funny housemate."

It took longer to go into his inner mind than it ever did before. The Weaver's words left him shaken and angry. The thought that someone deliberately did this to him, blurred his concentration and it took several lectures and much impatient huffing on the Weaver's part to finally get Art to calm himself enough to enter his inner mind.

Once inside the eerie place, Art looked around, completely confused. It was different. Before, when he entered his mind's eye it had always been in the broken temple. Where he was now was outside the structure. Yet, he would have been less alarmed by that if the temple itself did not look so different. Most of the roof had always been gone but now there was a tall roof, with archways and pillars. A broken clock sat on the building's face, everything covered in crawling ivy.

The spotty forest world around him was dark, so seeing nothing else to do, he headed into the building, pulling open a massive iron gate and pushing on the door beyond. The inside too was more intact, the floor still broken, the little river running through. However, the holes in the crumbling walls were repaired, even some glass hung in a few of the window frames. The ceiling above looked dark and black, but it was not the empty darkness of before. There was certainly form there now.

Unnerved, Art still wasted no time in looking for his mind's door. All the walls around him showed nothing, but he paused when he got to his Haunting Weir. A chill crept over him, sending hollow frosty air into the marrow of his bones. The whispering was much quieter than it had been before everywhere but near the Weir. Remembering the weight of the voice of the demon, he turned on his heel, not wanting to give it the chance to speak to him again. Real fear rippled through his blood and he set to his task anew, wanting very much not to dwell on the memories and the fact that he was so close to the thing now.

Art left the Weir and headed back into the main part of the temple. There he glimpsed an old broken staircase that had always been just pieces of a long set climbing upwards. Art had never gone up them because they had been too heavily damaged and they seemed to lead to nowhere. Now with the building more intact, Art could see they snaked around a wall.

Though still full of holes, he was able to climb them, following their ascent about the temple's outer wall, until finally they ended at a small door. Little with a rounded top, it was green, accented by amber. Curious, Art pulled the handle and gasped when he found the Weaver on the other side. Beyond, the man he could see the room in which they were sitting, even see himself, entranced, sitting across from the man.

"Ah!" the Weaver smiled. "Finally." He got up and headed towards Art, but the young man had to do a double take. Though the Weaver had gotten up, his body also remained sitting, eyes closed, unmoving. It was as if a double of him had seamlessly separated itself from himself and was now free to enter through the door which Art had opened. "Let's go then."

The Weaver pushed past Art, telling him to close the door. Art found the experience dizzying. Though Weirimen worked inside someone's mind to battle a possessed demon, often doing combat there, it was usually like it had been in the pit. It was dark, formless, just exorcist verses demon. There was very little scenery or confusing surroundings. Art worried he would not be able to tell what was real and what was in his mind if these kinds of activities continued.

At the Weaver's insistence, he led them to his Weir and stood back, allowing the man to examine what he had come to see.

"Sit there, this could take a while," the Weaver instructed and proceeded to stand in front of the thing, one hand on it, facing away from Art.

Anxious, Art did as he was told. He knew he could not rush the process and would likely just be in the way if he offered to assist. He had no idea what the

Weaver was doing. He did not even know why he should put his faith in the strange person he had just met. He was beyond the Veil, let this person into his mind, and was near the Weir he knew he should not be messing with again after the last experience. Life events were turning out very differently from how he had imagined.

The thought brought back memories of leaving the Seminary. No one but Senny had even come by to talk to him about what had happened. From her short conversation it was apparent they were talking behind his back. He had never been too social but he had expected one or two of them at least attempt to inquire. If things worked out and he was allowed to return and graduate, would any of them even want to partner with him? Would he be considered broken or tainted now?

No matter how he tried to banish the dark thoughts from his mind, Art could not keep them from rising to the surface. Even with the looming threat of his soul being eaten and his life being taken, he could not put aside that the life he had worked so hard for might never materialize. What would he do with himself if he failed to become a Weiriman? He never even considered the idea.

"Ahhh there you are. Aren't you a beauty of a thing!" the Weaver suddenly exclaimed, startling Art.

The man's eyes were still closed, a smile over his lips. He dropped his head, the hand not on the Weir, but rising up towards Art. The Weiriman paused, uncertain what was happening until the world around him started to rumble. Scared, but uncertain what to do, Art watched as figures seemingly made of smoke and color materialized.

"People?" Art questioned aloud as the smoky figures moved passed him, clearly not real but some shadow of who they represented.

Calming more out of curiosity rather than anything else, he watched nearly a dozen figures come out of the archways lining the temple. They were dressed like Weirimen, though their style seemed older than what Art was accustom to. None of them wore the insignia of the Guild anywhere, but many of them had the signature mask up over their mouth and nose, like the one Art usually wore when working. Many demons emitted a tasteless, odorless miasma, known as Sin Breath that could affect the mind and induce fear. The specialized Sin Breath mask invented by the Guild, lessened the effects and most Weirimen, who did not have a natural immunity to the substance, used the facemask.

He wondered if this was a Weirimen hunting party. Was he watching the events of an old hunt? They spoke to one another, their voices only hurried whispers that Art could hardly hear.

"It is here," one murmured.

"Begin the ritual," another said.

Confused, Art watched as the blurry figures moved, placing a lantern down in the center of the temple, chanting, moving. It was unclear what was happening. The lantern started to smoke; the candle inside burning more brightly than any regular flame. Peering closer, he noticed it looked strangely like the soul lantern Cindervail had given him.

He wanted to tell the Weaver. Perhaps, ask about the lantern and if it had some significance to his condition, but something was happening among the figures. Someone was suddenly screaming and a body flew across the room. Chaos erupted among the group. Weapons were flashing, spells being thrown, and suddenly out of the darkness of the ceiling, Art saw it. The same demon imprisoned in his Weir was towering over the Weirimen, long arms swatting and repelling people and weapons.

Art watched in horror as many of them were slaughtered, despite their obvious skills. The demon was far too powerful. Its size changed and morphed as it roved through the room dispatching Weirimen and others, tossing and tearing them open like dolls. The great horned demon rose above the broken group, laughing. The sound rumbled through the walls, deep, guttural and made Art feel sick at the very core of his stomach. Glistening with fresh blood, the thing's maw looked even wider as it grinned, the empty eyes somehow conveying its glee.

"You will not contain me, mortals!" the voice was as foul as the laugh.

Art tittered to the side, bracing himself against the wall just as some of the group, who could still stand did the same.

"Now!" a wounded man on the floor screamed. "Use me, and do it now!"

A woman near him pulled out a long knife similar to the kind Art used. Dodging the grab of the demon, already bleeding herself from a previous injury by the thing, she leaned near the man. Coming together they starred at each for half a moment before she took her blade and plunged it into his chest. Art recoiled in horror and complete confusion; the demon reacting, similarly.

"You do my work for me now, woman?"

She turned, green amber rimmed eyes at the man, glaring, teeth clenched.

"Your 'work' in this world is finished, fiend!" Tearing the blade from the man, she lifted it over her own chest and drove it inside herself.

Art could only watch the milky figures, unable to take his eyes off the pair. The woman, near death, pulled the blade from her and slid it into a narrow opening in the lantern. Unable to do anything else, she fell back next to the man. Breathing ragged, the pair took each other's hands, but Art could no longer watch them. The lantern was shining and the demon howling, making a sound that could cleave stone from the earth.

He had no idea what was happening but the temple was shaking, stones falling. The bodies of the demon's victims were being swept up in the ensuing storm. He could see it and hear it, but he could not feel it. The smoky visual echo of whatever he was witnessing was peeling away from the real temple. He watched as the demon screamed, its form warping and wreathing in some horrific agony. Before Art could piece together anything more, the vision turned completely blurry, like reflections on a stormy lake and dissipated.

Art snapped his head to the Weaver who was now down on his knees, his face knotted in pain. Art started towards him when the man rolled his head up, snake like and suddenly rose to his feet. Art took a step back, instantly suspicious of the strange movement. The Weaver stood a long moment, unmoving. Art only waited, a hand on one of his knives. Then suddenly the Weaver turned towards him, his eyes springing open, completely black and empty almost like they had gone hollow.

"Ahhh," a voice rumbled out of the man like a cave echo, deep and fathomless. "Thought you could take a look in on me and I would not notice your presence. Even one as skilled as you must know if you look at such a moment in my existence I would eventually see you. I am ancient beyond the growth of the forest, frozen in the flow of time. Nothing rots within me but I am the rot that always takes those who wade too deeply into the abyss. When you look into the Void, it is through my eyes you view eternity and the extinguishing of hope and life."

Art's blood ran bitter. The Weaver had been possessed by the demon. He had to do something.

"Your name demon," Art spoke, but felt an awful pull on him like he had just slipped down an embankment. His demand carried no weight. He was fearful, not calm. He lacked the focus he needed to expel evil from another person.

The Weaver turned his face towards Art very slowly, the grin crawling over his mouth making the man look nothing like his original smirk. The expression was unsettling and Art tried to steel himself.

"Ahhhh, there you are again," the demon chuckled, his voice embedded with age. "Boy, we were not properly introduced last we met. I am...," the demon paused toying with a grin again, blinking his black eyes, teeth gleaming bright white. "Oh, but you know the power of a demon's name, don't you. How wonderfully amusing. You are a hunter, aren't you?"

"A Weiriman," Art corrected.

"Ahh, is that what they are called? How quaint. Much has changed since I have been gone from the world of flesh. But you have set me free, haven't you? I would very much like to reward you but," the thing crossed its arms, running one hand over the throat of the Weaver's body, "the last step of my release from this timeless pit is to consume your shiny, new soul. How convenient dinner has been laid out for me at my very doorstep. I never knew they were growing a meal for me."

"What are you talking about?" Art frowned, pulling his blade.

The demon laughed, but before he could answer the Weaver's body convulsed. The head snapped back, the body bending painfully before curling up and dropping to one knee. Art watched, uncertain what was happening until the Weaver's head rolled back up, his eyes having returned to their natural state.

"You need to go!" The Weaver commanded, his breathing labored. "Go back to your consciousness and leave here. He has not fully possessed me. I will put him back in the Weir prison but you must leave. I cannot do this with him feeding on your fear. Go!"

Art did not question the Weaver, knowing full well he could not exorcise this demon nor force its name from it. Sheathing his blade, he turned and headed for the exit of the chapel. He glanced back only once to see the Weaver enveloped with light, touching the Haunting Weir again. Even though he did not need to physically leave the temple to re-enter his body he was compelled to put as much distance between him and the demon as he could.

Running out into the strange courtyard that seemed to have developed a few twisted dry trees around it since he had entered, he forced himself to calm. He had to clear his mind and remind himself that even though he was not standing in the temple with the thing, and was no longer inhibiting the Weaver's battle, it was still all taking place deep inside him. There was no place he could run from the monster he now knew had to eat his soul in order to gain its much desired freedom. Art burned for answers.

Chapter Seven
Lucid

It was like waking from a heavy induced dream. Art's limbs were numb, his mind sluggish. His thighs and lower back were aching from sitting in the cross-legged position for who knows how long. Groaning under his breath, Art bent his head from side to side, listening to the crack of his fatigued body. He did not know inner mind experiences could be so taxing. He had awoken sore and hurting after his failed final test but he attributed that to the attempted exorcism and the battles between the Weirimen and the demon trying to take over his body.

He had actually been shocked he had not been more heavily injured than he was. Perhaps that had been due to the healers in the Seminary's hospital wing. The Weirimen did employ some of the best healing in the land. Wishing he was back there now, so one of them could work the aching kink out of his shoulder, he rose to his feet and stretched his arms over his head. The Weaver looked unchanged, still sitting motionless and Art knew better than to disturb his body. If some kind of inner battle was taking place he needed to let the man be.

Knowing there was nothing to do now but wait, he was about to remove his jacket, just to allow for more stretching, when something caught his attention. Art was not sure it was the breathing or maybe there had been movement, but his eyes snapped to a dark area in the small room, shadowed by a massive wardrobe. The moon was casting light in through the huge skylight above them and despite the deep shadows Art could still see it.

Smaller than him, thin but lean muscled, stood a figure. All dark, skin like black alabaster, the thing looked at him with pitch hued eyes, no color only white irises. It scanned him, glowing just a little like the moon's surface. Shaped like a boy, perhaps a teenager, its scruffy hair cut wild. It wore a loose-sleeved shirt, vest and pants cropped at its shins, held up by suspenders. Unusual dress for a demon, but Art dismissed it as his hand slid to the knife at his hip.

He shifted a glance at the Weaver who was still entranced, unmoving save only his eyes fluttering slightly. Art would have to defend him against this thing. Slowly, he started to pull the knife, watching the thing in its crouched position. Shifting and moving, its eyes on Art, it looked to the window, then to the door as if it was watching for something. When the knife made a noise, starting to come out of its sheath, the thing whipped its attention back to Art and hissed, barring teeth, equally black as its body but twice as shiny, long canine fangs gleaming.

Art drew the knife quickly, and suddenly the thing was in motion. Sailing through the air with cat-like grace, it leapt up onto the top of the wardrobe and hissed at Art again, clawed hands touching lightly as it landed. Circling the room, Art moved with it, drawing his other knife, keeping an eye on the Weaver and demon both. It came to the end of the furniture and paused, with eyes glowing, clicking its tongue irritably at Art.

Frowning, the young man only watched. As high as it was, he would be at a disadvantage to attack. Yet he did not want to wait for the thing to jump on him. He thought about using some of his abilities to topple the wardrobe over. He was a fairly powerful telekinetic and could move things of that size, though how the Weaver would respond to Art destroying things in his home gave the man pause. He did not want to end up in the demon pit again.

Suddenly, the creature's eyes went from Art to the wall behind him. Art did not want to take his gaze off the thing, but he had to turn just a little to see what had caught its attention. Something was moving, churning, and shaking as if the shadow was turning the wall's wood into a soft amorphous plaster. Alarmed, Art turned slightly, trying to keep both wall and creature in sight.

The creature looked angry now, though, its eyes transfixed on the thing now seeping from the wall like a huge goo of black oils. Flopping onto the floor, it suddenly rose, the goo having a humanoid shape and face twisting out to give an eyeless scream. Art suddenly knew what the thing was; a type of demon known as the Oil of Despair. It was created by an immense collection of negative emotion of extreme hopelessness, given life over a long period of time, urged on by suicide and strong emotional regret soldered with pain.

These kinds of demons were never from a hell realm like possession demons, and could be dealt with by Weirimen, Blackenmancer hunters, or Scarborough Knights. Art was trained in dealing with the like, as such things could appear in haunted areas where possession often took place. There was the problem of what to do about the pitch-black creature behind him while dispatching the Oil of Despair demon at the same time.

Even before he could make that decision though, something happened that dropped Art to his knees. Pain roared through him, originating from deep within. He cried out, trying not to drop his blades but the pulse was so strong his hearing dimmed for a moment. Suddenly, the Weaver gave a great scream, his head dropping back and his eyes opening only to reveal they were rolled completely into the back of his head. White eyed, mouth open, black smoke puffed out of the Weaver's open mouth.

Art was as horrified as he was mystified when the pain blurred through him again and he could not hold onto his weapon. Clattering to the floor, Art's gloved hands went into his hair and he let out another short scream of agony.

"Give yourself over to me!" The Pith demon's voice wracked him from within, deafening inside his head. "You cannot resist me, boy!"

Art grit his teeth against the onslaught of pain and terror the thing was inducing within him. He could feel it moving around inside his mind's eye, hurting him, trying to force him back up into the psychic space within.

"No!" Art refused, tasting blood. "You're going back into my Weir!" He bit each word out, trying to force the thing back into its prison. He was hoping that with his knowledge of exorcising a Weir he could apply the same pressures to force this thing back.

"You are not strong enough to defeat me!" It bellowed. "Give me your soul!"

Art screamed aloud in protest, but fought against the feeling of it trying to tear him apart. Suddenly he felt aid, perhaps the Weaver? He kept pushing it back until the pain started to ease. It was going back inside to its prison. Its screams pulsed and just as it had come upon him, it let up. Art was shivering, breathing hard.

He had no time to recover, for when he looked up the oil demon was on him. A great slick, shambling mess of wails, faces, and black tendrils reaching for Art. The man leaned back, but his strength was gone. He felt his knees give and he crashed to the floor, nearly unconscious. Panic was mixing with his fading mind and his last thoughts were of the demon on the wardrobe as it dropped down to loom over him, hissing at the Oil of Disappear. He wondered which one of them was going to eat him.

Something was pushing on his mouth. It was not hard or rough but something was definitely pressing against his lips. It was the first thing that pulled him out of yet another haze of unconsciousness. He had hoped that next time he awoke he would not be in such tremendous pain. Reality was brutal as his head hammered, his body aching.

Willing his heavy eyes to open, hoping the thumping on his skull was just a headache and not the symptoms of something worse, his attention went to his mouth. Awake, his lips were more yielding and whatever it was that was trying to push its way past his full lips clinked against his teeth. He could taste the slight flavor of cherry candy. Confused, Art focused on the figure leaning over him.

It was a boy, possibly a teenager, black hair, blue eyes and a face that looked oddly familiar. Frowning, Art started to sit up, groaning with the effort and the thing at his mouth withdrew. It had been the boy. He had been trying to push something into Art's mouth, and now the Weiriman understood. The boy was trying to aid him in suppressing the demon by giving him the candy he had gotten from the Shadow Confectionary.

"Why didn't you take that before I examined you?!" the Weaver's angry voice was suddenly behind him. "That thing almost killed me and you! Why didn't you tell me you had that Scarlet Extinction before?!"

"I didn't know you needed to know!" Art barked back, hating how the loud tone of the Weaver's voice was bouncing off his ear drums like the man was actually boxing his ears.

"Stupid Weirimen! They were always so stupid. I tried to teach them, but they just ended up being narrow minded, limited, and stupid!"

Art was rubbing the back of his neck to try and ease the dull pain flooding down his head when the boy was crouching next to him again. Wild-cropped hair and a handsome face with large eyes, he smiled at Art and held up the candy again, nodding. Uncertain what to make of the lad, Art took the sweet from him and starred for a moment longer. The boy proceeded to mimic the eating of it, seeming to think Art did not know what to do with the shiny red thing. Starting to crack a smile, Art experienced a recognition, looking at the boy's shirt, vest and suspender clipped pants.

"You're that black creature from before!" He suddenly exclaimed.

The events from shortly before he passed out came rushing back and he twisted around painfully to see what had become of the Oil of Despair demon. The only clue that it was ever present was a dark shadow on the wall, from which it had been hanging, and another in the spot Art had last seen it oozing its way over to him. Seeing his blade on the ground near him, Art reached for it, when the Weaver was right there, slapping his hand hard.

"What are you doing?!" The man snapped.

"Ow!" Art barked, pulling his hand back. "What are you doing?!"

"You attacked Lucid! You're not thinking about doing that again, are you?! I'll rip your head off right here and leave you for the demons beyond the Veil to find! You remember that, Weiriman!"

"I didn't attack him," Art protested. "I thought...," he looked to the boy who was still crouching near him, though he had moved a few feet away when Art had exclaimed. "I thought he was a demon that had come to attack us. You said this room is inside the Veil and I was warned I would be attracting demons now that my Weir is open."

"Well, we are and you do. We should get out of this room," the Weaver snapped, standing again, and running a hand through his silvery hair, still visibly irritated with Art. "But that's why Lucid is here. He was protecting us while we were in your mind. You were going to attack your protector, you moron."

The Weaver swept by him and blustered out of the room. Art sat on the floor for a moment longer, tired out by the events of the past few hours, days, and the antics of the odd man. Sighing, he turned his head towards the boy again, who had not followed the Weaver, but stayed with Art. He gave Art a smile and motioned again that he should eat the candy. Giving a slight, tired smile Art obeyed and popped the candy into his mouth. Flavor exploded on his tongue and he was surprised by the texture and actual pleasantness of the little sweet.

"Scarlet Extinction, this is called?" Art said to the boy as he got up.

Lucid nodded continuing to smile and coming to a full stand as well. He was the same as he had been before but his skin was no longer the rich ebony, like midnight. Now, he was pale, similar in skin tone to Art. He wondered if he also did not get out in the sun much. Art was notorious for staying inside to study, while others enjoyed the daylight hours. The boy's eyes looked mostly normal, with the exception that they were the lightest pale blue with a translucency to them that Art had not seen before. He was almost like an inverted version of the dark creature he saw before.

"Your name is Lucid?" Art asked and the young man nodded. "I'm sorry I scared you before. I thought you were something bad. I do appreciate you protecting us though."

Lucid gave him a big grin and stuck his hands into his pockets, looking pleased with himself. The simple act of the honest smile made Art do the same, though his was still small and tired. "Don't talk much do you?"

"He hardly talks at all," the Weaver snapped, reappearing in the doorway. "Get out of there, both of you before Art attracts another demon. And eat one of those candy twists. I won't be having demons attacking my house tonight. I'm already spent enough, dealing with that thing inside your Weirs. I never thought I'd see that monster again in this life time!"

He whipped back out the door again leaving Art to ponder the mess of cryptic things he had just alluded to. Cindervail had said the Weaver had been present for the one recorded incident of a Pith demon on record. Did that mean that the demon in Art's mind was the same as the one in the incomplete history? Brimming with questions, Art followed after him quickly, the boy in tow.

It took Art a few minutes to find the Weaver. His house was much bigger than it appeared from the outside, full of rooms and strange spaces filled with life and things Art did not have time to inspect. Ultimately, Lucid had to lead the way. The pair found the man in a low ceilinged back room. Twisting tree trunks lined the far wall under which were dozens of huge pillow seats. The Weaver was curled up in one, mumbling angrily to himself.

"There you are!" He barked as soon as Art entered. "Where have you been?! We need to talk about this."

Knowing that protesting that he had no idea where the man had disappeared to in a foreign house he had never been in, would only make the Weaver more unpredictably annoyed, Art said nothing. Moving past the hanging lights that looked more like vines and mushrooms than real fixtures, Art came to stand before the man. Not looking at him, the Weaver motioned for the Weiriman to sit down, Lucid taking to a chair in between them.

"So, you battled the demon. Did it possess you?" Art asked after a long moment in which the Weaver said nothing, only gazed out of the large round window sitting before him.

"It tried," the Weaver spat, still angry about the incident. "But, I'm not that easy to possess and the thing is tied to you. Had it been free of you completely, it could have had a chance at devouring me."

"Tied to me?"

The Weaver nodded. "It's trapped in your Weirs. The events you witnessed in your mind when I touched with the thing was the ritual performed to trap it."

"And you were there for this?" Art pressed.

"Not the actual ritual," the Weaver corrected, squinting as if trying hard to remember. "It was so long ago but if I remember correctly, I made the lantern. If we had that maybe…"

"You mean this?" Art took his pack off and pulled the lantern from the compartment he had it stowed in.

"Yes!" the Weaver exclaimed, sitting up, a smile spreading across his face. "Where did you get that?!"

"The Weirimen Guild had it stored in the Wine Vault at the Seminary."

"I'm surprised they could be counted upon to safe keep this all these years. I thought I left it with someone, can't think of who."

Art noted the Weaver, unlike most people, did not think highly of the Weirimen. He wanted to know the reasons. What had caused the falling out between the fey-descended and the Guild? But this was not the time nor the place. He needed answers about his problem first.

The Weaver took the lantern in hand and turned it over. Inspecting its condition and function, he placed it on the floor and watched as it transformed from hand lantern to standing and back again when he picked it up. It was then Art noticed the slot in the top of the lantern shaped as if to sheath a blade. The events of the imprisonment of the demon flashed back through his mind. This was the original lantern, the slot was meant for the dagger that had pierced the two Weirimen.

"I don't understand what happened." Art confessed. "I saw the lantern, the ritual and then the two Weirimen used a knife to kill themselves. With the knife and this lantern that somehow sealed the demon, right? So why is it inside me and not in this lantern? And why do I have an abnormal Weir?"

The Weaver was quiet a long time, thinking, rubbing a hand over his silver mustache.

"The lantern and the blade were only tools to help deliver the demon to its prison. The demon had to be housed inside at least two Weirs, but why it is in you and not inside the lantern with the Weirs…," he paused again and then grew wide eyed. "It's not possible!" He blurted out before rising and shoving the lantern back into Art's hands.

"What?" Art begged to know. "What are you talking about?! What's not possible?!"

The Weaver did not wait to listen, instead he was rushing out the door, Lucid right behind him. Screwing his face up with irritation and confusion, Art stuffed the lantern back in his pack and took off after the others.

"Wait!" He called as they disappeared down a hallway.

Art had to jog after them until they arrived at what could only be described as a workshop of the most strange. Several levels all connected with tree carved stairs and hanging baskets that moved up and down like lifts. A water wheel was half inside the room, bringing in water from a small stream outside, irrigating standing beds and hanging contraptions of all manner of plants. Fairies were at work, flitting back and forth, doing what Art could only guess at. Books, jars, cages, and an enormous variety of raw components such as: metals, wood, wire, and their like were neatly stacked, housed, and collected in shelves, bins, and any other form of storage Art could imagine. The Weaver lived up to his reputation as the greatest inventor in Haunted Weir Workings history.

Awed, Art said nothing, only heading to the Weaver, spying Lucid sitting high on a spiral stairs above them. He smiled at Art who nodded, but his attention went to the Weaver who was pouring over a book so large it would have been a two arm full just to carry it.

"Sir, what did you—"

"Shush!" The Weaver ordered and continued to look over his book. Turning many pages, he stopped at one with an illustration of the knife Art had seen used with the lantern. "Here!" The Weaver grinned, pointing to it. "This is Weir Hewn! I also helped make this blade. You will need this and the lantern."

"To imprison the demon?" Art frowned, looking at the long, silver and red blade.

"Oh no." The Weaver shook his head, looking serious. "Like I said before, the demon is fused with you, boy. You first must cut this thing from your soul. Only then will you even worry about containing it. Because now that your Weir is opened, it is only a matter of time before it gets out and you two will do battle for your body and soul. You'll lose, of course, at this rate. But that's not important right now."

"Not important right now?" Art's eyes were huge, his brow heavy with frown.

"No, the first order of business is to get the knife, and cut this demon from yourself."

"So, where is the knife?" Art was almost afraid to ask.

"Oh well, it's close," the Weaver said, not looking at Art. "I hid it in the Woods of Reaching."

"You did what?!" Art was trying not to sound too angry.

"It's a dangerous blade," the Weaver defended himself with no apology. "It has the ability to cut a Haunting Weir out of someone and other such uses."

"Why would you make something like that?!"

"It has practical uses!" The Weaver crossed his arms, looking boyish. "Look at you! You need it, don't you? Pretty glad I made it now, aren't you?!"

Art wanted to say he did not know about that since he had no idea how the lantern, knife, and his soul would work together to rid him of the Pith demon locked inside him.

"So I have to go into the Woods of Reaching to find this thing?"

The Weaver nodded. "It is located at the heart of the wood in a great tree known as the Willow's Unrest."

"Is it easy to get to? Do you have a map?"

The Weaver shook his head. "But Lucid can guide you. Come dawn, you two will head there. I hope you are a better Weiriman than you let on. Falling into my front yard trap makes you seem like a noob of a Weiriman, bottom of the barrel quality. Because if you aren't, this will be a short trip for Lucid and a very ugly end for you."

Chapter Eight
The Woods of Reaching

Art had never expected his quest to take such a dramatic turn. But as Lucid donned boots, pack, and a short cloak, the Weaver added to the growing list.

"When you get the knife, don't come back here."

"What? Why? I'll have the lantern and the knife so—"

"Don't interrupt as if you have anything of value to add to this situation, because you know nothing about anything."

"But you do," Art jumped in, growing tired of the Weaver's attitude. "And you've hardly told me anything! What do you know about this Pith demon?"

"I am getting to that, boy," the Weaver, glared as he stuffed food into Lucid's pack. Art noticed the boy's vest, shirt and even cap had an open hole in the back which seemed purposely sewn in that manner. The opening displayed a large tattoo, a circle twisted to form a giant dream catcher.

Curious, but having other issues, he dismissed it and went on to say, "Do you know the demon's name?"

The Weaver shook his head. "I never did learn it. If they knew it, they didn't tell me. Demons names do me little good. I don't exorcise people."

"But once I get this knife and lantern and cut the demon out of my soul, aren't you going to be exorcising me?"

The Weaver threw his head back and laughed. "Is that what you thought? Well, Weirimen really can be so stupid. Of course not. I'm no exorcist. I may have helped found the early Weirimen Guild, back then they were made of real grit and skill, but I'm not built for exorcism."

"But you exorcised the demon out of you!"

The Weaver dropped a look on him as if Art had said the most obstinate thing imaginable.

"I forced the demon, who was still attached to your soul and Weirs, back into your mind. It hadn't taken full hold of me. I'm not so vulnerable that I can't push something out of my mind when I don't want it there!"

Art did not really see the difference, since that was basically the first step of self-exorcism. But he decided to stop arguing.

"Well, if you're not going to exorcise me what am I going to do?"

"Worry about that later," the Weaver chuckled. "First you need to find the knife, second you must have the demon's name."

"I thought you didn't know the demon's name."

The Weaver blew air hard out of his nose, cocked a hand on his hip and saying with exacerbation, "That's why you have to find it, you dolt!"

Art chewed on the inside of his cheek. "Where do I even start to learn this thing's name? The Guild's library had no information, according to my professors."

"Go to the Consciatosium."

Art blinked, surprised. "That's a myth."

"It is not!" the Weaver chided.

"A great library of all knowledge of the world beyond the Veil and demonic information assembled by mysterious forces? It does not even sound real."

"It is real," the Weaver insisted. "I have been there."

"How do I get there?" Art asked flatly. "Is it close?"

The Weaver shook his head. "No, but you're resourceful. I can't remember the city it is in. But once there Lucid can guide you to its door. If you make it out of the Woods of Reaching alive, that should be your next stop."

"Great," Art's tone remained flat.

"Just concentrate on one task at a time, boy. You better be more talented than you seem. Someone so dull witted will never make it out of the Woods alive. The forces in there will be trying to eat you and your soul and that demon will be ready and waiting for when you become weak. So keep that in mind too. And for the sake of the Muses, would you use those Umbra Sweets if you need them? That's what they are for. But don't over use. You'll run out and that thing will eat you before you even make it to the library."

"Thanks." Art did not need the reminder.

"And you better take good care of Lucid. Don't let any harm come to him and don't let the Guild take him. If you allow the Weirimen to imprison or take him for any reason, I'll hunt you down and take your head. He is in your charge and will be kept safe at all cost. Do you accept this responsibility?"

"Why would they imprison him? The Guild is not in the habit of imprisoning people, some demons…." Art looked at the boy, who only blinked at him with his large pale eyes. "He can't be a demon, I would have sensed it by now. Surely, he is not possessed. I would know that too."

"Of course he is neither of those two things." The Weaver glared. "But, is he made of something that the Weirimen might not approve of."

"Made of something?" Art was confused.

"Lucid Dreamare is a dreamcatcher."

Art frowned. He had not heard of that kind of fey, fairy, or other reference other than an actual dream catcher: a tool used to trap nightmares. People often used them to keep tiny demons out of their dreams and sometimes Shadow Confectioners used their energy to make Umbra Sweets.

"Is that some kind of special fey?" Art asked, thinking of nothing else, but did note the tattoo on the boy's back was indeed a dreamcatcher.

"No," the Weaver explained. "Lucid is an actual dreamcatcher. I had acquired a great and powerful dreamcatcher many years ago from a Pitch Threader. Over time, it caught so many nightmares that it actually took on its own consciousness."

Art's eyes were huge. "It did what now?"

"I know it was remarkable!" The Weaver was grinning, looking at Lucid as if he were a prized child. "With all the negative energy and dreams something else manifested, something to balance the darkness."

"This boy is the balance to the darkness that the dreamcatcher caught? He has a soul?"

"More bright and more pure than yours or mine. Sometimes life answers the dark call of death or evil by giving the world a balance."

"But I saw him all black before," Art said remembering the scary form Lucid took with the onyx skin and long clawed hands.

"He has two forms. The one you see now, the dream form, and then there is the nightmare form. That is the one you saw before. Using the power of the nightmares within him, he is a great weapon against evil. He will be the only way you can sleep at night. You will be at greater and greater risk the longer you live with this demon clawing its way out of you. Lucid will protect you as you sleep from the things that come to feed from you. Even though you have an abnormal Weir, you are still bleeding life while it is open, boy. Lucid will protect you but you must protect him. The Guild might not look kindly on a boy with nightmare powers. They did not like items that developed a mind of their own, that were created from evil but emanate light. They never trusted that process. And for that I left them. Life is about balance, young Weiriman. Great good can be born out of great evil. We have often seen the reverse. But I believe the forces of good have just as much power against the darkness, and sometimes it is the only answer to the darkest of questions."

Art was staring at Lucid, who only blinked at him quietly with lagoon blue eyes. The Weirimen could sense nothing but good things from the boy, no demonic energy, nothing evil. Had he not seen the nightmare form himself, he could not believe this pleasant person harbored the darkest nightmare powers inside. But looking at the boy, Art could not see allowing any harm to come to him. He was a pure soul as any other a Weiriman should protect.

"You have my word, Sir. As a Weiriman I should have been, and as a decent man, I will protect him."

"Good," The Weaver nodded and turned to Lucid saying, "You will take good care of each other. You are brothers, all right?"

Lucid acknowledged, smiling broadly. He leaned in and gave the Weaver a great embrace. "Thank you, Father," he said in a gentle voice. "I will protect him."

"When you have the name and the knife, come back here," the Weaver instructed once they were outside and passed the pit. He bid a farewell and went back inside, not watching them go.

Dawn was just arching over the forest. Art had slept little the night before, still plagued by strange nightmares but it did not matter much to him yet. He had functioned just fine on less sleep, through some of the trials and tests at the Seminary. The words of the Weaver floating through him again and again as he and his new companion made their way through the Other Side Woods. He knew demons were far more active at night, but he had yet to truly experience what his new condition and midnight might combine to make.

The sun was not even half way through the sky when they exited the Other Side Woods, finding the country trail that Art had departed from to find the Weaver. It felt like a long time ago, though it had only been one night. He was tired all of a sudden, and knew that would not serve him at all.

"Let's have some lunch," Art suggested, which made Lucid grin widely.

Finding a nice spot near the side of the road, they sat. Lucid prepared the sandwiches and some fruit. Art only nibbled at his food, noticing he had lost most of his appetite since the stew lunch a day ago. Hopefully, it was temporary and brought on by stress but Art had a sneaking suspicion it was related to his condition. Noting that, he tried to eat a little more, despite his lack of hunger for it.

With the day nearly at the half gone point, it was hard to decide what to do. Going in the woods at night seemed like a very bad idea. The haunted place was dangerous enough in the middle of the day, but at night Art imagined it would be a great deal more like a layer of hell than a forest wood. Waiting half a day and another night did also seem like another very bad idea. He was on a timeline and there was no real idea how long he could withstand the demon. It was unclear how much he should risk.

The forest beyond was dimming, even though the sun was still casting more than enough light to penetrate the haze. The fog gathering around the skinny trees was definitely not natural. Art was frowning. The same whispering he had heard when he first passed the wood called to him once more. Only now, instead of just soft voices, he heard humming as well. It was haunting but also somewhat beautiful. His fist clenched. Either the woods had a special effect that made the sounds of evil temping or Art was being tempted because of the great evil in him. He had to fight against this change. He was not going to let evil seduce him.

Feeling angry, his stomach knotting so the nourishment he had just taken in tasted sour, he felt at a loss as what to do. Usually cautious, but not normally paralyzed by doubt, Art stood stressing over his next move when Lucid came up next to him. The boy looked at the Weiriman, then to the forest, and then back to Art.

Art hardly took notice of him, staring so hard at the forest his eyes were starting to brim gold. Lucid, frowned slightly with worry, thinking for a moment to himself. Then, as if all had been made clear, the boy smiled and started into the woods. As he passed, Art was jogged out of his frustrating thoughts to see the boy heading towards the woods.

"Hang on," he called, gathering up his pack before pulling his hood back up.

Lucid slowed a little but did not wait. Art caught up and seeing the confidence in the boy's eyes, allowed Lucid to lead him into the forest.

The border of the woods was felt, rather than seen. Instantly, the temperature difference could be felt and both Weiriman and boy shivered at the sudden loss of heat. The fog gathered in great billowing puffs of slate tasting breezes. Had Art not walked into the wood in the middle of the day, he would have thought it was an ashy evening, everything a slight teal gray and muted.

Art did not wish to linger and hurried them along the path that was quickly narrowing to something more like a trail of dried dirt made for fleet footed creatures, rather than booted travelers. The trees were growing ever denser, blocking out more and more sunlight with their shriveled black and brown leaves. Art could taste the taint in the air like old tin. The place was heavily touched.

"You know where we are going, right?" Art asked Lucid as they turned at a crossroads of strange and twisted little paths.

Lucid nodded and pausing for only a moment, pointed in a direction and beckoned Art to follow. Art wanted to know how the boy knew where they were going, but the close narrowness of the woods and the growing feeling of being watched kept him quiet. They just needed to reach their destination as soon as possible. He hoped they would not be woods-deep by the time the sun winked its last light out of the sky and the night opened the world up to all array of ugly possibilities.

Moving along, their boots rustling in the growing thickness of the underbrush, Art thought he heard an odd sound. It had been quick and had it not been for the thick silence of the wood, he was not sure he would have noticed it at all. Before his senses could tell him to dismiss it, the sound happened again, a strange sort of hollow slap. Art slowed his stride just a little, reaching out to Lucid and tapping him on the shoulder. The noise happened once more, and the boy heard it too.

Lowering his head just slightly, both man and boy scanned the woods, caution driving their breathing to quiet even more.

All the talk of the woods being full of the kind of mysteries that killed travelers, ensnared Weirimen, and led fully aware adults to disappearance, trickled back to Art's memories but he tried to shut them out. Giving into fear would only make him vulnerable, but a touch of it just might spark his instincts to save his life. He had to maintain the balance.

Again, the sound drew their attention but it was almost recognizable like a slap of a hand on something hard. It happened again, loud and deliberate, and close. Getting antsy now, Art finally spotted something that only gave rise to a whole new set of terrifying questions.

Nearby stood a tall, thin tree. It looked sickly like all the others, its form bent and twisted as if by some blight. But it was not its pathetic shape or the droopy branches that had Art looking horrified and confused. On the trunk of the dull wood were sets of pale, almost white blue hands. They were just gripping the tree tightly, the muscle almost too tense with the effort to hold on. Flexed but unmoving, Art thought there had to be two people standing behind the tree. But leaning back just a little to get a slightly different perspective, it became clear there was no one standing behind it. The hands were completely disembodied, seeming to grow at bent, awkward angles out of the tree itself.

"Oh, that's not good," Art mumbled under his breath, going for one of his knives.

Alarm panged in both Art and Lucid when another hand sprang from what appeared to be nothing and gripped the tree, the others moving and twitching a few moments before settling in place, one above another in some form of horrible totem pole. Art was unfamiliar with the apparition, creature, or some terrible combination thereof and, was not at all interested to find out.

Turning, he and Lucid started down the little path only to be greeted by the same phenomenon happening on another tree, now closer to them. Startled for a moment, the Weiriman frowned and Lucid tilted his head just slightly, looking curiously at the hands. But when he moved just a hair closer several more popped out, all wriggling and grabbing at the boy like maggots in a gut. Lucid yelped and jumped back in surprise, flashing white and black eyes and fanged teeth.

Art stepped forward and took him by the arm, his step falling into a jog as the trees around them all came to life with the gripping hands, flailing, clawing and grasping at the pair. Art let go of the boy who fell into a run behind him, allowing Art to draw both blades. The path all but disappeared and they were running through more waving hands than branches. Slicing and cutting, Art tried to get them through to a clearing.

"Which way?" He got out between blows and breaths.

Lucid, pushing and fighting off the hands trying to pull his hair and tear at his cloak, whipped his head back and forth a moment and then exclaimed, "Brother! This way!"

Art followed his lead cutting more hands which dropped onto the ground still wiggling, but not seeming to be made of flesh. They did not bleed. Climbing a small incline in the forest, the hands did not dissipate. Soon they were embroiled in them again, some tearing at their faces and throats. Lucid whimpered when one grasped him hard, nails digging into his neck. Clawing at his face, it started his change, pupils going white again, whites turning black.

"Don't fight them." Art was suddenly at his side chopping arms away, releasing both the boy's throat and clothing from their grips. "Just push on!"

Lucid obeyed and stayed close to Art who hacked his way to another clearing.

"We won't last long like this," the Weiriman took a breather, wiping a cut on his cheek. "Are we close?"

Lucid looked into another part of the forest, still full of arms but he seemed to sense something beyond them. He gave Art a grin and pointed, excitedly. Art returned the smile and stood again.

"All right, I'll start by cutting in. Guide me the best you can. I'll try to protect you."

Lucid nodded and Art was surprised by the easy trust that had sprung up between them. He had never worked all that well with people before. Yet, he had no time to dwell on the thought and started into the grasping, whirling arms to make their path.

Art was not sure how much longer he and Lucid could go on, when he felt a distinct chill rush over him like hot water on cold limbs. He physically shivered as they burst from the woods into a fog ridden clearing. The hands behind them stopped moving as the pair headed away from the woods. All sound grew strangely dull in the growing closeness of fog, air, and cold.

Cautiously, they went into the thick mist, a gray and white so dense Art could hardly see two feet before him. He still had his knives out, ready for anything, when Lucid grabbed his arm and they stopped. The fog started to dissipate and before them lay a small mote circling a great and terrible tree. Awing, the thing rose to massive height, bent, and twisted as if the willow had grown to a staggering size and shape and then suddenly lost its will to live and sagged back to the earth in strange and lazy forms of trunk and branches. The branches were rolling and contorted, making knots and odd shapes with their lamented growth.

"This has to be Willow's Unrest," he muttered, eyeing the thing. "So where is this 'Weir Hewn'?"

Scanning, he was disturbed by the lumps and shaping of the tree's roots and branches resembling bodies, even faces, in small ways. Trying to ignore the growing unrest rising within him, Art started to take a step onto the ice when a feeling flared up in him. He pulled his foot back. The ice was moving, just a little, or something just below its surface was. Seeing Lucid starting to do the same thing, he pulled the boy back.

"Wait, something is wrong." He pointed and Lucid took a step back even further.

It was not ice at all. It was an illusion, similar to the Weaver's pit. Art tried to suppress the smug smile at the corner of his mouth. He was not about to fall for the Weaver's trick a second time.

"Your father is not above using a good trick twice, hm?"

Lucid gave a wide smile and nodded. Art returned to thinking how much he did not really like the Weaver. He could have warned Art about the trap, but if the Weiriman said anything he knew the Weaver would take it as whining and likely make comment about how Art should be more talented, or observant, or maybe completely clairvoyant.

Putting that in the back of his mind, Art tried to assess what their next move would need to be. The ice mote completely circled the tree and there appeared to be no way around the thing. Art could not jump that far nor could he fly. Spotting a fallen tree, he had an idea. Going to the thing, he rooted in his pack for something as Lucid watched curiously.

Pulling out a device that looked like a rolled up whip, Art smiled saying, "This thing is called a Light Load. Wrapping it around what you are trying to move, it shifts the thing just slightly beyond the Veil. Their weight and matter feel different, so it, in a sense, lightens the load of what you are moving. Weirimen use it when trying to remove obstacles or dead bodies of demons and monsters."

Lucid beamed, nodding to indicate he understood. Taking one end, he and Art encircled the fallen log, and with some effort got it tied off. Energy glittered down the rope and seeped into the tree. After a moment Art anchored his boots into the earth and pulled. Much lighter than it would have been, the tree moved, nudging out of its shallow dip in the ground. Adjusting his grip again, Art heaved the thing towards the frozen mote, and yanking it hard, slid it out onto the ice. A flick of the wrist and the Light Load released and whipped back into its folded circle in his glove.

Art gave the thing a kick with his foot but the log, now back at its normal weight, did not budge. Removing his pack, his eyes mapped the best way he thought he should cross.

"Not bad, huh?" He flashed a smile at Lucid who returned it, nodding enthusiastically. "You stay here. I'm going over to that tree."

Before he went, Lucid patted him on the bicep then pointed to the dark knot only a few branches up the tree.

"What? Is the knife there? You can sense it?"

Lucid confirmed.

"All right. I'll get it," Art promised and climbed onto the fallen tree.

Steadying himself he headed across, being careful of the broken branches and his long jacket. All was well until about halfway across the log suddenly started to move. Alarmed, Art dropped to his knee for more balance as the thing started to shimmy and jump. Thinking that perhaps the tree had reaching arms starting to pop out, but then realized that was not the case.

Lucid called, "Brother! Brother!" over and over again and pointed to what Art was already looking at.

The frozen "water" was not water at all. It rolled and twisted, rising out and up like icicles. The higher they got the more their tops looked like heads until they sprang arms and gripped the tree. The one nearest Art twisted its strange top around, and his eyes widened as the thing's muddied gray face broke into a scream, empty eyes and huge maw.

Getting to his feet, Art broke into a run as the icy beings swiped and grabbed for him. Every place they touched the tree it turned to brittle ice, some even shattering as Art dashed across. He stumbled but caught his footing and diving the last few feet to avoid a large creature, he leapt onto the island of dirt the Willow's Unrest occupied. He rolled over and looked back, the creatures continuing to wail in frustration.

Breathing a little hard, Art did not waste time, worrying they might be able to come out of their frozen mote. He sprang to his feet and started to climb the tree. Its bent and strange form made it easier for Art to find footholds and before long he was at the knot Lucid had indicated. Uncertain what to do, but driven on by the wails of the creatures below, he felt around the thing with his glove until he felt something move. Drawing his hand back, the knot seemed to slip just a little in the tree and a trick door in the wood opened. Peering inside, Art saw the glint of a blade in the little alcove.

Uncertain if he should reach in, he made a rash decision and stuck his hand inside. Half expecting it to get bitten off, Art was extremely relieved when he pulled both hand and weapon out unharmed. It looked just like the drawing Art had seen at the Weaver's, but even more beautiful. He pulled it from its sheath to inspect it. Undamaged by time, the long knife gleamed along the silver metal, a blood red vein of colored gem or shell woven in.

Knowing this was the wrong time to be admiring the coveted artifact, Art stuffed it in his belt, making sure it was secure and headed down the tree. The creatures were tossing about the water madly, angry, and agitated. The log was still laying across the mote, patches of it in treacherous ice. He could not see how he would make it across again with the things fully awake and all waiting for him.

Thinking hard, Art went through every lesson, every drill, anything he could think of from his schooling. He had not read anything about creatures like this, not knowing if they were demonic or some other form, but he did have an idea. Inching closer, he neared the one closest the tree. It roared at him, sending cold air icing over his face, but smelling slightly sour and rotten. It made Art think these things might be touched or tainted in some way. This gave his idea even more merit.

Standing just out of reach, first making sure the creature could not grab him where he stood, Art centered himself. The whispering of the woods had dimmed in his ears since the reaching arms had come to life, one demonic presence over shadowing another. This aided him now, able to hear nothing but his own thoughts. He started to bring up his own energy, his own life force. Weirimen could control the flow of their own life's spirit.

Just as he felt his focus come into the perfect alignment with this goal, Art heard a deep voice ripple through him like a hand over his cheek. It spoke his name, gently, cooing-like. A wave of sick passed over him. It was the demon. He had to ignore it.

"I can taste the rise of your life within you." It continued the rumble of its voice making his gut tremble. "Release me."

Art ignored it again. He went back to his task. He had to focus. Suddenly Lucid yelled to him and Art's eyes opened just in time to miss a piece of the log narrowly sail past his head. He could not afford to stay there. They would tear his bridge up or actually hit him with it.

"Release me, child," the demon cooed again, the soft tone contrasting with the ugly slime of the voice.

"Leave me be, demon." Art grit his teeth and forced the voice from his mind. It took more effort than he wanted, but he went back to his task again.

Focusing his life's energy, he removed a glove and held his hand out towards the creature before him. It could almost be seen, just the whisper of spirit move from man to monster. Slightly gold hued, it hummed as it poured over the thing and out of Art. He shut it off quickly and waited to see its effect. Almost instantaneous, the ice the thing was made of turned liquid and the monster broke into a cascade of water, running into the others, causing them to also melt.

Art knew he did not have much time. He had not shared enough life to dispel the demon for long. Running up and onto the log, the first creature was already taking ice form again as his boot passed its reaching arm. He dashed across the log-bridge, the thing breaking and crumbling under him; ice patches cracking and bursting, making it even more unstable. Trying to be careful but quick, Art ran across as the monsters were coming back to ice, roaring and wailing angrily.

Just at the end his boot slipped on an ice patch and caught in the tree. Falling forward he righted himself quickly. He was so close to the other side. Tangling with his boot, an arm of ice reared up, crashing down towards him. Lucid was suddenly there. Combining efforts, man and boy tore Art's boot free of the tree's pit and they flung themselves out of the creature's reach.

Breathing hard on the other side, the pair watched as the creatures howled their frustration. Then suddenly, like a vacuum, the cold mote seemed to suck them up, making a clean, perfect, and undisturbed circle of ice once more. The tree lay in pieces and ruins, the only evidence that anyone had breeched the treacherous field where the ice monsters lay in wait, now once more in their prison.

Chapter Nine
Deadly Forest Knight

Weir Hewn was a marvelous weapon. Art pulled it out of his belt as he rose and brushed off the dirt and dead leaves. Slightly longer than his other knives, its balance was perfect; the blade sharper than anything he had ever seen. It could likely cut a single hair out of the air. Art tried not to grin. He had never seen a blade so finely crafted or anything that fit in his grip so well. He could not help but say the name aloud.

Lucid was next to him, eyes pouring over the weapon as well, smiling as Art was.

"Want to see it?" Art offered and the boy nodded, taking it carefully in his hands. His fingerless gloves allowed him to touch the stunning detail of the designs on the sheath, admiring, as Art did, the craftsmanship.

"Your father may be a loon, but he sure does make beautiful things."

Lucid chuckled and agreed, handing the blade back to Art. The man, having recovered his pack, started to place it inside next to the lantern when he had a thought.

"Do you know if I'm allowed to use this?"

Lucid nodded vigorously, shaking his wildly cropped hair and bangs up and down with the motion.

"There won't be anything bad that happens? I'm allowed to wield it like a normal blade?"

Again Lucid nodded, mimicked a slicing act with his hand and then pointed to Art with even more nodding. Art took the boy at his word and standing again, removed his more dominate knife and slid Weir Hewn in its place, fastening it to the waist-high holster. Again, he went to put the knife in his pack but had another thought.

"Can you use this?" He looked at Lucid who cocked his head a little to one side. "Do you know how to fight with a knife?"

Lucid looked at the blade and then with both hands pushed them together, leaving a small space between.

"A little?"

The boy nodded.

"All right, well why don't you take this? I know you have abilities, but having a weapon is also good too." He leaned down and fastened it to the boy's belt. "If we have time on the way I'll show you a few things. I'm good with a blade. I'll teach you."

Lucid seemed overwhelmingly happy and surprised Art by saying out loud, "Thank you, Brother!"

Art chuckled and nodded. "Why do you call me Brother? You can call me Art."

Lucid's face became very serious. "We are brothers. We are very alike."

He said no more and Art decided it was enough for now. Perhaps it was just another odd thing the Weaver thought, and his words had a heavy impact on the boy. He never did learn Art's name so perhaps that's all he gave to Lucid when he made them traveling companions. Art did not think them very similar.

"You are coming with me now, right?"

"I go with Brother, yes," Lucid nodded, looking happy again, which made Art smile. The boy would be positive company, something Art felt he would be sorely needing before long. A shiver ran through him again thinking of the demon and before they planned their next move he retrieved the Umbra Sweet twist and munched it down. Both the encounter with the demon in his mind and the ice moat had left him feeling more tired than he would have liked. He hoped the candy would help mask his Weir's scent as they progressed through the haunted wood.

"Any ideas on how to get out of here?" Art said once he had finished his candy and replaced his gloves.

Adjusting his cloak and hood, Art glanced at where Lucid should have been. The boy was no longer by his side but standing just beyond the reach of the arm-filled trees. Crouching, animal-like the boy's attention was on something in the woods. Walking up to Lucid, he peered into the forest. The darkness had rapidly fallen and the haze of the day was now a mixing fog and twilight.

"We have not been in here that long," Art murmured. "It could not possibly be nightfall."

"The moat and tree," Lucid spoke softly, "it holds time."

Art was confused at first but then recalled the "holds time" term from his classes. Some places in the world had pockets that time either traveled faster or slower. Often they centered around places of great magic or great evil. Being at

Willow's Unrest had robbed them of the day and now they were on the verge of night. Art had hoped they would be out of the woods by the time night fell.

"We need to get out of here before the demons of the night come out," Art said, his eyes scanning the area for an opening with less arms.

"Too late," Lucid said before doing something that made Art step back a foot.

Peeling out of his cloak and pack, Lucid hunched forward, rolling his shoulders. The dreamcatcher tattoo on his flesh flexed with the movement of his muscles but then took on a motion all its own. The woven strands of thread and twine that made up the circular form of the design lifted and started to unwind from one another, as if Lucid's back was a screen for a moving motion picture. Astonished, Art watched as the threads traveled up and over the boy's shoulders before spreading all over his body in growing black sketched lines until Lucid was completely wrapped in them, like a thread mummy.

It was only a moment more before all the threads fused together and blended into his skin like water colors on an artist's canvas. When the boy opened his eyes again his skin was onyx black, his iris white. He had become the nightmare form of himself. Fanged teeth and black hair, Lucid turned his handsome face into one, that now bore such a haunting look.

"Run that way." He pointed with a long clawed hand. "I will follow after. The path will lead out."

"That's the opposite of the way we came," Art protested before he heard a pack of low growling, rumbling up through the woods. The hands on the trees in the direction in which Lucid had been looking had disappeared, pulled back into their tree trunks.

"That way. Go now." Lucid said nothing more but turned towards whatever was now rushing through the woods at them.

Art obeyed, hoping the boy knew what he was doing. He snatched up Lucid's cloak, rolling it before attaching it to his bag. Pulling his blades, he rushed into the woods cutting arms that grabbed for him as he went. He heard a fight start up behind him: growling, snapping jaws, the wrestle of bodies in the leaves. He hated leaving the boy. But he had to trust him, knowing he might be a hindrance to Lucid.

The narrow path was barely visible in the darkness of the wood. Pulling up his facemask, Art whipped out a pair of goggles from a side pocket on his bag and pulled them on, cutting his way through more arms. Flashing red before dimming again to just red glass, the goggles enabled him to see better in the low light. The arms were starting to thin and he had only received minor cuts and clawing on his way out. Art was counting himself lucky. The forest might be coming to an opening or an end soon.

He was right. The space between trees grew and soon he burst out of the woods into the night, running at full sprint through a meadow bathed in moonlight. The heaviness of the forest was leaving him, the whispers dimming. Art was smiling behind his mask and starting to slow when he entered another wood.

It was not like the Woods of Reaching. He felt no malevolent presence, heard no voices. He wanted to stop there and wait for Lucid but there was another problem. It was fast, so fast that Art had just barely enough time to duck and roll before a large beast leapt at him from the trees. Blades ready, Art jumped back to his feet, steadying himself, eyes on the creature.

It was huge, much bigger than a normal bear, its head strangely deformed. It had only a slight resemblance to what it used to be, before a demonic force infused with it making it the grotesque thing it was now. Drooling a yellowish smile, the thing glared at Art, eyes sickly and white blue. The teeth were most prominent, almost swollen too large for its mouth but sharp and lethal. Art had no confidence he could take on a monster of this mass and speed. He would die quickly facing this thing.

Growling, an odd clicking in the back it its throat, it sniffed the air. Art knew it was smelling him, his Weir.

"Yeeessss," a voice hissed from within the beast's throat. "There is the flavor, do you hear the melody?"

Demons. Art could sense them embedded deep within the thing, which was likely once a ram-bear. Perhaps the thing had been caught and infested with them, lumbering too close to the Woods of Reaching. It was now a perversion of nature, just a flesh wagon for the demons to move from one place to another, looking for souls. Without aid, he would be unable to exorcise this poor beast, to at least set it free from the suffering it was enduring. He wished he had a Scarborough Knight from the train ride with him now. This was the kind of things they dealt with.

There was nothing he could really do and eyeing the woods behind him, he turned and sprinted into the thickest collection of trees nearby. The creature roared and the demons inside it wailed and commanded it forward. Dropping into a dead run, the thing headed after him, busting through trees and other forest growth that got too close for its width to fit through unimpeded.

Art was cursing, knowing there was little he could do, other than to try and find a place to hide or run until the thing tired of the chase. Climbing a tree would not stop something that could fell one by smashing it down. Running blind, Art had at least a small lead, the closeness of the old forest slowing the thing down a little. His breath was labored before long. His lungs and legs both screaming at being pushed so hard. The howling of the beast behind reminded him he had to go on, despite his body's limits.

He was certain he was going to have to do something other than run when the Demon Touched gasped a horrific cry. Trees were still breaking, the sound of snarling and growling indicated the massive thing was struggling with something. Art slowed just a little until he was certain something was doing battle with the monster. He hoped it was Lucid.

Finally the thing went still, its huge body making a tremendous thud, echoing through the woods, sending birds out of the trees and into the night's sky. Art waited for a moment but when the boy did not come to him, he headed towards where the fight had taken place. Broken trees, and sickly black blood splattered the area but the Demon Touch was dead. Art could feel the small demons inside wailing and crying in horrific sounds.

Not seeing Lucid, he knelt by the monster. He knew he should exorcise the demons for they could possess another animal or person nearby. He tried to slip his mind into that of the demons, the realm which they were floating about, angry at losing their vessel. He could sense them, a little cluster of six lesser demons and they were sensing him.

"A Weir is open!" One hissed.

"The flavor!" Another bayed.

Art did not listen but proceeded to press his will down on them. They all screamed at the pain and pressure it caused.

"Your names," he demanded. They screamed and tried to claw at his mind with their own but they were no match for Art's skill. "Your names!" He demanded again.

They were going to speak, going to tell him, they could not compete with him but there was something else. Art suddenly felt it. It was as if in the corner of his mind, watching this whole time, the demon within him had been curled up, waiting. It could almost see behind his eyes, it rose out of the darkness, twisted horns smoking and gleaming, bellowing his name. Pain shot through him and he pulled back from the little demons who flushed themselves into the night, taking the chance to escape the Weiriman.

Art's body writhed with pain as the demon within him loomed as if in his face.

"Give into me, boy, release me!" Its voice shot through him like liquid fire and Art screamed again, blades dropping, hands going to his head. He had to push it back. His struggle would attract all kinds of things.

"No," Art screamed and mustered all the strength he had to pull the bottle of Scarlet Extinction from his pack and force a candy into his mouth. The sugary flavor poured over his tongue and the pain started to subside. The demon withdrew but not before whispering it would not be long before he would succumb.

Panting, Art gathered his blades and pushed himself to his feet. He swayed on them a little, stomach churning, but he knew he had to get out of there. The foul odor coming off the beast was threatening to make him sicker. He knew it was disintegrating, as all Demon Touched creatures did when demons vacated their bodies and they were set free of the suffering, but the process was foul.

Staggering into the woods, Art sheathed his weapons and wandered without direction. He hoped Lucid would find him soon. He was so tired, so sore again. He hated that he had to take another candy so soon after having had one before. He could not take them so close together, he would run out before he completed his quest. But the demon was so strong. He had no idea how else he was to keep the thing at bay.

Wandering through the woods at night, still so close to haunted ground, Art knew he would be attracting more demons soon. The evil inside him and his cracked Haunting Weir were like the scent of fresh cooked meat to a hungry man. He then had a thought, remembering the lantern Cindervail had given him. It was the one used in the ritual, but he also thought it might give him some slight protection against evil. Other soul lanterns could emit such an aura, he hoped this one did too.

Stopping for a moment, he went to remove his pack, when Art felt something. Deciding he should not stop, he started into the woods again, pace quickening. The feeling did not relent and soon he was sensing the presence again, until finally his eyes caught a glimpse of a dark form rushing through the shadows. Almost part of the trees, Art was uncertain what he saw. A second glance made him think it was possibly part of the forest.

Yet, Art did not think this was a demon, it was different, cleaner somehow; a presence like a whisper of soft autumn wind. An elf. Only those creatures closest to the earth, to the life stream of the world, had that feel about them, ancient, wild, and pure. The knowledge did not slow Art's feet though. He had escaped the Wood of Reaching but he might not be in any less danger.

Elves could mean a lethal end to his desperate dash through the woods, just as any demonic presence. If he had stumbled into the territory of an elf that did not care for mankind, he might dispatch the man like he would a dangerous demon or predator. The world had not always been such a dark and dangerous place. Many elves placed heavy blame on man for inviting the evil in, with their dabbling in other worldly practices. Not all worked within the world of men like the Scarborough Knights. The elves of the wild were unpredictable, and in their own lands could do as they pleased.

Art had no idea on whose land he was in, so he kept moving, knowing a Weiriman, or one that smelled like he should be one, had an equal chance of being slain by an elf as he did befriending it. He hoped that his run and his general state of panic might dissuade the elf from putting an arrow in his skull. The deeper he plunged into the wood, the greater Art's concern grew. The elf was still tailing him, though why and for what purpose Art could only wildly guess. He had no defenses up, if the elf had wanted to kill him, it would have been easily done by now.

Not knowing what else to do, Art slowed his gait to a jog and then to a stop, breath ragged. He bent to his knees for a moment, trying to slow his heart all the while listening for his pursuer. Silence. Elves could be almost untraceable, even expert hunters could miss them, but Art has senses most men did not, and he knew the elf was nearby, very close.

"Look," he spoke softly, not wanting to end up dead should he offend or startle the elf. "I know you're there. I can sense you. Why are you following me? I hope I have not trespassed into your wood. I was just fleeing the Woods of Reaching and this forest was where it let out. I'll be on my way if you'll only let me pass."

Art's voice suddenly fell silent as part of the wood moved. He stifled a gasp as what he thought a dark mass of shadows and branches, took the long elegant form of an elf. Strong, but slim, lank but toned, his clothing was deeply green, nearly black, subtly textured like vines, leaves and bark. A dark hood shadowed his face, but it was to his long arms and beautiful hands Art's eyes were drawn to as the elf held a large bow, an arrow strung and knocked.

"I really hope you didn't reveal yourself just to shoot me with that." He quirked an eyebrow and the elf's hood shifted a little, seeming to notice Art's fear of the bow he carried.

There was a pause and Art felt perhaps the elf was deciding whether or not to kill him.

"Really, I mean to be on my way, I didn't mean to disturb your wood. I—"

"This is not my wood," the elf spoke, his voice low and smooth.

"Oh," Art muttered when the elf did not go on. "Then, can I ask if there's another reason you have your bow drawn?"

Again, there was a moment of thought on the elf's part. Then the tension went out of his arms and he drew the arrow out of the bowstring, before sliding it back into his quiver. Fastening the bow into his pack, he turned and dropped his head slightly to pull the hood. Art knew he would be stunning. All elves were beautiful beyond most of the races of man. High cheek boned, with hair of black green, he stared intensely at Art with eyes emerald as summer foliage. Perhaps some kind of Tree Elf, Art speculated but he did not know much about the different races of the elves.

Art removed his goggles as they stared at one another, seeming to size each other up. The elf was close to his height, only slightly smaller. Hair flowing around him, some tied back in small braids here and there. His clothing was hard to make out in the darkness but seemed meant for travel and Art frowned.

"If this is not your wood, I can't help but wonder what your business with me is." He did not mean for it to sound so straight forward, but having just escaped with his life more than once this night, he was in no mood to play games with a stranger, elf or not.

"I too have traversed the Woods of Reaching. Yet, I was not as successful as you and did not acquire what I know you have at your hip."

Art's heart jumped into his throat, his foot instinctively taking a step back. His hand went to Weir Hewn.

"You mean my blade? You were after it too?"

The elf did not answer but Art did not need him too.

"I require it for unique purposes." The elf dropped his gaze heavy on Art.

"I also need this blade for unique purposes," Art said cautiously.

The elf's eyes narrowed to two almond shaped slits. "I will have it and no man, not even a Weiriman, will keep it from me."

Chapter Ten
Elf and Dryad

Facing off with an elf for the Weir Hewn blade seemed like at least number three on a great list of things Art never wanted to do, but it was right in line with the way his night had been shaping up. Tired, spent, and getting angry, Art put his hand on the blade, which in turn made the elf narrow his eyes, menacingly.

"I have fought tooth and nail for this thing and need it as a matter of life and death. I will not be handing it over for any reason."

The elf stared at him for a long moment, his beautiful face almost unreadable but there was a hardness in his eyes that made Art very nervous.

"I require it for reasons just as dire."

"I know elves are not in the habit of stealing from people." Art leveled the insinuation at him, causing the elf's expression to twitch. Questioning his honor was the only way Art could think of dousing the growing friction between them.

"You are correct," the elf's voice dropped, his hands going to the bow he had just placed back in his pack. "However, for her I would sully more than my honor. I will have the blade, Weiriman, or I will have your life."

Art barely comprehended the full weight of the elf's threat before he had drawn out the bow and knocked an arrow faster than Art could even draw Weir Hewn from its sheath. He was dead; he knew it. The arrow would pierce his skull before he could react. Unable to even close his eyes, Art's heart stopped in his chest when suddenly a cry broke into the night. The elf halted his arrow and Art blinked, breath shuttering out at the fact he was still alive.

"Stop!" the female voice cried again and the elf lowered his bow.

Confused, Art's eyes moved around the forest, the elf, and anything else he could see, looking for the source of the voice. When he saw no one, he frowned deeply about to speak, when a light rose out of the elf's body, ghostly shimmering like glowing frost. Awed, Art stared as the light softly took on shape, folding and rolling like sheer curtains in a breeze until the form was recognizable.

She was beautiful, the most dramatically beautiful thing Art had ever seen. Her skin was like lit porcelain, hair in blowing waves of white, tinted with yellow and soft fuchsia. The billowing dress, like long petals, fell around her form making her look like a flower blossom. Her face a perfect jewel in the whole of her appearance, heart shaped, crowned by two deep plum colored eyes, they opened, blinking in long lashes. A glitter of light shimmered off her as she took a breath of the night's air.

Art stood dumbstruck, staring, not knowing what she was, not caring for she was a vision, ghostly, or other. Her form was gossamer and slightly transparent, floating in the night like a lantern against the trees. Her dress and hair moved with unfelt air. Eyes roaming over her, Art noted a wisp of white, like a tether, between her and the elf. She was somehow linked to him through the whisper of light.

"Please don't, Ever," she spoke, her voice like music. "This is not you. He is right. You would never steal from someone. You would never take a life like this. You are a Knight. I could not bear for you to sacrifice your mighty morals, please! You have already given up so much for me."

She was hovering before him, her arms out stretched. He looked up at her, his summer colored eyes swam with sudden emotion. His hand lifted to hers but as they were going to touch her form shifted as if turning to milky mist and their fingers passed through one another's. She was not physical. Art could only stare, as the pair looked on one another with such longing, such sadness, that he was almost tasting the emotion on the night's chilled air.

"We must have the blade, my flower," he said softly in Elvish.

Art was glad he had been forced to take all the major languages.

"But we cannot do evil to another who has not earned its wrath," she spoke back to him. "I would rather be this ghost for the rest of my days than harm another in this way. Please, do not do this."

As Art watched he was starting to get more of a sense of the pair. His inner eye was seeing something, sensing something, and then he suddenly knew it the way he had been taught to sense such things.

"Her Haunting Weir is within you!" He said aloud, surprised.

The elf flashed his eyes back to the man. "How is it you know this?"

"I can sense it. Your Weir and hers…they are somehow fused?"

Slowly the elf nodded and the woman smiled at him. "You can sense this in us because you are a Weiriman? Perhaps you can help then?"

"We have seen other, Weirimen, Orchid. They could not help us." The elf's voice was empty, unhopeful.

"But perhaps he is different. He has the Weir Hewn blade."

Seeing that this issue of blade and owner might be resolved without bloodshed, Art cautiously asked, "What is it that you need with the blade?"

"That will require an explanation and she should not do it here. My camp is nearby. We will be safe there through the night. Come," the elf ordered coolly.

Art hesitated but the woman, who's ears were long and tapered much more so even than the elf's pointed tips, smiled at him.

"I promise Ever will not harm you. He does not truly want to. Even if you cannot help us, I promise no harm will come to you, stranger."

Her eyes were so large, so beautiful, their color even more glorious than Art had thought, a mixture of dark purple and gold. He knew he should not so easily trust someone who had just threatened him, but he could not help but believe the ghostly beauty. He would have to be careful but nodded and followed Ever and the ghostly tethered Orchid into the woods. His thoughts were on Lucid as he glanced one last time at the forest from which he came. He hoped he was all right and they would somehow find each other again.

The woods were not quiet. Things moved through the underbrush; small animal screams perforated the night, making Art jumpy. His mind was racing, wondering about Lucid, thinking perhaps he should not be following this strange elf and his ghostly companion, and worrying over the strength of the demon inside him. His head buzzed with everything that had happened in the last few days, all of it feeling more heavy with the fatigue of his body. He needed sleep, rest, and food but he worried he would not be getting any of that soon.

They were nearing a campsite, when suddenly something burst out of the bushes beside Art. The elf had heard it coming and pulled his bow but Art, mind lost somewhere else, had been unready and took the full brunt of the creature's body against his.

"What the h—" but he stopped mid word when the smiling face of Lucid looked up at him, large blue eyes wide.

"Found you, Brother!" he exclaimed and Art could see out of the corner of his eye the elf relax. Orchid had hidden behind her solid partner, her glow very soft now, her eyes large.

Art was suddenly glad the elf had not shot Lucid but wondered if he had not protected the Weiriman purposely. It would be easy to take the knife off a man's dead body. The fault would have been Art's entirely. Dark thoughts aside, Art returned his attention to Lucid.

"You found more friends, Brother?" Lucid looked to the pair and gave them a nice smile, which seemed to further put the pair at ease.

"Well, I think so," Art murmured as he and Ever exchanged a momentary glance full of question and suspicion. "But are you all right? Are you injured?"

Lucid shook his head, standing up to show he was intact. His clothing was more dirty, some dry blood on his hands and forearms but it did not appear to be his own, as it was black and deep brown. Demon blood likely, though Art really did not know what color Lucid bled, if at all. He had no idea what to expect from a dreamcatcher. The Weaver's insistence that Art keep him safe did indicate the boy could at least come to harm. Regardless of the color of his blood, Art planned to keep his word and Lucid had already proven he was willing to protect the Weiriman. He continued to be surprised by the youth.

"Come," Ever commanded. "We should not linger in the woods like this. It is unsafe."

Art nodded but Lucid stopped him and pointed to his pack slung over Art's body. He had forgotten he had taken the boy's things and nodded handing them over. As Lucid pulled his cloak on he motioned with his hands, acting like he was eating and then pointed to Art.

"Oh, I haven't eaten tonight yet." Art shook his head. "Are you hungry?"

Lucid shook his head and leaned over to reach into Art's pack. The man let him, thinking it would be the easiest way since the boy had gone silent again and was surprised when he withdrew a candy twist. He held it up to Art and the man took it having forgotten he should take one. It would help him get through the night.

Their encampment was tucked away near a huge rock face. Ever had assured them it was safe and well fortified. At this point Art had ceased to care. By the end of their walking he was colder and more tired than he had ever been in his life. The past few days seemed to have all piled on him at once and all he wanted was to sit and maybe sip something warm.

"You look so weary, stranger," the beautiful ghost leaned over him shortly after Art had collapsed by the low light embers elves used for warming night encampment. They were rare in the towns and Art had always thought the Weirimen should have brokered more deals to make them a standard issue in their equipment. Full fires at night were so dangerous.

"I am," Art mumbled out as he watched her float in front of him, her ghostly figure ever connected to the elf who was seated opposite of him, watching. Looking at the pair together, it was clear she was not elven. Her ears were too long, her form different. There was something even more outwardly to her. "Are you a fairy or fey of some kind?" Art did not mean to ask the question but his fatigue was weighing on his judgment.

She gave him a soft smile and floated back towards the elf. Her hand graced over his shoulder but she was unable to touch him. Art noted how his eyes followed the movement but he did not reach for her.

"She is a flowering dryad," Ever spoke, his voice low but silvery.

Art glanced at him. He had heard of dryads but never a "flowering" one.

"I doubt you would have heard of my kind," Orchid smiled. "Flowering dryads are just a more rare form of dryad. We have other abilities."

"I'm sorry, I'm rather uneducated on the matter."

"I suppose Weirimen only study the darkness." Ever's voice had an edge in it that Art did not understand.

"It is the rudimentary core of our function, so yes, we are well versed in the study of the darkness."

"It has been my experience that the Weirimen have little interest in the lives the darkness affects. Their only care is for the cleaving of that darkness, regardless of the cost. All I have seen is a private war with the underworlds."

Art had never heard anyone speak so negatively about the Weirimen. His mood was not improving.

"I find this fairly offensive, coming from someone who just tried to rob me."

The elf's handsome face turned dark, his lip curling slightly when Orchid was suddenly between the pair.

"We are sorry about that, stranger. It is not something Ever would normally do. He is just desperate to help me."

"You said that before." Art leaned back, not realizing he had sat forward, his finger pointing rudely at the elf. Trying to recover some of his manners he said, "And my name is Art Storygrove."

"What a lovely name!" Orchid's face broke into another beautiful smile. It was so lovely it almost made Art feel better just looking at her, "I am Orchid Sarathone and this is Ever Nahrwel."

"Lucid!" The boy popped his head up and pointed before settling back down, playing with a strand of yarn, folding it in and out of unusual forms between his hands and fingers.

Orchid smiled at him but turned back to Art.

"I promised you an explanation. As I said, Ever would never truly hurt you. He is a Tree Elf, after all."

Art chuckled deep in his throat and crossed his arms over his chest, wrapping his coat about him for some comfort to his aching body.

"That was not my impression this evening, and not what I have heard about elves. They can be dangerous to men, should they enter their territory. They are not always known for their mercy."

"How like the races of men," Ever interjected, looking stone faced. "Your kind is given to exaggeration and misunderstanding so easily."

Art tightened his lips but Orchid spoke before he could go on, "What I mean is Ever is a Scarborough Knight. While many elves do not mix their business with races of the towns, Scarborough Knights are often credited with helping anyone afflicted by Demon Touched beasts."

Art looked the elf over, noticing much of his clothing was similar to theirs but it did not look exact. He lacked the full uniform, something rarely seen among the Knights.

"If he's a knight what is he doing out here away from his garrison? I did not know them to travel alone."

"She means to say I am formally of the Scarborough Knights."

Orchid looked suddenly sad, her eyes drifting to Ever for a moment but he did not return the look.

"I've never heard of a Knight leaving the service either."

"They rarely do," the elf confirmed, his voice portraying little of what he might be feeling.

"Let me explain," Orchid said moving towards the low light embers which were casting enough light to put a thin color on the rock face near them. "Once there was a flowering dryad. She lived in a beautiful tree in the Farahgall Woods."

She extended her hands and a flourish of ghostly petals came forth to cast shadowy shapes on the rock. They twisted and bent until they formed the depiction of a tree and female figure. Lucid sat up instantly, completely enamored by the shadow play.

"Many happy years passed and there was nothing but the beautiful cycle of changing years." Her shadow figures moved, the tree flowering, dropping tiny leaves and then blooming again to show the passage of time in her tale.

"Yet, as you know darkness haunts our world and danger is rampant. The forest near her small wood spawned a patch of haunted ground and many animals were poisoned by this evil." Again her image changed, morphing into monstrous shadows, echoes of the twisted animals that suffered in these places just like the touched ram-bear Art had encountered.

"You know the longer these animals fester, the less like an animal they are and more like a demon. After a long time of fighting with the animal inside, the demons take over and hunt others to feed its demonic appetite. This was what brought the pack of Demon Touched to my tree one day." The image showed animals that looked more like huge misshapen dogs than anything Art had seen before. They attacked the shadow tree and the female figure.

"I would surely have perished if a band of Scarborough Knights had not been tracking this pack. They battled the beasts, but demons are illusive, vapory creatures. In my grave wounded state, I was vulnerable to one that slipped out of its animal prisoner." The scene first showed a group of elven knights engage the monsters, then the shadow Orchid terrified as a demon loomed over her, its hands plugging inside her head. "It was in the process of breeching my Weir when Ever got too close to us, still battling with the animal this demon's group occupied." Her shadows followed clearly what she was saying, imagery still disturbing though only in tiny play-like shadows.

"It is unclear what happened next. The mortal battle going on inside me and the raging battle going on above me somehow crossed, the demons tried to escape into me, Ever not letting them go with his own will and might. He was able to protect me but my Haunting Weir and my soul were now inside him."

"Wait, how did that happen?" Art was confused. He had heard of accidents happening, Weirs being broken, altered, even removed on very rare unexplained occasions, but all these normally took place during exorcism. "Scarborough Knights have never been known to exorcise. I've only heard they release the beasts who are afflicted. If they engage the demons early enough on in the possession, sometimes the demons leave on their own accord driven out by the elf's purity."

"That is a form of exorcism, Weiriman," Ever spoke, his manner slightly condescending.

"Purity of soul is not enough to drive a demon from a possessed person," Art added, feeling a little defensive. "It requires great strength and aggression of spirit, training of psychic skill, and control of the mind and Haunting Weir, and of course the demon's name."

"The Demon Touched are not the same as a possession," Ever explained. "Early enough in the possession of an animal a Knight may drive the demons from it. There is no clear mind for the demon to infect, animals are neither good nor evil and therefore cannot be corrupt."

"Oh," Art's brow popped up, the new knowledge seeming to rob him of his hostile feelings. "That makes perfect sense. We never learned such a thing in the Seminary as we rarely deal with Demon Touched animals."

"By the sounding of it, your curriculum could do with some additions."

Art knew the elf was being condescending once more, but he did not disagree and instead said, "I agree with you. I feel Weirimen could benefit greatly by the study of much more than just the narrow field of our profession. We should know all things demonic and the combat by which they must be fought."

Ever said nothing but his eyes did portray a moment of surprise. Perhaps if Art worked at this he could gain a working relationship with the cold-shouldered elf, though to what end he was not sure of yet.

"Anyway, Orchid," Art turned back to the dryad, "that incident is what led your Haunting Weir to be within his?"

"It is not just my Weir is inside his," she tilted her head, looking a touch whimsical as she spoke. "It is more that I now reside within his psychic space, his mind's eye. My soul, my consciousness is, as you know, attached to my Weir. My soul followed my Weir."

"Yes, of course." Art nodded, his brow sinking low with thought. He had never heard of a case similar. "Your only recourse has been to find the Weir Hewn blade?"

Ever sat up, looking irritable. "Not the only, it is the last. We have been to healers of many kinds. They could offer no aid. All they could do was heal her body and her tree, but they were unable to separate her from me."

"They did move my tree to the garden at Ever's home, but with me unable to return to my body it did little good. My whole life will be spent inside Ever's mind, my body locked within my tree in ever slumber."

"Did you not seek out the Weirimen? Surely they could have—"

Ever's eyes took on the glow of the embers and angrily he said, "Ah, we have been to the Weirimen, several in fact. The solution they have offered us is to purge

Orchid from me as if she were some encroaching demonic force or a parasite. In doing this she will perish."

"They say I am now a foreign soul within him, a ghost and should be exorcised and moved on to the next world. My attack by the demons was my death and they say it is only natural the process be completed since that is what would have happened had this accident not occurred."

"But your body lives," Art protested, appalled by what he was hearing.

"Not just her body. She lives," Ever said darkly. "Her whole being lives, her body, soul and Haunting Weir. Though two are separate from the one, she is no more dead than I. I could no more condemn her to death now than I could if I had just happened upon her loveliness in the woods. The thought is repugnant."

Art agreed though he should not have been completely surprised. Though highly respected and sorely needed, the Weirimen were known for harsh judgement, and if the possessed could not be saved they would be put down. This fact Art had always known, but it had been only recently that he understood the full harsh reality of it.

"They said it was natural and I should do this so that I might live and return to my life as a Knight."

"With a foreign soul inside him, the Scarborough will not allow him to work as a Knight." Her eyes cast downward, the windless float of her flowing dress seemed to slow as her feelings of guilt etched over her pale face. "They say it puts me in far too much danger and could compromise his judgment."

"I would give up that calling if we could find a way to liberate you from my mind's eye," Ever's voice softened, his eyes portraying emotion rarely seen in elves.

Art could not deny he was moved by their story and he could not bring himself to agree with his Guild. An accident had severed Orchid's soul from her body. If steps could be taken to restore her, he fully believed they should be pursued. The idea that they would want to put her down, when clearly both her and the one she was attached to wanted to find another way to save her, seemed a rush to judgment and a waste of a life.

"So what is it you need my Weir Hewn for? You still have not explained that."

"The last person we visited knew of a special blade, one that might have the ability to separate my Weir from Ever."

"Was it the Weaver?" Art was already frowning even before he asked the question. Sending Art after the blade he had already sent the elf and dryad after, seemed like something the Weaver would do and either not think to mention it or not care to. Art did not even try to understand the oddity.

"The Weaver, no." Ever shook his head, smoothing back long bangs of his deep green hair. "Though we would likely seek him out once the blade was in hand."

"Well, it was the Weaver who sent me after the blade. But am I understanding correctly that you do not know how to use the knife then?"

The pair shook their heads.

"I suppose that is why you were going to go to the Weaver after you found the knife? Makes sense."

"Father cannot use the blade," Lucid suddenly spoke. "He does not use his prizes. He is just an artisan."

Everyone was looking at the boy now but Lucid had gone back to playing with his string, which he was weaving into amazing designs in ways Art did not think possible.

"What do you mean, Lucid?" Art tried to coax an answer but Lucid only blinked at him and pointed to Art, before making a slashing motion with his hand. "I don't understand."

"Your father is the Weaver?" Ever asked and Lucid nodded.

"Well, I don't think that's entirely right," Art interjected. "The Weaver is like a father to him, but not actually blood related. Lucid was born of something else."

"Something else?" Orchid tilted her head.

"He told me he was a dreamcatcher, but I really don't know too much more than that. He told Lucid to come with me, to aid me." After hearing how the Weirimen Guild might react to Lucid, Art was weary to share his full origins just yet.

"But, he calls you brother."

Art nodded. "He did that of his own accord. We're not related."

"He is my brother," Lucid said plainly, unfazed by the group's confusion with his origin.

"But if he was built or created from a dreamcatcher does that make him a thing?" Ever's brow was lifted high, inspecting Lucid's appearance. "I have never seen a golem, creation, or homunculus as such."

"Lucid is a person." The boy looked sharply at the elf for a moment before going back to his string.

Art strangely felt the same way. The boy was a person to him and no artificial creation.

"I believe he is correct. He is a person. I feel a Weir and a soul within him."

"Remarkable." Orchid smiled. "The Weaver lives up to his legends. Yet, the boy says he could not help us even if we were to bring him the blade."

"He seemed to imply you could help us, Storygrove."

Art stared at the couple realizing Lucid could have been indicating that. "Well, I…I only just got the blade myself," Art confessed. "I really don't know how to use its special properties."

"Then what is your plan for the blade?" Ever asked, looking skeptical of the young man once more.

Art did not want to divulge his situation to the elf. He still did not fully trust him, even if Orchid had rather easily persuaded Art he was innocent of any dark intentions. The lengths to which the elf was willing to go to save her, gave Art misgivings. Honorable as elven Knights might be, their goals and beliefs could set them at odds with the morals of other races. Art had already seen that. Ever could have convinced himself Art was a man and not worth as much as the life of a flowering dryad. Whatever his reasoning for nearly killing Art, he did not want to give him further reasons. Harboring a Pith demon would likely insight fear and mistrust.

"All the Weaver told me was I needed to cut something from my soul but I don't know how to do that. I had to get the knife and visit the Consciatosium and then I return to the Weaver. Hopefully, he'll tell me what I need to do next."

Clearly, Ever and Orchid knew Art was avoiding explaining his predicament but they chose not to press him.

"Perhaps you as a Weiriman could cut my Weir from Ever without killing us both." Orchid looked so hopeful.

One of Art's eyebrows dropped a bit and he gave the pair a half smile. "I am skilled with a blade but this is new to me. However, if I am able to do it, I will help you both. Despite your experience with my brethren I still feel that is my duty."

"I am no possessed or afflicted, Storygrove. I will not allow you to purge her." Ever warned in a gentle but heavy tone.

"I assure you that is not my intention." Art felt himself growing sleepy. He did not want to drift into nightmares that he knew awaited but his body and mind were so tired. "I'll help you. If you want to accompany Lucid and myself to the Consciatosium and then back to the Weaver, I'll do whatever he suggests to free you both of your situation. It's my duty. You may not be traditionally possessed, but you are afflicted. Weirimen should aid you. It's our charge."

Art knew he was rambling a little but sleep was over coming him. The last thing he recalled was Lucid moving to sit next to him, as if a sentry. The Weiriman found himself wondering if Lucid slept. Would he watch over him all night? His cracked open Weir could draw trouble. Worry was not enough to keep the young man awake and before long Art was drifting into black, watched by the eyes of his inner evil.

Chapter Eleven
Wivenguilder

The smell of fresh death woke Art from a dream in which he felt like he was being chased, strangled, smothered, and consumed. A blur of ugly images and sickly feelings gave way to wet, sticky coughing and a stiff neck and back. Looking around wildly he saw dawn breaking through the forest as the tall Tree Elf from the night before loomed over the Weiriman.

"Awake, Storygrove?" His silvery voice hinted at a foul mood.

He said nothing else, before taking a step over the log Art had propped himself up against. Cranking his neck, Art spotted the source of the foul smell. A large dead beast, warped and twisted from whatever it had formerly been before it was Demon Touched, lay nearby. The elf was retrieving arrows and cleaning them when Lucid was suddenly in Art's face.

Art jumped back surprised, but Lucid only grinned and offered Art some food and an Umbra candy from his pack. Art ate less than the boy wanted him too, but his stomach felt sour, his mouth tasted bad and no amount of drinking from his canteen was washing it away. He was grateful that he had not actually spoken with the demon in his dream.

"You look unwell, Weiriman," Ever said once they were packed up. "Did you not sleep well?"

Art noticed a heaviness in the elf's question, as if Ever had already known the quality of his sleep. Perhaps the man had been fitful and the elf had watched along with Lucid.

"Nightmares," Art mumbled, annoyed, but knowing he had not told Ever of his issues, the elf was taking the moment to remind them both of that fact.

They headed towards the edge of the wood. Lucid seemed happy to pick up the couple for the journey. He kept bouncing around Ever looking for Orchid until the elf told him she had to rest at times since her soul was weak due to their situation. Pouting, the boy left him alone.

"We saw an unusual number of demons this night past," Ever said just as they were clearing the wood. "Perhaps it was providence I joined your odd band of two. You slept through the night and did not take a shift of watch. I assume this is due to some…condition you suffer from?"

Though well worded, the question had not been subtle and Art truly just wanted to ignore him. Knowing he would not be able to do that, he stated shortly, "Yeah."

Some satisfaction bloomed in him when Ever shot him an irritated look. Art was thankful for the aid, but not happy that he had slept through the night and left Lucid to deal with what his Weir had drawn. Despite the issues it might cause, Art still planned not to tell the elf about his problem for as long as he could. The reaction his own Guild had displayed left him distrustful and leery, though he could not blame them. He truly was walking about with a danger inside him.

"Do you know where we are headed?" Art changed the subject.

Still looking cross, Ever nodded and extended an arm to point across a set of small rolling hills.

"We should head towards the town of Crestbelth."

"That's not a town that has a Weirimen Guild." Art frowned having had memorized nearly all the places that had one.

"It does not, but it will have an airship that can transport us to Wivenguilder."

Art knew of the largest city on the outskirts of the Wyld Lands, which they were in. It was host to one of the largest Weirimen Guilds in the network. Being on the edge of the Wyld Lands that hosted a great many haunted grounds, people were often afflicted by wandering demons and spirits. Those killed in these areas harbored a greater chance that a soul would become a wandering spirit or leave a piece of itself to haunt the place of death.

Art sometimes wondered why people chose to live in some of these dangerous places. He suspected several of his graduating class would be stationed at Wivenguilder because the demand for exorcism was higher. Being on the outskirts of the Wyld Lands meant for encounters with Demon Touched and that brought another whole set of demonic and evil inflicted maladies. The thought of running into his newly graduated classmates after the rapid rumors likely circulating made Art's stomach twist up. He hoped none of them had been transferred yet.

The trek to Crestbelth was easy, though it took nearly half the day. The elf's pace was faster than Art was accustom to, but he kept up and Lucid seemed unbothered. Stopping for lunch, the group exchanged little conversation. Art suspected that without Orchid, and with Lucid only speaking when the situation was dire, he and the uncomfortable relationship with the Knight might stay tensioned for quite some time.

He was most relieved when the afternoon wore through and Orchid appeared, floating out of Ever like a shimmering billow of white mist. Lucid was extremely pleased and after some pleasantries, the atmosphere lightened and Art started to feel more comfortable. They were all sad to see her disappear when Ever said it would be best when they entered the nearing town.

Crestbelth was larger than Art expected and as they hurried into the town, Ever explained he worried they might miss the last flight of the day. It was far too dangerous to fly at night. Great demons rose out of the woods on all sides of the town attacking airships under starlight. Arriving at the airship docking station, Ever inquired about the last flight, happy to find it still had seating. Ever paid for the lot, not even asking Art for coin before beckoning them to board.

Seated, Art watched as Lucid, excited and interested in everything, took the window seat and waited impatiently for the ship to launch.

"Will there be lodging at your Guild or should we look for rooms when we arrive in Wivenguilder?" inquired Ever.

Art had been distracted by the light whispering he was hearing from the other passengers. It could have been his slight use of mind reading or perhaps his control to keep the voices out that had been fatigued by the demon's pressure. But the voices sounded so sinister and strange, not like the thoughts of regular people. He was concerned they were leaving behind a group of demons somewhere that he should be looking to root out before leaving the town.

"Storygrove," the elf commanded Art's attention back. "You do not look well. Do you not take flying in stride?"

Art had not even noticed the ship had taken off and they were now gliding at great speed across the massive lake that separated the Wyld Lands from Wivenguilder.

"Oh, no, no I'm fine with flying," Art answered, noting his face felt cold and to his surprise his lip was damp with chilled sweat. He dabbed it hastily from a handkerchief in his pocket and tried to turn towards the window Lucid was dominating.

Something was definitely wrong with him though. What the demon inside him could be doing now, Art was not sure. He had not heard the thing's voice all day and though it brought him comfort, it also worried him. Was the thing doing something more insidious now? He would have to be on his guard.

"Tea?" The elf offered when the beverage cart came around.

Art gladly accepted and sipped the smooth warm liquid, hoping it would settle him as the elf eyed him cautiously.

The tea did help and before long Art had settled into the small comfortable booth they had reserved for the flight. It had a nice window and a good view of the rest of the ship. For a while, Art watched the other parties, some well dressed on obvious holiday, but mostly they were weary travelers and commuters. He wondered what kept people so close to the dangerous parts of the world. The threat of evil, possession and being attacked was dramatically real. The thought turned amusing when he thought of himself. He, of all people, could not question such a life. He had chosen to be a Weiriman after all.

"Do you hail from a large city, Weiriman?"

Art had not expected Ever to make conversation and had thought the flight would be as quiet as the day's travel. The questions about his origin were equally surprising but then he had the thought perhaps the elf was trying to gauge him. They were nearly complete strangers, trusting one another, though much mystery hung between them.

"The Weirimen Seminary is in a fairly large city, but I grew up in one of the surrounding nine villages that was much smaller."

"You do not strike me as a village boy. Though I suppose the moral promise you made to aid Orchid and I should have guided my assumptions of you otherwise."

"Your experiences with Weirimen cannot all have been bad," Art offered, watching the elf's gaze linger on the passing world outside the window Lucid was so interested in.

"They have not been all bad. My garrison rarely dealt with them. We were often in the deep of the Wylds, protecting elven and fey settlements as well as animals of the woods. I was not one of those that worked on the outskirts of the cities of men. Yet, even so, I was taken back by their solution to Orchid's condition. It has soured my opinion of your brethren."

"I don't blame you for that," Art half mumbled not meaning to sound so concurring.

Ever's eyes returned to the man and after studying him for a long moment said, "It is rare to see one of you out alone. Do you not travel at least in pairs? We know the boy is not a Weiriman. Will you not share with me something of your sojourn so that there might be some trust between us?"

Art had expected to be called out eventually, but had expected the elf to wait a few days, or maybe witness one or two events with Art before doing so.

"It's not something I want to share just yet," Art confessed, hoping truth would win out over the suspicion. "We did not exactly have the most cordial of introductions." He meant what he said but gave the elf a friendly side smile, sweeping the long bangs from his eyes. His shoulders ached and he was still feeling ill but he did see the reason to make something of an effort with the tree elf at least in manners.

Ever, still looking guarded nodded. "You are correct, I did strike the first mark against the trust between us. I will give you time and ask you no more, less you give me reason to do so again."

"Unless I give him reason, huh?" Art's thoughts were sour. He feared that would be happening sooner than he liked. He could feel something at the back of his mind, like an itching in a wound he knew he could not scratch, less it infect and bleed constantly. A whispering was just beyond his hearing, present, but not audible, hinting at words, licking at ideas. Art tried to suppress the feeling and block out the voice. He did not want the thing to talk to him. He did not want to feel its presence again, though he knew it was the source of his growing fatigue. He had hoped symptoms of the threatening possession would have taken longer to overcome him. But the thing inside him was powerful and fully conscious of its affect on the Weiriman. Art would have to be on his guard. Blinking a few times and settling his back hard against the cushion of the booth, he tried to get comfortable and pretend nothing was wrong. Perhaps a meal and thoughts about other things would distract.

After a server came around to take their order and the light food was being served, Art felt a tug on his sleeve. Turning to Lucid, who had only ordered cake and crumpets, he was greeted with the boy holding up another umbra sweet. He was glad Lucid had an understanding of such things because Art kept forgetting to eat them. He wondered if that was him or perhaps the demon was at work in the back of his mind. The thought unsettled him and he chewed the candy down before taking to his dumpling soup.

The flight was smooth and uneventful. Before Art realized, it they were docking at the Wivenguilder side lake terminal. Disembarking always took less time than Art expected. The ship and crew were well organized to get everyone off in a quick and efficient manner. It ran nearly as well as the railway.

Before long Art, Ever, and Lucid were heading into the grand bustling city of Wivenguilder. Different from the city Art had spent the last six years in, the enormity of its size. Mixes of new and old buildings were blended together, lining city blocks and hugging street corners. Everything seemed at least three stories tall, brick and stone and wood, making an attractive but eclectic appearance of new and old world coming together to accommodate a bustling population.

"Do you know where we are going, Storygrove?"

Art did not say anything to the elf, but pulled out his compass and its needle spun wildly until it gave him a heading.

"I'd say we should head this way. Only the Guild should have such a strong demon energy reading as it should be the only place housing relics, demons, and the afflicted."

"In a city such as this, I do not know if that is a true statement."

Art tilted his head towards the elf, looking for explanation.

"A place such as this is likely to have an underbelly of black market trade as thick as the night is cold."

"Let's hope you're not entirely right about that," Art mumbled.

He had heard of black markets that sold and traded in demonic relics, demon fused, or touched items, even those possessed. Blackenmancers and Weirimen alike tried to root out such corruption. He had always thought such a large Guild as the Wivenguilder sect would have a good handle on the black trade of its own city. Ever seemed to have a different opinion of their capabilities.

Saying nothing more on the subject, the small group headed into the city. Lucid was fascinated by nearly every street vendor and shop. Before long, Art had to take a firm hand to the situation and explain they needed to get to the Guild before night. Pouting a little, the boy understood and begrudgingly followed the two others with a frown.

All pouting was forgotten when they reached the Wivenguilder Weirimen Guild House. Lucid stood in awe at the collection of buildings before them, towering over even its tall neighbors. Great gates stood sentinel, a work of scrolling black metal. Art approached and was greeted by a guard, dressed similar to him, hooded and wearing the Weirimen insignia.

"What is your business here?"

Art produced his temporary license and stated his name.

"I seek use of the library resource. These two are my companions. I would like to bring them in with me."

"You'll have to produce proof of Shrouding before you may use the facility or seek further permission, brethren," the guard warned but opened the gate and allowed Art and the others to pass.

Art had been to several Guild Houses in his training years, but none as well fortified as the Wivenguilder. Tall walls of silvery gray stone, bound together with great arches and thick doors. Grand, beautiful, but also powerful and warding. It stood like a cathedral against the world's darkness, judging all who passed by its tempered glass panes and iron gated grounds.

"Your buildings are cold, Storygrove," Ever said coolly as he followed behind Lucid.

"Our world deals very rarely with warmth that is not brought on by fire of hell," Art's voice was dark, "and you'll find the deepest fire burns cold. Weirimen are not close to the organic world like the elves."

"Evident." Ever dropped a look on Art when the man looked behind him.

He wanted to be offended by the elf's passing judgment on the Guild, but he too was feeling the chill in the air. The way his Guild had threatened him was weighing on his mind again, more so than he had planned to allow it. A voice inside him said he would have to tread lightly because he was not among friends, though these people were supposed to be his brethren. He wished the dark thought had been voiced by the demon within him, but he worried more that it was from his own mind, and that carried much more fear with it.

Passing into the large courtyard, they were greeted by a pair of guards who questioned him just as the front sentury had. Art knew what they were doing. The front gate was not the real test at all. The courtyard was an area intruders could easily be captured, rigged with traps, and watched carefully. Young or dim demons, hoping to infiltrate a Guild, sometimes tried to wander in hidden within a person. The Weirimen were not easily fooled and Art knew while he spoke with one Weirimen the other was scanning him with her abilities, looking for possession and trickery. Anxiety started to fill him, knowing he carried darkness within him and he started to reach for a letter Cindervail had given him to offer other Weirimen when the woman lifted her hand.

"This is him, Knifecaren, this is the man the Crimson Dispatch spoke of: Art Storygrove."

Art fell silent. He was unaware a Crimson Dispatch had been sent about him. Only the most important news was sent by this special letter, received by all the Guilds, concerning only the gravest and most dangerous of contents. He suddenly felt he might be taken in custody at that very moment. Perhaps Minevur had won out after all and gotten the others to side with him rather than Cindervail and Art would be condemned.

"You must not let that happened. Do not let them take you now. You have a real idea how to cleanse yourself. You could destroy this thing." Art felt his jaw clench as he watched the pair glance at him before nodding to an unseen observer high in the rampart of the walls of the Guild. He knew they were signaling one another, maybe even talking through Shrouded Telepathy that he could not hear. "You must not let yourself be condemned and destroyed! You have only just begun your quest. It would be unfair to try and stop you now."

Another pair of Weirimen arrived, a very tall slender female and her partner, short and petite, both wearing Sin Breath masks similar to the one the hung at Art's neck. More shrouded thoughts passed between the four. Their faces gave away little of what was being said and Art grew all the more nervous.

His hands were itching to be on his blades. He wanted to be ready if they attacked him, wanted to be able to slit throats and use bodies as shields when the arrows started to rain down on him as he tried to escape. He would need to take the large one first, he would make the best shield for...

Art stopped, completely shocked at his line of thoughts. His mind had raced through a whole scenario of who to kill in what order, which traps would be triggered, how he would need to avoid them, and what he would have to sacrifice between the elf and the dreamcatcher to make it out with his life. His mouth went dry. Though he often thought out his moves, his escapes, his plans for how he would execute an operation, he had never done so in such a brutal manner. He had never thought about killing other Weirimen, nor betraying allies such as Lucid and Ever.

He could feel a cold inkling in his limbs and he tried to control the trembling when he felt the black eyes of the demon within staring. It was laughing, mocking him, grinning and Art felt nauseated. It had slipped thoughts so seamlessly into his mind he had thought them his own, long after he should have known better.

Shaken, but trying not to show it, Art forced his attention back to the Weirimen just as the smallest of them was approaching him, pulling down her mask and pushing back her hood. He was stunned to be greeted with both a smile and a familiar face.

"Senny Greiventine?" Art managed to waft out.

"Don't sound so surprised!" She gave him a wide smile with full lips and sunny brown yellow eyes. "You knew we were getting our assignments. This is my post. And this is my partner mentor, Heavykel, Korfa Heavykel." The taller women acknowledged him with her eyes, but did not remove her mask.

"I didn't know you would be sent way out here on the frontier," Art admitted.

"Me either, but I'm excited. We've already had our first serious exorcism."

"Did it go well?"

Senny had been all smiles but when Art asked the question her face darkened.

"Not everything is like classes," Korfa Heavykel spoke before Senny could answer. "Many out here are beyond our aide. The darkness is thick here, the haunting grounds many. We are much nearer the core of darkness."

"The Wyld lands are not the source of darkness, Weirimen," Ever spoke. Art had almost forgotten he was standing behind him.

"But they are greatly afflicted by it, elf," Heavykel spoke back, tone edged. "Here it runs as ramped and unchecked as any of your kind."

Art did not have to turn to see the remark offended Ever, but the elf stayed silent, leveling nothing back at the Weiriman other than in icy stare.

"Come, Storygrove, before you are allowed access to our library you must be seen by our Grandmaster, Felvase."

"Don't worry, Art," Senny tried to comfort as they followed Heavykel, the other pair of Weirimen watching the whole time. "Our Grandmaster has been briefed on your situation."

"That's what worries me." Art thought to himself as they led the trio through the huge doors of the Guild's great house.

The hallways were never well lit but not dark enough for Art to use his goggles. Weirimen could operate in lower light than most men and they preferred to keep the Guild user friendly to only those with the gifts. Art knew an elf could see in even deeper darkness than they and Lucid could function in pitch black darkness. But it was not their comfort he was really thinking of, it was their company.

Weirimen worked with Scarborough Knights from time to time but only on larger operations and only in areas of the Wyld they already patrolled. For him to be with an elf and an unidentifiable creature such as Lucid was somewhat taboo and at the very least highly unorthodox. He was hoping they would not be seen as further complication to his already overly complicated predicament. Cindervail had told him to go alone on this quest.

Passing through many stone walled hallways and finally through a gallery of art depicting Weirimen and their many battles with darkness, they came to a figure at the back of the room of portraits. Art was expecting to get questioned again but the man turned around sharply and started to speak.

"So you are Storygrove. I am Borne Felvase, Grandmaster. Can't say I'm pleased to have you show up at our doorstep, as you are, bearing evil and towing strangers. But with Minevur's dramatic announcement about the dangerousness of your state, I truly half expected you. We are on the edge of the wild and if you are to cure yourself of this unique affliction to this cursed place, I expected you to come."

Towering over Art's already tall form, the large man of flaming red hair and blue orange eyes struck quite a figure in his black and brown layers of Weirimen dress.

"Now what it is you're looking for in my library and what can I do to get you on your way because I do not want Cindervail's prized, but afflicted, favored pupil in my camp any longer than you have to be. Should you break down into full possession, I would hate to have to face her if we be the ones to put you down."

Art was surprised and affronted by several things in that statement. Never had he thought he was favored by any of his instructors. But to hear Cindervail would be upset should he die did bring a small measure of comfort.

"I need to find a place," Art explained.

"What place might that be?"

Art hesitated. He had always been told the place he was looking for was a myth.

"Out with it, boy, what's this place?" The Grandmaster urged, his broad, bearded face screwed up with impatience.

"The Consciatosium."

For a moment the Grandmaster stared, then dropped his face into a flat, sneer.

"Awe, hell, Storygrove, I knew you were trouble the moment I sensed your presence here."

"I didn't think it was real," Senny spoke, her and Heavykel having not been dismissed but having stayed to listen.

"Oh it's real all right," Felvase blustered, thick hands on his hips. "We just don't tell everyone it's real because the place is damned dangerous and somewhat taboo for us to visit. You could be corrupted by it, you know."

"Corrupted, sir?" Art frowned.

"Yes, boy, the Consciatosium is a very real place. It exists on the edge of worlds, saddled in the center between ours, the Veil, and the Demonic. It is a library that hosts all the knowledge of demon history."

"Surely, such a place would be useful to Weirimen," Senny said, sounding excited. "Couldn't we use it to learn all the deeds and names of all the demons we face? It would not be such a struggle then to research the names of great demons."

"And this is why it's knowledge that shouldn't be known," the Grandmaster turned large, darkening eyes on the young woman. "It holds great secrets, much knowledge, and in truth, it has everything we need to do our work. But this library is alive."

"Alive? What do you mean alive?" Art cut in flatly, his nerves starting to dance at the ferocity with which the Grandmaster spoke about the place.

"This place has a mind all its own and it favors no one, man, elf, demon or fey. It tests you, weighs you, toys with you, all at its leisure. And it had been known to corrupt, turning righteous to darkness or darkness to wanderers. In our history, many Weirimen who ventured there never came back and some who did were no longer themselves."

The man's grim face was a testimony to their possible fate in the Consciatosium. He did not trust the Weaver in the traditional sense. He was a crazy man in the woods who had put Art in several situations that very easily could have killed him. But he had enough sense to know the Weaver had been correct and clear about what Art needed to do or he would perish under this great evil.

"I have to go," Art mumbled tightly.

The Grandmaster looked hard at the man for a long moment and Art could hear whispers of his thoughts. The man was remembering times spent with Cindervail, how much he valued her skill, opinion, and for some reason she placed great trust and value on Art. The man would trust her recommendation to aid him.

"All right," Felvase agreed. "Take him to the library. You can shroud the minds of your companions from our secrets, can you not, Storygrove?"

This is what the guard had meant by passing a Shrouding. Often when non-Weirimen were let into the Guild their minds were shrouded from things the Weirimen did not want the public knowing. There could be weapons, secrets, displays, and books in the library the Guild would not want Ever and Lucid to see. Should Art come across one of those, he was to hide it from his companions.

"Yes, I can do that, Sir."

The Grandmaster waved his hand, "I need to see no test of skill from Cindervail's finest. Now go."

Art nodded his thanks and followed Senny and Heavykel out. Though surprised himself by the Grandmaster and much of what he said, he had not missed that both women too were taken back by his faith. Art had never been aware that Cindervail thought anything special about him, though he knew she had been close with his guardian, Evendale. Did Cindervail know more about his past then she had let on?

Chapter Twelve
Insidious Talk

If Art had another chosen profession, he would have been a librarian. For all his skill with blades, aptitude with demons, and psychic abilities Art's greatest love was to read. The library at Evendale's home was his favorite room in the house and contained the fascinating things from demonology and history books, to epic adventure stories and references of most interesting subjects. He spent most of his youth soaking up all he could from her books, especially since her work often took her away from home for long periods of time. They were his company and he always felt like time spent reading was productive.

The second greatest thing about actually qualifying for the Weirimen Seminary was the library. Vast, finely furnished, and packed with the rarest most fantastic stories, histories and terrifying truths of the world, Art spent nearly every night until midnight in the place his whole first year, going through everything he could get his hands on. People thought it was his drive to succeed, be the best among his peers, but the truth of it was Art just loved knowledge.

In the shadow of everything that was happening to him, Art felt more than a pinch of relief when joy spread over him at the sight of the magnificent library rising up before him. In stacks taller than any he had seen before, they were so large they traveled up to the second story of the grand room.

"Yeah, I thought this would make you happy." Senny was at Art's side smiling.

Surprised that she knew anything of his love of books and libraries, he blinked in slight embarrassment. She said nothing more, just followed Heavykel into the room, beckoning Art and his party.

"Let Senny know if you should require anything else, Storygrove," Heavykel said once she had led them to the area which the Grandmaster indicated they should look. "Be sure to keep your companions out of the restricted books and away from the historical weapons displays. I expect you both to Shroud anything they should not be seeing."

Ever's expression clearly indicated he did not like the Weirimen and their guarded secrets but he said nothing. Lucid was entirely unaffected and took to a large comfortable chair near the stone hearth nearby the shelves they had stopped at. It did not seem that he was going to aid in the research as he curled up in the warm spot, dropping instantly off to sleep.

"So he does sleep," Art murmured as Ever came up beside him.

"He watched over you every time you slept. He is due the rest."

Art nodded, feeling suddenly grateful for the boy's silent and tireless support. He had never been close to anyone, never relied on his peers. It was odd to have companions now, even an old classmate was at his side, aiding him for no other reason than his need. Even though the Weirimen had been clear on their fate should he fail, Art was still finding a small comfort in the kindness.

Yet kindness was nothing and would not last. Should the demon take him over, no one would hesitate to end his life and send the demon back to its depths. It could even be what they were planning before he left. Perhaps that was why they left him with a familiar face. With Senny around, he might drop his guard and it would be easier to take him then.

Art stopped. He had bent over a book of maps Senny had given him when his mind had raced into darkness again. He did not have to look for the demon's influence. He knew his thoughts had been soured by it again. He would have to find a way to distinguish his thoughts from the ones planted by the thing or he could be acting on what he thought were his own ideas, but in truth were all guided by evil.

"I can't believe this thing is real," Senny remarked as she, Art, and Ever were into their third hour of searching through books, records, and maps for a sign to the location of the Consciatosium.

"That remains to be seen," Art grumbled as he pushed aside yet another thick, leather bound tomb large enough to strain his arms in just lifting. "We have very little to go on other than it's near the Shard Lakes, which I have yet to find as well."

"I believe it exists," Ever commented, unrolling another map he pulled from a huge case of tubes holding maps new, aged, and some nearly in pieces. "However, I do not know if we will find it in this place."

"The Weirimen have the greatest libraries in the world," Senny defended. "If it exists, it will be here."

"If that were the truth, then we would have no need to travel to this great demonic library."

Senny gave the elf a slightly sour face but said nothing else. Art found himself almost chuckling. The elf had rubbed him the wrong way several times with his opinion of the Weirimen but he was finding it did not bother him so much anymore. Their eyes met for half a moment and Art recalled he had been witness to everything that had happened with Grandmaster and the mentioning of the Crimson Dispatch. He was certain the elf would have questions, but surprisingly Ever had said nothing, only aided them with the research. Art knew he would owe him an explanation later.

"Ah, what is this?" Ever drew everyone's attention and the pair of Weirimen gathered around to see the map the elf had spread on the table, his long finger near large shard shaped lakes, over a strange symbol and faded lettering reading Conscia---um. It was missing several letters but something in Art's gut told him this could be nothing else.

"You found it!" Senny exclaimed. "Good eye."

Ever lifted an eyebrow slightly, almost as if he were going to remark on the excellent vision of elves but he said nothing, only gave her a slight smile.

"This has to be it!' Art was grinning. "Look! The lakes are even there; those are the Shard Lakes."

"Where is it located?" Senny asked, leaning over a bit more when Ever rolled the map up.

"I think it best if we keep the location secret. Only Art and I should know.

Blinking very fast, a frown forming, she responded, "What? Why is that?"

"Your Guild has been less than friendly to Storygrove. I feel that it is best, until our quest is at its completion. We should leave the Weirimen out of it. Come, Storygrove." The elf tucked the map into his pack. "If they will give us lodging here we should turn in and leave at first light. I shall keep safe the map."

Senny was visibly offended at the elf's statement, but could not bring herself to say anything about it. Instead she angrily stepped in front of Ever and pointed to the packed away map.

"Who said you could take that?!"

"It will be alright, Senny," Art tried to sooth her. "I'll take responsibility for the map. Thank you for your help, but I think he's right."

She wanted to say more, wanted to ask something but Art only nodded at her and set off in fast steps towards the exit, Ever following and Lucid suddenly at his side as if the boy had been listening the entire time.

Several Weirimen were in the front of the library and the adjoining hallway when Art made his exit. Some said nothing, watching with wondering and judgment filled stares. Others were whispering, clearly not caring that Art could tell they were talking about him. He could sense the thick hang of disapproval as he passed, his mind reading needing only to graze over the lot to know the most of it. He did not want to stay the night in their care.

"Ah, find what you were after then?" Grandmaster Felvase was suddenly at the juncture between the inner halls and those that led to the exit courtyard.

Halting his pace that had become increasingly quickened, Art tried not to frown so deeply. Taking a sharp breath, he nodded.

"Yes, thank you, Sir. We'll be of no more trouble. I'll take my leave and—,"

"Nonsense," the Grandmaster squared his eyes and peered down at Art, his expression hard to follow. It made Art nervous. "Night is upon us. You should stay here and depart tomorrow."

"It was clear you did not wish Art's company longer than necessary," Ever spoke.

"And I was quite rude about it." Felvase gave the elf a grin that only seemed to set Ever on edge. "But Storygrove is very nearly a Weiriman. Cindervail made it clear she wanted him treated as such. Tonight he should stay, despite my manners before. I do apologize. Your situation is rather a sticky one."

Art knew the elf wanted to slide him a glance but did not break the stare he had with the Grandmaster. Art was curious as to why Ever was holding such a strong appearance of loyalty to him. They had not been comrades long but his defense of Art was giving the Guild a different impression.

"We've prepared a room for you and a spot of dinner." The Grandmaster's tone was less an invitation than it was a push and Art said nothing more. Having the Grandmaster himself show them to their room was further proof that Art had little choice unless he wanted to openly decline and disobey.

"They are planning to imprison you."

Art knew this was the voice of the demon now and it made no attempt to hide its cold presence, licking through Art's mind like a frigid slime on hot skin. There was a sense of fear in the thing's warning. It did not feel it could defend itself against so many Weirimen. It knew as clearly as Art, that they would not take pity on the young man as his judgment council had. They would kill Art to deport the demon back. The thing was not strong enough to deflect the lot without first consuming Art's soul. Its transparency did nothing to quell Art's nervousness. Threatened could mean the beast would be more dangerous.

"Here we are," the Grandmaster announced when they had traveled high into the fortress' levels to the sleeping chambers. "This room is unused and set aside for guests that are not of the afflicted nature. Though you fall into the category, I can expect you will not display any of that behavior, will you, my young man?"

Art's eyes were rimming amber color at the direct shot at his condition. He wanted to mouth back, shout at the man. His stress flared open and he was annoyed they would not let him leave.

"This is more than adequate for our needs," Ever said as both he and Lucid passed between the men. "If we might, could we supper here?"

"Dinner is served in the hall," the Grandmaster said stiffly. "We will see you soon then."

He dropped a look at Art, eyes hard. Art wondered if Felvase noticed his very sudden, very near loss of control. If he did, he said nothing and closed the door, leaving the group alone.

"You have some explaining to do, Storygrove, and I would make haste before we are expected in the hall."

Art felt anger rising in him again, a bitterness he had tried to suppress since this all started but he was feeling hot, flushed with emotion and reeling at the imbalance in the world.

"I…," he started, voice edged and sharp when he felt a tug on his sleeve.

Lucid smiled up at him, an Umbra Sweet in hand. Art stared, first vastly irritated. As the boy continued to smile and made the motion that Art should chew, the man's anger started to ebb. Hand slightly trembling, he took the candy and lowering his eyes put the sweet thing into his mouth, gnawing slowing. As the sugary taste spread over his tongue he started to calm, feeling foolish and a touch bewildered.

"You are possessed?" Ever said very quietly, as Art slumped into one of the large comfortable chairs by the window, dropping his bag as heavily as himself.

Art was silent a long moment and Ever waited. Lucid, looking between them, shrugged out of his own gear and took to one of the beds in the room, pulling his legs up as if to watch the conversation unfold.

"Yes, and no," Art finally said, the candy consumed. He felt slightly better, though he could still sense the presence of the demon watching the words float out of his mouth.

Ever's brow arched but Art was not looking at him. His eyes were on the setting sun, casting golden light onto the vast city before them, chimneys billowing gray smoke into the evening.

"Can I ask you something?" Art turned back to the elf. Ever said nothing but tilted his head indicating Art should go on. "You defended me today, aided me, even though you knew there was something wrong with me that I didn't want to tell you."

"I did," the elf confirmed.

"Why?"

Ever gazed at Art as if he did not want to answer. As the moments dragged out into uncomfortable silence a glow appeared around Ever. Lucid perked up, grinning as Orchid appeared, billowing out of Ever like glowing petaled wings. She seemed to take a deep breath, though if she could smell the air or not Art had no idea. She did seem refreshed when she opened her yellow and fuchsia eyes, giving him a radiant smile.

"I'm sorry to suddenly appear, but I feel your question deserves an answer and Ever, likely, will not bring himself to do so."

The elf dropped a stern look on the ghostly dryad but she shyly gave him a little smile and glided over to Art. He sat up just a little as she stopped before him, her long hair weaving about her spectral form.

"We are moved that you would help us, Art. Where we have been met with mostly ideas of release and death, you shared Ever's revulsion at the idea of moving me on."

"Killing you, Orchid," Ever corrected. "Do not use their terms. It was a sentence of death, not release. Art saw it for what it was as well. Just because evil forced us into this situation does not push you into the same realm as a demon invading another soul. I resented the implication and the comparison."

"He was moved that you saw things differently from your kindred. You said it was your duty to help, even though you were under a cloud yourself. The races of men do not often inspire a Scarborough Knight."

"I never claimed he inspired me, flower," Ever popped one brow at her.

She only smiled and returned her gaze to Art.

"Your pledge has caused us to make one of our own. We will aid you as well, Weiriman. Please share your plight with us so we can do all we can for your cause as you said you would do for us."

Art looked into her beautiful face, watching the light move through her transparent form like sun on water. He did not trust easily, but it was hard to see anything but honestly in Orchid's eyes. Ever, though still stern looking, had softened his gaze on the man. Lucid's ever pleasant face was the last note Art needed before he settled back against the chair and relayed the events of the past few days, hinting at his life and aspirations before the demon's discovery, finishing with his time with the Weaver and the retrieval of Weir Hewn.

After his story, a long moment of silence webbed between all in the room and Art's down cast eyes glowed with worry. In telling, all he might have accomplished was to rob himself of the only allies he would hope to garner in his predicament. The Weirimen were unlikely to continue to help him as he exhibited more and more symptoms of the possession. Though Lucid would help him, he was not sure the boy was up to the task of protecting him when they traveled into more haunted ground country. His cracked Weir was going to draw the most awful of things.

"Seems providence we found one another." Ever was the first to speak. "Our goals are uniquely suited. We will get you to the Consciatosium, Storygrove. You just concentrate on holding that demon within your Haunting Weirs. Now, let us to supper. We should eat, rest and depart this place as soon as the sun is up. I do not trust the Weirimen."

"Except Art," Orchid added, her ghostly tether drawing her after him as he moved across the room to remove his gear and weapons.

Ever did not say anything but did give a small grunt. Art tried not to smile.

Art had run through a list of horrid, agonizing things he would rather be doing other than going to dinner in the Weirimen Hall. Though it consisted of things like taking his Weiriman entrance exam again, battling a demon blindfolded, allowing his instructors into his inner most thoughts, and the week long physical training test that ended in a broken arm and forty three stitches down his shoulder, back and thigh, Ever still insisted they needed to go.

"You and I both know refusing this 'request' from the Grandmaster will only generate fear and misgivings. You are well aware of my suspicions of your brethren, but in the shadow of your story, I have even greater worries."

Art did not need to ask what Ever meant. He was also fielding the same concerns. The Grandmaster's back-peddling on Art's presence in the Guild House, combined with the demon's clear warning of capture, had the Weiriman believing there could be something other than goodwill behind Felvase's reasons. Their chief mandate was to rid the world of demons hiding inside others' souls and Art carried the promise of the most dangerous kind.

"I know," Art mumbled, wishing he did not have to leave his gear and jacket behind in the room. There was no reasonable expectation for him to show up at dinner dressed to run, though he was at least relieved he could wear his blades. Weirimen were expected to be armed at all times. He felt self-conscious though without the hood, knowing everyone would be staring at him.

Lucid had been inspecting the room's every nook and cranny when Art removed his long coat and ran a hand through his hair. The long slightly waving strands of dark blond laying heavily into his eyes on one side, while the under part, sheered very short, took on a deep goldenrod. Art had a habit of wearing his hood up and pulled tight over his head. The boy was suddenly at his side, inches away from his face inspecting the hairstyle he had seen little of.

"Woah, Lucid!" Art blinked surprised by the boy's sudden movement. "What are you doing?"

Not answering, Lucid looked at Art's hair and reached out touching the small exposed shaved part, before poking the long strands that covered most of Art's head. Curiosity satisfied, Lucid grinned and then headed towards the door, completely unaware his behavior might be socially awkward. Art frowned and blinked a few times before looking at Ever and Orchid. The dryad giggled but Ever only shrugged.

"What was that about?" Art rubbed a hand over his light mustache and goatee, checking his knives and running his hands down his shirt nervously for at least the fifth time. He really did not want to go to dinner and be seen by even more of the Guild.

"Perhaps, he has not seen an under-cut hair style before?" Orchid offered.

"I don't think it's that usual. I've had my hood off before."

"Perhaps he has just noticed." She gave a light smile as she watched the boy poke at a hanging lantern on the wall, the ornate swirls and curves of the black metal causing him to run his finger over the loops.

"I hope he doesn't do anything like that at dinner." Art grumbled as he followed Ever out the door, Orchid disappearing before she could be seen by anyone passing by.

"It will be a good distraction for you. Try not to look so concerned. Your brow is knit so deeply your face could be mistaken for tree bark." Ever dropped a judgmental glance.

"Thanks," Art droned sarcastically, but did try to smooth his expression.

The hall was busy. Art had not seen so many Weirimen in one place before. Even for a city as large as Wivenguilder, he had not expected the numbers. The profession was rare and dangerous, but he supposed he should have known there were more than he expected. Demons were prevalent but not taking over the world so there had to be a significant force standing against the darkness.

The large hall was filled with beautifully furnished tables and chairs, as grand as any other part of the compound. The Weirimen did live well, though Art knew the majority of their fortune did go to the equipment, training, and defense of the Guild. Many a dangerous thing was contained within the Guild House's walls.

As Art started towards a table on the edge of the room all eyes were on him. Whispers of thoughts, hushed voices and heavy staring bore into him and he sat, back to the corner. He would rather have not faced them but he could not bring himself to leave his back vulnerable, feeling paranoid.

"Would you like a menu, sirs?"

Art glanced up at the server. The Guild employed a great many who were not Weirimen to work in the kitchens and take care of the other chores.

"Thank you." Ever nodded and took the menus, handing them to Art and Lucid.

Art did not care what was for dinner. He was struggling to ignore the eyes on him, the talk. He was getting bits and pieces about what they had heard, what had been said, the mandates about what was to be done about him should he start showing signs of possession, and how they all were directed to be leery of him.

"Art," Ever commanded the man's attention back.

Art had started to rub his hands together roughly, his expression growing more and more intense.

"You need to ignore them and order some food." Man and elf looked at one another for a long moment; Art felt as tightly wound as a ball of metal wire. Then, blinking twice rapidly, licking his full lips, the Weiriman nodded and snapped open his menu, forcing himself to read the words and ignore the thoughts.

"Lucid, what would you like?" Ever asked, after layering a heavy look on Art's nervous behavior.

"Can't read." Lucid grinned at him. "Want cake and toast."

Art glanced at the boy and cracked a tight smile. "Don't you eat anything else?"

Lucid cocked his head before shaking it.

"Just nightmares. I like cake and toast though."

Ever and Art both smiled a little. Perhaps the boy did not really need to eat. Art had noticed the only thing he ate out of the food he had were biscuits, crackers, and peanut butter with honey sandwiches.

"I'll have steak," Art said, suddenly craving the meat.

Ever glanced at him, watching Art closely but the man did not feel his stare was like the others. He never expected to become so comfortable with his new companion so quickly and at such a time of adversity. He wondered why he had never made fast friends with the other novices at the Seminary.

Art managed to make it through his meal. It helped that the food was good and Lucid was so enthusiastic about the many different dessert and toast options available to him. Before long, Ever had dropped into interesting conversion about his forest home and Art was feeling almost normal when someone approached their table.

"So you are this 'Storygrove' we have heard so much about?"

Art knew the tone and it only coiled his hackles. The person, whomever he was, was only out to make trouble. A loner and gifted in a dangerous, competitive profession had given rise to many occasions Art had encountered bullies, trouble makers, and those seeking to prove themselves or test their peers. Knowing he would be looking into the eyes of someone he knew without ever having encountered them before, Art did little more than tilt his head up a hair's width and slide his eyes over.

"I'm not here to socialize," he said coolly.

"That is some truth there," the man spoke his hands on his hips, his tall muscular frame enhanced by the four others he had brought with him. "None the less, I am Joss Lirecolden, one of Grandmaster Felvase's chosen elite. It is my business to see the source of so much talk and the reason for the Crimson Dispatch."

"I think you'll be disappointed at the effort. I'm not much to see." Art tilted his head up more, his amber green eyes bright. He did not want to show weakness but gave the man an out to leave him alone. He hoped he would take the hint and leave Art be.

"Not even out of the Seminary and you've already fallen prey to the darkness. Such a waste. Grandmaster Cindervail spoke so highly of you to Felvase. Must be hard for her, putting so much time and effort into a prized pupil only to have them succumb to darkness and failure so quickly. Everyone knows she left the field to teach. Cannot help but wonder now if there was not another reason for her retirement from combat. Perhaps she's not as good as they say she is, producing new Weirimen such as yourself."

Art knew Lirecolden was only trying to rile him up. He knew he was testing him to see the hold the demon had over his emotions. Those possessed had lower impulse control and could even lash out violently as a result of their subconscious mind trying to fight off the demon within. Knowing all this, Art could still not suppress the flush of anger that shot through him. He felt the demon's chill, riding the heat of his emotions, its thoughts molding with his, whispering Art should defend himself against the accusations, defend his instructor. Art could show them what he was capable of, how skilled he could be, how he could cleave their Weir's right out of their bodies with the new blade he had acquired through no small act of skill and courage. It would be easy, and the spilling of warm blood would soothe the aching cold he was feeling in his hands.

Art's heart rattled suddenly at the dark thoughts that had all too easily flooded his brain. He was not sure when he had risen from his seat. He heard little of what Lirecolden and his allies had said. The smiles on their faces and the jeering laughter told Art it had all been mockery.

"Enough," Ever suddenly spoke, rising from his place, Lucid doing the same. "I will not sit here and watch those who claimed to be of a good and honorable profession ridicule and mock one who is afflicted, by his own fault or not. Who placed you in the position to judge his torment and to lay bare before a dining hall of your peers his trial? Should he fail his very life will be forfeit to the malady. Your jeering is nothing but a show of the honor-less pack of coyotes your kind can be."

"Here, elf, you are a guest in our house and you talk to us in such a manner?!" the woman next to Lirecolden bit.

"I speak when it is necessary, a tradition your kind should exercise more often. We will retire for the night, as the company has soured the wine."

Steely eyed, Ever headed toward the exit, Lucid grabbing Art's forearm and pulling him along with them. Art glared at the group, some smiling, others scowling back, but he said nothing else and followed elf and boy back to their chamber.

"Bullies," Ever spat angrily when they returned to the room.

Art hardly heard him though. He was embroiled in his own thoughts. So many times that day the demon had inserted itself into his thought stream, as if it were just another fish in the river. It did not seem to matter if Art was conscious of it or not, he could not stop the current and was swept along with the dark and violent thinking of the thing.

"Storygrove?" Ever called but Art ignored him, going to a chair near the window, night starting its fall.

He had thought he would have had more time. With the aid of the Umbra Sweets, Art had expected to have better control over the beast.

"Storygrove!" Ever was standing over the man now, frowning down at him with concern. Beside him Orchid floated, her lovely face also a mask of worry. "Are you all right?"

It took a long moment but Art finally looked up at them, his brow a knot of concern, his hands in tight fists.

"Is it the demon?" Ever asked, trying to sound gentle but there was fear in his voice and Art hated that he could hear it much louder over the concern.

"It…it speaks to me," Art said almost against his will. "Its thoughts are like my thoughts, but I don't want to be thinking them."

Ever said nothing for a long moment, taking a controlled breath.

"From what you have conveyed to us, this thing is of an ancient malevolence and cannot be contained while it is still within you. You must resist its pull until we learn its name for exorcism. There is nothing else to be done. You must resist."

Art felt a pang of anger. "You think I don't know that?!" His voice growled, his eyes turning dark. "I have been trying but it gets inside my thoughts!"

"You must not allow it to gestate doubt within you," Ever pressed. "You must remember who you are. When darkness forces its will on you, cling to your own identity and fight that beast within you."

"I am trying!" Art's voice pitched loudly, his desperation in the volume.

"That is all you need to do, Brother." Lucid was by Art's side, handing him an Umbra Sweet.

Art stared a long moment, face screwed up, his confusion tinged with fear. He did not want to lose the fight to the thing even before it forced its way out of his Haunting Weir. He had to find a way to hold on until he could learn its name. He had to maintain his strength or he would never be able to battle the demon once he had separated it from himself. Should it consume or weaken him too much, cutting it from his Weir would only free it to take him and then unleash itself on the world. Having consumed a powerful psychic soul, the Weirimen would then have to banish it back from whence it came, taking Art's soul with it. That would be a fate worse than the death they would deal him should he fail to learn the thing's name. Art looked on the approaching night feeling the weight of his ebbing life much like that of the darkening sky.

Chapter Thirteen
Uneaten Nightmares

Sweat, breath and Art was suddenly sitting up, panting and shivering. His dreams were dark swirling images of the demon sealing ritual he had witnessed. The thing was so massive and powerful, a darkness unfathomable. These two people had given their lives to seal the monster and it had stayed imprisoned for an untold number of years, so long ago no one in the Seminary had known of it. But why was it within him? Had someone put it there? Had it been his guardian?

Art's mind raced back to his childhood with Evendale. She had been a strict woman, but always loving, always patient with him. He had never felt anything but acceptance from her.

"See her as your mother, do you?" Art felt the demon's voice ripple over him and he tried not to feel the cold. "Yet, how could she keep secrets from you? How could she not tell you of your fate? She must have known."

"Shut up." Art grit his teeth, trying to block the thing from his mind as he would a telepathic thought he did not want to hear.

"Cover your ears boy, but you will always hear me."

Art felt something behind him and, eyes widening, he realized he was not in the bed in the guest chamber, but sitting on a stone slab in his mind's eye. Panicked and confused, he rose up only to be confronted with the demon standing before him, billowing smoke and ash. Art turned away, unable to look into the eye sockets filled with black abyss.

"Don't turn away from me, boy!" The thing bellowed in his mind. "Succumb to me now! You have always been mine! You should never have been. You are an abomination, just as I!"

Art was sitting up again, panting, coughing, heart racing so hard he felt like a horse on its death run.

"No…!" He shuttered into the black of the room, his fingers digging into the meat of his arms, the pain bringing an odd sort of grounding comfort.

Once his breathing had slowed, Art noticed Lucid sitting in a dark corner of the room, eyes glowing in the darkness. He was unsettling at first, moving like a cat he slipped off the chair and came to stand before Art.

"Dark are your dreams. I can't eat, too much evil."

He sat down next to the man on the bed. He did not look at him but gazed out the large window into the night of the city. Art started to wonder what he had meant, when he recalled Lucid had said he ate nightmares.

"My dreams are too dark to eat, huh?" he whispered, not wanting to wake the elf in the adjoining room.

"Demon is too real, too strong," Lucid said. In profile he did not seem like a mystical creature, just a youth of wild ebony hair and pointed ears like the Weaver. He seemed distressed that he could not aid Art. He wanted to function as a dreamcatcher and be a protector. If Art had to choose a word to describe Lucid's expression it would have been frustration.

The man could easily identify with that. All his life, all his effort had been about doing what he thought he was born for. His natural gifts told him he could have been nothing else but a Weiriman. His guardian had wholly approved of his choice and encouraged him with help and praise. But that had all been snatched away and a darkness billowed up inside, haunting his life, robbing his purpose and setting him against a path of dark conclusions. Hope was illusive. Yet this boy, who likely had a life of comfort before joining with Art's company, sat next to him, feeling the same emotions, burdened by being unable to perform his true purpose. It brought a small comforting feeling of connection to another person Art had rarely felt.

"I sit with you, Brother." Lucid mumbled, shoulders slumping a little.

Art nodded, not saying anything, but grateful for the company. Lucid understood what was happening to him, understood the darkness that loomed; he understood everything.

Dawn was not golden but a murky haze of humming light and exhaustion. Art's eyes felt like two balls of cooled steel. Heavy and cold in his head, they felt his inability to sleep again that night. Every time he had started to nod off, the demon's face met him in the darkness until he was seeing it even before his eyes closed. Fear, feathered with alarm, kept him awake. He was glad Lucid did not sleep, for the boy was the only comfort in the ruddy night.

Lucid was sitting before Art on the bed after the man had dressed and started to pull his long Weiriman jacket on. He made a motion that Art should eat, but his stomach felt sour and he shook his head.

"I don't have an appetite. I can't eat."

Lucid made a face of disapproval when Ever appeared, looking well rested and refreshed.

"You should try to abide something, Art. You will need your strength." Orchid floated out after Ever, their tether shimmering between them.

"She is correct," Ever concurred, gathering his gear to him and pulling his own cloak on. "We should stop in the dining hall before we depart."

Art hated that idea, but knew protesting was not worth the effort and followed them down, saying little.

There were few Weirimen about but they were able to get service from the kitchen.

"It would seem that this place is always open," Ever commented, serving Art eggs and toast, which he looked at as if they were made of sawdust and mud.

"Weirimen have an usual schedule. We go when and where we are needed. The hour plays little part in it."

Art could feel the elf's eyes on him, weighing the tone of his voice and expressions. He tried not to be irritated. He knew Ever was just being careful, that the demon inside him was a real threat and should Art lose his hold on the thing, it would kill everyone around him. That very same demon was likely making it hard to control his temper. Art hated that he was not stronger.

Weak. His thoughts were as bitter as his mouth tasted.

Taking only a few bites of his toast and a spoon full of eggs, they were ready to depart. Lucid offered Art an Umbra Sweet but he refused.

"I don't have very many of those left," Art half hissed. "I'll be fine."

Frowning, the boy put the candy back in Art's pack but re-emerged with the Scarlet Extinction.

"I have even less of those." Art was trying to keep his voice even but he was snapping at Lucid and he knew Ever had noticed, likely Orchid too. He was glad he could not see her at the moment. He had enough eyes on him, judging him.

Insistent, Lucid held the bottle out to Art, eyebrows raised expectantly. It only further angered Art but before he could respond in a way he would regret, a voice drew his attention.

"Leaving us now, are you?"

The party turned to see Grandmaster Felvase descending the stairs.

"Yes," Art's voice was cold, "thank you for your help and your hospitality."

The man nodded, but there seemed to be something in his eyes. There was a whisper of thought but Art could not quite make it out before the man's mind swallowed it back up. Art was frowning but he said nothing else. Ever and Lucid both nodded their thanks and took their leave.

The Grandmaster watched them go, following them to the courtyard, but stopping at the centuries, silent. The whole experience had Art on edge. His eyes darted around the ramparts, half expecting an ambush. It would be the perfect place to take him if they were going to. His palms were itchy. He wanted his blades in his hands. He felt hot inside his jacket, but cold in his legs and feet. Everything felt wrong.

"Storygrove," Ever's tone was hardly above a whisper, "you must calm yourself. You act as a caged beast."

Art's lips pressed firmly together, he could feel his teeth behind them set hard against each other. He knew the elf was right. The caged animal was not him, it was the demon. It did not want to be captured and deported. It had waited such an expansive amount of time to enter the world. In the nest of Weirimen it knew it could be turned back just as it was about to taste freedom. Art closed his eyes as they neared the front gate. He had to will the thing's emotions apart from his own. He had the soul, he was stronger. He could force it back. He had to.

"Farewell," the guard at the gate said, but Art barely heard him. He sounded far away, as if in a tunnel. Ever answered as Art, glassy-eyed, stiffly shuffled passed.

He remembered very little of the trek out of the city. So many people created so many voices and feelings. Art was losing himself in the hum of their thoughts. Never before had his abilities overwhelmed him so dramatically. His mind reading was usually a whisper and only when he sought out the thoughts. They had increased. The air ship flight had first shown that. But he had never experienced anything like the static hum and chatter clamoring between his ears. It could have been due to the demon; perhaps its powers were allowing Art to experience a higher level of his own abilities.

Regardless of the source, he was so intensely relieved he let out a great sigh when they cleared the final city walls and were out on the open road. His chest felt tight as if he might have been holding his breath the entire exiting of Wivenguilder. Art paused for only a moment, eyes on the city, truly surprised they had allowed him to leave. He expected to be detained. Even now that the demon's presence had died down, he still felt the anxiety.

"How convenient you've stopped for us here," a voice Art had only just come to know, came out the woods. A shadowy shroud of concealment spells fell away, and before them stood Joss Lirecolden.

Ever already had an arrow knocked, his expression showing he was greatly threatened that the Weiriman had used a shrouding spell to hide his presence until he was close to them. Orchid, who had emerged, shimmered turning even more translucent, hiding behind the elf.

"And what is this? Your companion is haunted by a most beautiful ghost. Something you did not share with the Grandmaster. You should have told us, elf. We could have exorcised her for you, since it seems your Weiriman is incapable."

Four more Weirimen came out of the shrouding spell. It had to have been such a large and perfectly crafted spell to fool a Scarborough Knight's senses entirely. It could only have been constructed by a master of the art. Art knew instantly Grandmaster Felvase had to have been the caster. He ground his teeth in anger at the betrayal.

"Come near her Weiriman, and I will put an arrow through your mouth." Ever said, his voice gravel deep full of malice.

"Such odd companions," Lirecolden smirked. "And what's with the boy? He doesn't look elven or man. Fey maybe? An odd mix of rabble for a partnerless Weiriman. But I guess one possessed might do things unlike one's kind."

"What do you want, Lirecolden?" Art grit out, his hand on Weir Hewn.

"I've come to take you back."

"The Grandmaster let us go."

Lirecolden did not try to mask his condescending attitude. "That was for show. We did not want the entire Guild to see us take you down. There are some who have sympathy for your plight and trust Cindervail when she says she believes you can exorcise the demon from you. And while you are not so afflicted that we can take you legally now, you will be within its clutches soon enough and Grandmaster Felvase sees little point in waiting to hunt you down. Who knows what damage you will do while the demon occupies your body, what heresy you will inflect or what innocent you will harm."

"I would take my own life before that happens! Cindervail knows this," Art spat, offended.

"Well, no one has faith that you'll do the right thing, Storygrove. So I suggest you just accept your fate now and come with us. We will put you down humanely, without the violence and bloodshed that could ensue should this demon get out. You know it could happen even if it takes just partial control of you."

"You will not take him while I am here," Ever cautioned.

"We have no qualms with you, elf. I suggest you leave. I don't know why you're with him or what he's promised or paid you for your aid, but by your look you are a Knight. You should have nothing to do with this afflicted. We will take care of our own."

"I would hardly place Art akin to your kind. Lying, backstabbing thugs! To even think I could be bought and paid for like some underbelly hunter…!" Ever's beautiful face was a mask of contained rage. "Now, step back or I shall draw first blood."

Surprised, the other Weirimen, though clearly about to draw their weapons, looked to Lirecolden. His eyes locked on Ever as he started for his blades when suddenly Lucid sprang from behind Art. Fully nightmared and completely black, he jumped on the man so rapidly the others were shocked into stepping back. Man and boy fell to the ground and Lucid clamped his clawed hand around the man's throat.

A black length of thread appeared on the flesh and Lirecolden's eyes rolled into the back of his head.

"Sleep!" The dreamcatcher commanded and Lirecolden's lids fluttered before his whole body went limp and he lost consciousness.

The black thread around his throat spun, moving on the skin like a liquid tattoo. It rolled and twisted until it formed a braid of many tangles. The thing settled into a slow unraveling, like a clock counting down. Lucid had cast the ability so fast that he was sliding backwards after he was finished, avoiding the lunge of the next closest Weiriman.

"Lucid!" Art barked but the boy, more acrobatic than Art had realized, rolled backwards in a perfect arch, rolling on to his hands, then belly and finally his feet.

Weapons drawn, a Weiriman took a step forward and Ever raised his bow.

"No!" Art yelled, pushing Ever's arm.

Confused, the elf glared at him but Art was not paying any attention. He had already drawn both Weir Hewn and his other blade, stepping between Lucid and the group of Weirimen. He had faced combat with more than one opponent before but the skills Art displayed when the small squad attacked surprised even himself. Blades flying, body spinning, his ability rivaled any training evaluation he had performed. It was as if something else was moving him, almost like he could see his opponent's strikes before they happened.

His blade narrowly missed the throat of the woman closest to him and Art abruptly realized the source of his sudden great agility. It was the demon. The demon was using his body somehow or feeding information directly into his mind and muscles. It was giving him the tremendous dexterity and a lethal edge rivaled only by the most skilled of elves.

He was going to kill the whole party if he did not stop somehow. He had to pull it back, had to regain control. He focused his mind, shutting out all other thought than taking back his body. He did not want to die, but he did not want to kill these men and women even more. The pure rage of being used inched the thing's control over him and the fight inside his mind slowed him down.

"Art!" Ever yelled and came between a Weiriman's knives and Art's back just in time. Parrying the man back with his bow, Ever pulled his long sword, slashing and finally landing a boot to the man's knee, knocking him down.

There were too many of them to just deflect and Ever could not stop them all without killing, which Art clearly did not want. Another, moving past Lucid who was trying to protect Art as well, dove at the man. Having collapsed to his knees, Art was trying to hold the demon off inside. He could feel it overwhelming him, icing up his muscles, clawing for control.

"Will you not defend yourself, whelp?!" The thing screamed in his head. *"Let me take them! Let me kill them! We will both live! Would you die here like this, hunted by your own?!"*

"You're not killing them!" Art screamed back, his whole brain on fire. "You're not killing them using my body! I won't allow it!"

The man was upon him now, blades ready, when Art and demon together locked up, eyes a blazing red and gold, issued a burst of fiery rage, exploding off of him in a wave of energy. The man yelled and was thrown back. Everyone around Art, Ever and Lucid included, were flattened to the ground.

"You useless sack of meat!" The demon bellowed inside Art when the people started to move again. Disoriented and dazed, but very much alive. Art had held back the thing's power enough so that its energy did little more than stun the group.

Ever was the first to recover, moving to Art's side, hauling the man up roughly by the arms and setting him on shaky feet.

"Steady," Ever ordered. "Lucid!"

The boy got to his feet and shook his head, nearly teetering over. He was dizzy but seemed unharmed. He knew what the elf wanted and was at Art's side, dragging him away as Ever covered their back. The Weirimen were in worse shape and were just starting to roll over and rise to shaky knees as Art, Ever, and Lucid disappeared into the woods just outside the city's main road.

For the first mad dash into the forest Art was unsteady, breathless and barely conscious. After a half mile of Lucid dragging him along through the woods, Ever stored his bow and hoisted the man into an over shoulder carry. Elves had great strength and though Art was tall, toned, and heavy, Ever was able to carry him with little effort. Elf and boy raced through the woods, light footed, leaving very little of a trail to track, putting much distance between them and Wivenguilder.

Chapter Fourteen
Catatoran

Art was in pain when his eyes forced themselves open. The demon inside him was close, leering, burning him from the inside out. Hardly conscious, he did manage to hear Ever barking orders to Lucid. There were creatures nearby. He could hear growling, combat, the wailing of wounded beasts and cutting of flesh by metal.

They were in the woods but Art had no idea what was happening until suddenly something was being fed past his dry lips and the sweet cherry flavor exploded on his tongue. Art coughed dryly but managed to chew a bit before swallowing it more whole than this throat liked. The pain started to ebb, his muddled thoughts beginning to clear and the demon still full of rage melted back into the ache of his mind.

"Get him up!" Ever was ordering Lucid, who was under Art's arm and hoisting him up.

Still disoriented, Art tried to rise, eyes focusing on the beast Ever was fighting nearby, a great hulking thing, gnarled teeth and twisted jaw. He had no time to ask when Orchid was suddenly before them.

"Lucid, take him out of here. Dark is almost upon us. Ever and I will find you."

Lucid was in his nightmare guise, smeared with strange blood not his own. Questions raced through Art's mind. What had happened? Where were they? How long had he been out? Fragments of nightmares and words from the demon flooded him as the boy helped him amble away from the fight, Orchid's glowing form disappearing behind the trees as they went.

"Lucid, what's happening?" Art's words were slurred. He felt sick and weak, the demon must have been trying to drain his energy, another sign he was losing to the possession.

"Your Weir, it brings Demon Touched," Lucid answered as the trees started to thin and Art could smell the sunrise just before them.

"Is everyone all right? I feel awful."

"Many days you fight the demon," Lucid said to Art's alarm.

"Many days?!" The time lost to him gave a rush of ugly dreams blurred with pain. Some of what had transpired between him and the thing inside him, surfaced in sickening after taste and muddied images. He pushed the memories away. He did not want to recall the details of what had happened in his unconscious mind. Miraculously, he seemed to have battled the thing and still retained his mind and soul. That was enough for the moment.

The strength in his legs was starting to solidify again and he tried to lift himself off of Lucid and take his own full strides. His body ached as badly as the first night his Haunting Weir had been opened but he ignored it, knowing they had to get out of the woods urgently. Something had caught Art's scent and he too could smell the foul beast nearby. Lucid was already wide-eyed and growling.

"It's fine," Art tried to reassure. "The sun is coming up; we'll be out of the woods soon. I don't think it will pursue us. Just stay with me."

"Leaning fairly hard on your companions, aren't we now?"

Art felt the voice of the demon within him, but it was not as foreign and cold as before. It had been less demonic, even friendly. The change in its communication with him brought more alarm than the evil voice had. It could have meant the thing was closer to claiming his soul than before, blending with his voice, it was starting to become him.

The thing laughed, *"Even after all you have been through, how much of your mind I tried to consume and subdue, you still see clearly what is happening to you. Such a rare thing you are, Art Storygrove. You would have made a splendid Weiriman. How many of my brethren would you have expelled back to the depths had I not eaten your soul?"*

"It's not supper time yet, demon. Now leave me alone."

It chuckled darkly, clearly amused. Art was completely dismayed. Even though the thing was still locked inside his Weir prison and he had just eaten Scarlet Extinction, it could now openly talk to him. He was progressing too rapidly. He had to put it out of his mind. He had to ignore the thing. Now he needed to get out of the woods, and make sure Ever, Orchid and Lucid were safe. He needed to figure out where they had to go next. While he was still alive and thinking he could not let the thing win out over him. There were no other thoughts to be had.

Clearing the woods, they emerged atop a hill looking out over a road leading down to a large town. It was older, less modern than Wivenguilder. Narrowing his eyes to see better in the low light, Art pulled his mask up. The filtered pure air would help clear his lungs of some of the demonic Sin Breath he likely inhaled over the last few days. It would help cleanse his mind as well.

He knew this city, the front archway over the main road was unmistakable.

"Catatoran," Art mumbled to himself knowing this was home to one of the oldest Weirimen Guild houses. They had traveled a long ways in Art's lost time. The man felt cold down to his gut. What a burden he had been on the little group. Just how deeply had the demon worked its way into his mind? He would have to be even more careful until he knew more.

"Don't just stand there!" Ever was suddenly bursting out of the woods at full elven speed.

Art had not heard him coming, lithe footed as elves were.

"What's wrong?" Art asked as the elf blurred past him. Orchid in tethered tow, like a glowing balloon on a string, her eyes wide on where they had come from in the trees.

"Run!" Ever called over his shoulder as he took to the road.

Lucid obeyed, pulling Art by the forearm. The man glanced over his shoulder, eyes bugging when he caught sight of the thing Ever fled from. A great gray figure made of misty black shroud, embedded with whirling hands and arms, streaked through the trees, moving through the trunks completely without form. An incorporeal of such a size Art had never seen before, but by the chill of cold and fear melting off it, he knew it was likely a wraith or a conglomerate of angry vengeful spirits.

Scarborough Knights could do little against such monstrous creatures, as they were immune to all physical attack. A Weiriman could dismantle it and send it back to the Abyss. But Art was in no condition for such an arduous task. A wraith was one of the most dangerous incorporeal creatures and took great mastery and skill to defeat. Most Weirimen could not battle such a thing on their own. Truly the only remedy was to run.

Usually the thing would haunt only a specific area, attacking only when things came into its haunting grounds. Art knew when the creature emerged from the woods, it's shifting distorted body turning towards them, blue and gray hands grappling desperately, that is was after him and his cracked Haunting Weir. It was outside of its normal behavior. Sunlight would weaken the thing and send it back to its grounds, but even so close to dawn it charged after them, hovering over the ground. Near the top of the formless mass of arms and clawing hands something resembling a head, pushed its way out of the mess and wailed after them. Eyeless, with only a gaping hole of a mouth, full of jagged teeth, it screamed. Art could feel its pull. The thing was definitely after him. The elf, ghost, and boy were all unimportant. The thing could almost taste the living soul of Art's Weir.

Slightly fearful but more struck with awe at the horror of it, Art willed his jellied legs to run, his body protesting with every step. Before long he could see the sky lightening and glancing back again, he saw the wraith shrink from the coming light and start to fade. The thing wailed and wailed its frustration, many voices issuing out of the thing as if all the souls it had consumed and held prisoner within it cried out in sheer anger at losing such a tasty prize. Art turned back around knowing the thing's form would disappear and it would return to its territory. They were out of danger, but still he ran on until they reached the archway of the city just for safe measure.

"I have never seen a wraith behave in such a manner," Ever said, sharp green eyes on the thing as the sun turned it translucent and it finally disappeared. "I believe it was drawn to you and I just got in its way."

"Oh it was," Art wheezed, taking in huge gulps of air, his tired body completely drained from the short, terrible sprint. He felt like he had been sleeping for a year and his body had forgotten how to function in a vertical position. "It could smell my open Haunting Weir."

"Are you all right? You have not been conscious for days!" Orchid's ghostly face swam with concern.

"Yes, we have had the most inconvenient time hauling your unconscious, open-Weir body across the countryside." Ever added flatly. His normally immaculate appearance looked slightly disheveled, though not as worn as Lucid. It was clear they had been through an ordeal.

"I'm sorry." Art chewed his inner cheek. He felt guilty but also grateful and Ever, seeming to read the expression, said no more, only turned his gaze to the city.

"Orchid, you should hide yourself. This is a town of Weirimen."

She did as she was told, glancing at Art, concerned again, before disappearing into Ever's form.

"We should find what we came here for and quickly." Ever's eyes scanned the still sleeping town. "The last town we stopped in had a wanted declaration for you already posted. The Weirimen have put a notice for you to be captured for 'attacking' them. I believed they used the incident outside of Wivenguilder to move your status to officially possessed. You are being hunted now, Storygrove."

Art had known, even if he escaped Lirecolden's gang he would be a fugitive to the Guild. He would receive no more aid from the Weirimen. He would have to rid himself of the demon before his Guild caught up with him or suffer the fate Professor Minevur had promised.

Ever had used the map they had gotten from Wivenguilder to get them to Catatoran, but from there the map had given little clue as to where to find the Consciatosium.

"I know about this town," Art explained after they found a small bistro that was open early and mostly empty of patrons.

"Is this a good idea?" Ever interrupted him in a hushed tone, eyes glaring up at the door every few moments. "I am certain your wanted notice is here. People will be looking for you, not only Weirimen. The reward for information is a prominent motivator. I feel you could be discovered here."

"We could be seen anywhere," Art responded, sipping his tea and taking a large bite of his sausage. He was certain the demon's presence was making him crave meat, but he ignored the implication. He was just glad to be hungry rather than feeling sick. "Let's just eat and then move. I think I know where we need to go."

"How so?"

Art pulled out his demonic compass. "I can track demonic energy with this, but what I meant by I knew of this town is it is famous for their ancient catacombs in the city's underground. My gut feeling says we should head there and use my compass. It will just be a matter of finding the entrance to the catacombs. I don't know where those are."

"I am hoping your 'gut feeling' is more accurate than your taste in what you fill it with." The elf eyed the sausage with a brow raised in disapproval.

Art smirked. "What's the matter, you don't like sausage?"

Ever turned his nose up slightly and Lucid shook his head as well, a mouth full of coffee cake.

"Not a sausage made by the races of men. I question the quality of the meat."

Art laughed. "Well, I don't care at this point. My body needs the protein and I crave the meat."

"You know that is a sign of—"

"Yeah I know," Art cut in. "I don't care. Let's find this thing and end my problems rather than discuss them."

The elf could see the wisdom of Art's words and finished his breakfast along with Lucid, who seemed unbothered by Art's carnivorous appetite.

"We still lack a means of finding the entrance to the catacombs. I hesitate to inquire with anyone; it could draw attention to us. Your notice does not name us as wanted, but does list us as possibly associating with you. I think we shall be noticed."

"Yeah but this town is large. Exploring it will take too long. Maybe, we should check the town hall."

Ever dropped a heavy look on Art before speaking in a flat irritable tone, "The town hall is the last place wanted folk should wander for information."

"All right, that was stupid a suggestion," Art admitted. "It's not easy to get information on an ancient place like this. They don't do tours or anything in this place, because it is said to be haunted."

"Why has it gone on un-cleared? Certainly with a large Weirimen Guild in town it should not pose a threat." Ever questioned before giving coin to Lucid who went to pay for their meals.

"It has been, several times and it is maintained, but I believe it sits on a Hell Mouth, deep in the catacombs. A hole into the underworld can never really be cleared. They just have to keep turning back what comes out."

"And people live in this place," Ever scoffed. "This whole town is likely saturated in demonic energy."

"I'm sure people wear masks, and there is a large Shadow Confectionary here to compensate. People adapt, Master Elf. Your kin would not just up and leave their home because it was near a haunted ground would they?"

"I doubt such a corrupt area would ever exist so close to a settlement of my kin," Ever answered smartly, gathering his belongings before they all exited.

"Let's wander a bit," Art suggested. "Perhaps we will happen on what we need. I'll try using my compass."

"You are proposing much risk again."

"You have a better idea?"

As the elf did not, he pulled his hood up and fell into step behind Art, stone faced and suspicious of every passerby.

Lucid, was back to his usual curious self and had to be told more than once to keep his hands to himself and not to engage the towns folk as shops opened and street vendors set up their wares. Pouting a little, but understanding the circumstances, he shuffled along behind Art for the better part of the afternoon.

Standing before yet another Shadow Confectionary sweets shop, like the one Art had visited before he began his quest, he ran his hand hard through the long strands of dark blond hair, frustrated.

"We are going to have to talk to someone," Art sighed. "There's not enough demonic energy in the air for my compass to give a clear reading. Likely, the Shadow Confectioners gathered it on a regular basis. The only places my compass seems to lead us to are Confectionaries. They are the strongest concentration of demonic energy above ground. This is getting us nowhere."

"If we ask someone they might alert the Weirimen."

"I know." Art rubbed his hand over his light goatee and grumbled. "But we have to do something. Come on, we'll ask in here."

Ever looked uncomfortable but said nothing, only followed Lucid and Art in. The little shop was not nearly as impressive as the Bohurst Confectionary in Riftenshire but it smelled equally as pleasant and was filled with sweets.

"This might be a good time to restock your Umbra Sweets," Ever suggested.

"I can't." Art shook his head. "Cindervail said only the ones I got from the Bohurst Confectionary would be strong enough. How low am I?"

Lucid stopped and turned slowly. His expression looked alarmed, apologetic and scared all at the same time. Worried, Art went for the two bottles in his bag and found them nearly empty. Even the Scarlet Extinction was down to only three candies left.

"It has been a very difficult passage for you to get here," Ever explained as he watched Art's face turn from panic to sickening realization. "Lucid had to give you some just to keep you sane and present. You were battling the demon for your body. Do you have no memory of this?"

The mention of it flashed through Art's mind and he tried to suppress it.

"I only remember bits and pieces and want to keep it that way for now. I understand what you did for me, Lucid, thank you." He tried to hide the fear bubbling up inside him as well as the laughter from the demon within.

"Running low on the little candies that keep me at bay. Whatever will you do when they are all gone? I do wonder."

Art ignored the jab and tried to quell his fear.

"It will be all right," Ever reassured, even though his eyes betrayed a note of fear himself.

"Let's just get what we came for," Art mumbled, eyes flashing to the shopkeeper approaching them.

"Can I help you?"

Art's inquiry raised suspicion with the Confectioner, but he did take note that Art appeared to be a Weiriman and Ever looked like a Scarborough Knight. Whispers of his thoughts did reveal he was a little confused and slightly wary that the pair was working together. Knights on occasion worked with Weirimen but usually in the Wyld and were almost never seen fact-finding in town together. Art also appeared to be partner-less, another oddity. His eyes glanced at Lucid, knowing the boy was no Weiriman, his pointed ears leaned him towards a fey. The group was abnormal and it heightened the Confectioner's suspicions.

"Are you here with the Scarborough Knights garrison in town, Master Elf?" The Confectioner asked before answering Art's question.

Ever looked surprised. "There is a garrison in this town?"

"Yes." The Confectioner nodded. "They are following a pack of touched beasts that came dangerously close to several towns. This place always has scares like that though, due to the catacombs. Why would you lot want to go there?"

"It is a matter of some urgency," Art said pulling out his license and flashing his Weirimen seal. The badge shimmered crimson in a way only shields of the Guild could. Only a tiny spark of those with the ability of a Weiriman could make it glint and the shopkeeper seemed to accept Art's authority and divulged the location of the catacombs entrance.

"We need to hurry," Art muttered as they exited the shop. "We may have gotten our information from him, but he is suspicious of us. If he reads the newspaper I saw on the front counter we will be exposed."

"The newspaper is of worry?" Ever questioned as they quickened their pace down the cobblestone street.

"I saw a red notice in the folds of the paper. It would appear I am serious enough to be put on a leaflet and slipped into local papers."

"You cannot know this notice is about you. That would be more serious than anything I have heard before," Ever protested never before hearing of Weirimen issuing Crimson Dispatches to the public.

"The best of the Weirimen Seminary could not put this demon down without killing me. That's unheard of. That in itself is pretty serious. After spending time with this thing I can tell you its plans for me and what it will do in our world. They are harrowing enough to print a notice and send it out to Weirimen towns and cities."

"You are recalling your memories of the past few days?"

Art's face darkened. He was now. He recalled some of the visions the demon had given him: the death and ruin, the plans the demon had to infiltrate the Weirimen and destroy their order. Just its magnitude of power and blood lust alone were enough to alarm his whole Guild.

"I think Felvase was doing more than just giving us room and board. I think he was poking around in my head when we were together and maybe spying on us. He had some psychic abilities I couldn't read well. He might have seen what this thing has planned. I'm sure he doesn't want to chance it eating my soul and gaining a permanent body in our plane. He'll hunt me down. He's got to be behind the public relations push to find me."

"We must hasten to the demonic library."

Art nodded quickening the pace but not before he noticed the Shadow Confectioner rush out of his shop and spot their party disappearing around a corner in the road. Even at this distance he could hear the man's thoughts.

"Special Notice by the Weirimen Guild. Wanted: Art Storygrove, possessed and dangerous in league with Pith demon. Urgent! Any information pass directly to the Weirimen Guild. Ample reward."

Art knew exactly where the shop owner would be headed next, and it would take very little time for the Weirimen to be swarming through the city heading to the very place the Confectioner had sent them.

Heading to the area the Confectioner had directed them to, Art pulled out his compass hoping to narrow down the exact location.

"Are we close?" Ever's voice was doing little to hide his annoyance. Too long had they been wandering through the city following Art's compass.

"It's a compass," Art stormed back. "It doesn't give me foot unit destination information."

The elf shot him a look but Art ignored him. He did not appreciate Ever's attitude anymore than the elf liked his, but they were both stressed and had every reason to be on each other's nerves. Only Lucid did not seem to be bothered and followed along, ignoring things that would normally interest him. He too understood the serious nature of finding the catacombs before the Weirimen found them.

"We are getting close," Orchid's voice suddenly echoed out of Ever's body.

Startled, Art did not know she could speak through him without being physically separate or without his mouth moving.

"How do you know?" Ever asked.

"I can hear the call of the voices from the catacombs."

"Ghosts?"

"Yes," she answered. "I can hear them."

Art felt a chill. She was right. He could sense it too: a cold dampness at the edge of his skin, traveling up his limbs and into the warmth of his neck. They were close to something souls had passed through or occupied.

"She can hear the voices of the dead?" Art asked as they made their way across another street towards a cluster of tall stone buildings and an especially old looking block.

"She is closer to the side of the dead than the living," Ever confirmed. "While in this form she can hear the call of those across the Veil and of the underworld."

Art did not have to be a mind reader to see how much it disturbed Ever. He would have to press the Weaver for a solution for the pair.

Just as Art was wondering if the Weaver would be the right place to go for information, recalling how unhelpful with details the man had been on his prior visit, a voice called to them from the street they had just crossed.

"Halt!"

Art turned just a bit to get a glimpse of the Weirimen. Cursing under his breath, man, elf, and boy all broke into a run towards the older district of buildings.

"Where are we going?" Ever barked, leading them as his run was far faster and he was more jogging than actually running.

"There! Head that direction!" Art pointed before glancing back seeing the two pursuers. He knew he had to put some distance between him and them before they started to employ all the other things he knew Weirimen used to catch fleeing prey.

"Here, Brother!" Lucid suddenly said, grabbing Art by the neck of his coat and pulling him down an alley way, Ever spinning to follow.

"This is the wrong way!" Art growled but the boy was already at an old iron gate, chained closed blocking off a long dark alley before them.

"Come!" Lucid urged and put his hands together indicating Art should use it as a foot hold.

"I can scale the gate," Art protested but Ever gave him a shove and the man was putting his foot in the boy's hands before he knew better.

Art hardly had time to think, when suddenly Lucid was lifting him and the man was not only scaling the gate, but he was flying over it at a height Art's screaming mind could not comprehend. Ever was near him, having run up and used the side of the wall to scale the gate easily, giving himself as much height. Man and elf sailed well over the gate and towards an old stone balcony of one of the buildings. Art yelped, but Ever had him by the arm, pulling the man down with him into a landing. Art skid and hit the wall of the balcony hard, but mostly unharmed. The elf, effortless in his grace, turned to catch Lucid as the boy flew through the air after them, having as much agility as the Knight.

Panting and totally bewildered at being flung through the air, Art peeked over the side to see the two Weirimen glaring up at them, equally stunned.

"Storygrove!" Ever urged, having spotted a ladder leading to the roof.

Art nodded and looked at the Weirimen again, who were scrambling below to get through the gate or find another way to the building the trio had just scaled.

"Where are we going?!" Art asked once they arrived on the rooftop.

"Which way to the catacombs?" Ever ignored Art's question.

The man looked to his compass and pointed confidently.

Elf and boy started in that direction, running towards the edge of the roof, both grabbing Art by the arms.

"Wait!" The man protested wildly, but could do little more than scream as the pair leapt from one rooftop to the next, pulling Art along with them.

The landing and roll was rough again, and Art was lucky he did not roll an ankle. He managed to shake it off and follow the pair, climbing down another ladder, then heading towards an alleyway below. Art was visibly grateful they were leaving the rooftops. Without Ever and Lucid he could never have made the huge leap.

"They'll find us," Art wheezed, slightly winded once they were on the ground, his shaky legs glad to be earthbound once more.

"I know," Ever said, "that is why we must move quickly."

Nodding, Art pointed the way and the group headed off at speed, boots slamming cobblestone.

Rounding another corner, Orchid's voice rang out that they were very close. Art's eyes darted around for a doorway, opening, or something that might indicate the entrance to the under-city. He knew the Weirimen would be along soon and likely with more. They had little time.

Suddenly he saw it. Curved and bent into the base of a building was a huge stone door, carved and aged with symbols of death and demons. Faces resembling gargoyles decorated the pillars framing the door which was set at an angle, leaning back into the earth as if it were the cover of a large hole rather than a doorway.

But before they could head towards it, Art heard the sound of foots steps and the flex of bowstrings. Turning, alarmed, he was greeted with a group of tall, armored and well-armed Scarborough Knights, bows drawn, arrows ready.

"Wait," their commander ordered, a gloved hand pointed at them, even as Ever stepped in front of Lucid and Art.

Chapter Fifteen
Elves and Eyes

Outrunning a group of Scarborough Knights would have been as impossible as Art twisting his body into a loop and rolling down the road like a wheel. He knew their dexterity, agility, and stamina was superior to the races of men but he did not know just how impressive they were until Ever had scaled the gate as if popping over a bump in the road. Coupled with the knowledge that he had helped carry Art across the countryside during his unconscious demon battle to the city they were now in, suggested combat against a dozen trained Knights was foolhardy at best and suicidal at worst.

Art felt his gut tighten, his heart spinning in his chest as the leader of the group approached, hand on his blade but not drawing.

"You are Everther Nahrwel?"

Art and Lucid both looked to the elf, who seemed perplexed at the inquiry.

"I am." the elf lifted his chin slightly, eyes stern on the advancing captain.

The leader turned and motioned for the elves to stand down. In unison, they lowered their weapons, but kept them at the ready, eyes on Art and Lucid.

"I am Dahnaren Finnafor, leader of the Birchwood Garrison. I saw you on the market street and gave pursuit. I seek words with you." He was as tall as

Ever, but his hair was silvery gray, eyes a deep brown, and his skin a porcelain cream. He did look very much like some kind of birch tree kin.

"Why would the Birchwood Garrison be in search of me?"

"Ever, there's no time," Art hissed knowing the Weirimen would still be on their tail and could appear any minute in force.

"I am sorry, Captain Finnafor, but I am currently—"

"Forgive me, but I believe I am aware of your situation. Many in the Scarborough Knights know of your plight, Nahrwel, and know of your reputation prior to the incident with the dryad. My condolences on those happenings. We of the Birchwood Garrison are sympathetic and find your sacrifice of your position for her life a noble one. That being said, I am not in understanding of your association with the Weiriman his Guild is now hunting. I have been privy to the wanted noticed and its mention of you. For this issue I had to seek you out."

"For what purpose?" Ever narrowed his eyes.

"That would depend on your reasons for associating with this afflicted."

There was a moment of silence where it appeared Ever weighed if he felt he needed to explain himself to the other elf. Then, taking a slight breath, he spoke.

"This man, Art Storygrove, is afflicted but he is a good and honorable man, a better Weiriman than all I have encountered before. He has promised to aid me in removing the dryad from my Haunting Weir without harming her. He has the skill and the tool but we are in search of the proper method. In this endeavor, a second quest has emerged and that is to remove the demon afflicting him, which can be done with the same blade that will aid my plight. We must get into the catacombs in order to attain this knowledge."

"The dispatch says he is beyond aid and must be brought in."

"This information hails from the same people who deemed the spirit inside me a ghost affliction that should be exorcised and moved on, essentially killing the dryad. Weirimen are quick to judgment when a difficult situation presents itself that is in connection with ghosts, demons, and afflicted of any manner. They are singular in their desire to rid the world of such things."

"This is not a negative thing, Nahrwel. The world is plagued by evil forces and the Weirimen are a great force against that invading tide."

"Yes, but not all touched and afflicted are to be dealt with only a singular set of monochrome rules. Discretion and preservation of life is also essential to that fight. I tell you this man is not beyond hope anymore than I, myself am."

Finnafor stared at Ever for a long moment, brown eyes looking hard into the green. Art felt himself bunch up into a knot inside hoping this was not going to be a longer conversation than it had already turned into. They were so vulnerable to the Weirimen finding them Art might as well start walking back to the Guild house. Then, as if the breaking of spring on a winter pond Finnafor's stoic face broke into a smile and he nodded.

"Where is it you are headed?"

"The catacombs!" Art blurted out causing both elves to look at him. "This door here."

"The catacombs can be very dangerous and dark," Finnafor warned.

"I have a soul lantern!" Art could not help but smile with relief and he fished the thing out of his bag. "It will help against both wandering spirits and the dark, two in one. Can we leave now? The Weirimen are close."

"You will need it." The elf eyed the lantern in Art's hand. "Go, my Garrison will wait here and move the Weirimen along when they come. Should you find your way soon we will still be here. Should night fall, you can find us at the Silver Whale Inn for the next day. Seek us out and we will help smuggle you out of the city."

"Thank you for your aid, Finnafor."

"We are brethren." The commander smiled again as he clasped Ever by the wrist and they shook hands. "Now go, I hear a group approaching."

"Yes, boots on the street at a run." Ever confirmed as he and Art pulled open the aged heavy door. "We will seek you upon our return."

Art's lantern blazed to life as the darkness poured out as if made of smoke.

"Thank you." Art looked up at the other elf, who stood on the slope above the pit that was the catacombs' entrance.

"Everther Nahrwel is a great Knight among our ranks. If he trusts you, Weiriman, so do I."

Art nodded his thanks and followed Ever and Lucid into the underground network. The elves closed the door behind them and the bleakness of the catacombs set in. While still near the surface, the light of two front window holes allowed some illumination in. The place was somewhat diminutive, carved out of rock many long years ago. There was little sign of upkeep or even recent entrance. Dust thick along the stone floor and walls, cobwebs, and stale air greeted their nostrils.

Art started to lead the way when Lucid gripped his arm. Turning, the man started to question when he was greeted by the boy's eyes, completely black and white.

"What's wrong?" Art frowned, wondering why Lucid would be touching on his nightmare form.

"Evil down here."

Ever and Art exchanged a glance but knowing they had no other choice, Art patted the boy with his gloved hand.

"I know, but we have to go down there."

Lucid's black and white eyes bore into him. Art wondered what he might be thinking, but in a few blinks, Lucid's eyes returned to their natural blue. Perhaps the thought of going too deep underground unnerved the boy. Art was not sure. Before they went on Lucid tapped Art again and when the man turned he made the motion of eating and then pointed to Art's pack where he kept the Scarlet Extinction.

"I don't have many left," Art cautioned.

Lucid's eyes were unwavering.

"Perhaps you should do as the boy says," Ever advised, his face pointed towards the darkness before them. "Should the demon be drawn out in such a place, it could likely lead to your end."

"The calls of the damned grow ever stronger," Orchid's voice rose out of the elf and she once again appeared in a flourish of light.

"What do you hear?" Ever asked, watching.

With eyes closed, she listened to voices he could not hear, feeling things he could not sense. "The cries of lost souls, tormented, hungry. There is also something else, demonic voices. They are quiet though, strangely. It is the cries of the dead that have lost their way here that are the most prominent," she explained, coming to hover before Ever, his hand going to hers even though they could not touch.

Art had noted this interaction between them often. How hard it must be on the couple to have fallen in love post this odd tragedy, having never been able to touch. It was one of the things ghosts craved above all and often a reason they lingered after death, refusing to cross over. The pull to touch and feel a loved one once more, was a strong temptation to seek life once again. Art was trained to mostly exorcise demons but Weirimen were often called upon to remove a ghost, spirit or presence from a person, place or thing. Orchid was seen as just a thing by his Guild, but watching the pair interact Art could see beyond that reasoning. With her body still alive, she was not just a wandering spirit longing for life. She was not like the strange things that likely wandered the haunted tunnels before them.

Art pulled his mask up again. In his condition, he could not afford to breath much more of the touched air. It would weaken him to the demon within him, as well as the voices and things he would encounter. Weirimen dealt with things that came out of the catacombs and attacked people, but he could sense now there was something deep and old about the place. There was no way to clear an area this touched. It seemed an appropriate place for the entrance to the Consciatosium.

"Take the candy," Ever insisted as he passed the man, his eyes scanning the steep sloping stairs before them.

Not wanting to, but knowing the youth and elf were right, Art pulled his mask down and retrieved the candy before repositioning his pack and following Ever and Orchid.

"What is the function of that thing on your face?" Ever asked as the light from the windows started to wane, their descent on the stairs quickening its dimming.

"Demons and haunted ground give off a demonic miasma. We call it Sin Breath, that races of men can breathe in, like a pollution that effects your soul, mind, and weakens your Weir. It makes us more susceptible to evil, possession and dark thoughts."

"Elves are immune to such things. I would think living in a city like this, the Sin Breath would be fairly thick. Is that not unwise to make such a place your home?"

Art could hear the judgment in the elf's voice and found himself chuckling a little rather than being offended. "I supposed you're right. However, we have measures against it. These masks filter it and people can eat different kinds of Umbra candies to counteract it. Shadow Confectioners are usually present in towns like this. They keep the people healthy from Sin Breath. Weirimen are less affected by it, but we always have the mask as a precaution. But down here I thought it best to put it on, especially with my…"

"Condition?" Orchid offered the word and Art nodded with a slight smile.

"Interesting profession," Ever added. "Did you ever consider Shadow Confectionary opposed to the more dangerous one of a Weiriman?"

"Like Weirimen, you have to be born with a talent to deal with demonic energy and Sin Breath, not to mention you have to be able to cook and create the candy. The latter doesn't come easily to me and Shadow Confectioners do see some danger themselves, though nothing like Weirimen of course. But I never considered another profession. I was born to be a Weiriman."

Ghost and elf gave Art a glance but said nothing, their thoughts on Art's conviction already known by their actions and faith in him.

Directly after the stairs was a wide corridor lit by a strange reddish light, so low it was almost harder to see in the ruddy hue. Stepping off the stone steps, Art's boots splashed in the thin layer of water covering the ground. Musty air whistled softly through the corridors beyond, carrying with it a faint singing: high and airy.

"What is that?" Ever's voice was low.

"Ghostly singing. It's often heard in haunted places like this. I never really knew why, but some tormented sing to themselves, especially old ghosts trapped for many, many decades."

"It comforts them," Orchid suddenly said, floating between man and elf and then into the corridor as if drawn by the voices. "Singing translates their pain and anguish more than talking. It carries their emotion as well as their meaning…"

"Orchid!" Ever said sharply and she turned to him startled. Her eyes were a strong, bright yellow, lacking all the lovely hued plum that illuminated them so softly before. She looked strange, more transparent, her glow dusky. "Do not listen to the songs of the dead."

She stared at him a moment, her eyes glossy but starting to return to normal. Art suddenly understood Ever's fear. She was closer to the dead than to the living in her present state and it was entirely possible she could slip away to the other side whether or not he released her. The pull of the other dead could be a serious threat to the beautiful dryad.

"What's this red glow?" Art asked purposely changing the subject. There was little more they could do for Orchid than watch her closely.

"Afterlife stone," Ever informed. "It is rock infused with the energy of the dead. It glows when it interacts with the energy of the living."

"I should have remembered that," Art mumbled as he led the way into the wet corridor.

The red lit hall opened up into several hallways and Art drew out his compass for direction. The needle spun and spun but would not focus. After a moment, Ever glanced at the Weiriman, an eyebrow raised.

"Is there a reason for the unusually long consultation of a relatively simple device?"

Art slid the elf a flat glance, followed by a worried look. "I'm afraid there might be too much scattered demonic energy. My compass won't focus."

"I thought the Consciatosium would have the strongest collection of energy and would pull your compass as this very location did."

"For whatever reason that does not appear to be the case."

"I feel it, Brother." Lucid was suddenly right next to Art, his skin black as ebony again, his eyes white and glowing. "Follow."

The boy turned down a corridor quickly. Art and Ever had to break into a run after him not to lose sight of the boy in the ever-growing darkness of the catacombs. It was not long before the light of the red hued hallway was completely gone and they were wholly reliant on the luminance of Art's lantern.

Deeper and deeper they followed Lucid, the walls growing high and low at the different shapes of the tunnels. It was becoming colder and though the group had glanced moving shadows, strange forms and whispered movements just beyond the scope of light, they did not acknowledge nor discuss what everyone knew were wandering souls, ghosts, and other apparitions. It was no good bringing attention to something they desperately needed to pass them by.

Art did note that Orchid, though glowing and luminous, more so than any ghost Art had encountered before, her light did not illuminate the catacombs. The only thing she seemed to light up was herself and Ever. Her glow cast no light on anything else.

Finally, when Art was starting to wonder if they were going to the very center of the planet's core, they reached a strange tunnel: stone walls stretching so high into the darkness the lantern was unable to reach their ceiling. What was far more alarming than the height of the walls, were the narrowness of the tunnel itself. It was just hardly wide enough for a man's shoulder width to pass untouched by the old stone. It made Art feel squeezed and slightly claustrophobic.

"Here," Lucid said, his form returning to normal. He stretched an arm out and pointed.

"Down this corridor?" Art asked, holding the lantern up as something glinted in its light at the end of the long, narrow passage.

Lucid nodded.

Art was certain it was his imagination, but the passage way seemed to grow even tighter as they headed down it, single file, Art's lantern light leading. The air felt thin, smelling of dust and wet stone. Finally, after a long, unnerving trek in the dark they came to a very small aged door, iron hinged, wood worn and tried. Frowning, Art lifted the lantern inspecting it to find a very small window near the top.

"What have you found, Storygrove?"

"It's a tiny door," Art answered bending so that he could peer into the hole.

"Be careful," the elf warned, but Art knew there was little to do other than to scrutinize.

It was in an awkward position to his height and he had to bend at his waist and knees to get down to it but soon he was looking into the slot of the door. Inside was a stone face, startled at first, Art pulled back as suddenly a pair of eyes opened, red, glowing and pupil-less.

"You seek knowledge of the darkness, the world behind the Veil, forbidden and secret, things that should not be known?" The voice was deep, odd sounding, as if the thing were in a huge auditorium bent to allow sound to bounce and resonate.

"There's a hole here with a red-eyed glowing thing inside asking me a question," Art reported as both the elf and Lucid tried to see over his shoulder, the space too narrow for them to come up beside the man.

"What did it ask you?"

Art repeated the question and the elf seemed puzzled. "I am uncertain how to properly answer this question. Could be some kind of strange trap? Or a spell?"

"I had the same thought," Ever admitted.

"How will we know?" Orchid asked, peeking over Ever's head. Even though she was not physically limited like the others, she appeared to find it off not to stand in line as they were all doing.

"I'm not sure." Art had not expected to be greeted with a puzzle.

As he thought, Lucid seemed to grow impatient and suddenly started wiggling his way past Art. Bewildered, the man tried to move but the space was too narrow and they ended up struggling awkwardly until Lucid was pressing Art against the wall just so he could get his face to the little window.

"Lucid! What is wrong with you?! What the hell—"

"Yes," Lucid said into the door's slot.

"Passage will require reflection of one's self. Should you be willing to face the mirror you may enter the Consciatosium."

"Lucid!" Art scolded but the door's handle clicked and the little entry opened slowly, creaking loudly. Lucid wriggled past Art, who cursed and glared but the boy ignored him going to the black opening of the door.

"Wait!" The others all said at the same time but Lucid disappeared.

Cursing even more, Art went after him, careful not to bang his head on the very low frame. As soon as he stepped in, there was no need for his lantern as a large ornate chandelier lit up made of cast iron, hanging lowly in the room. The space looked much like a cell hewn from the rock itself. Eyes scanning, Art tucked the lantern back into his pack before he caught sight of Lucid on the other side of the room standing before three enormous and dirty mirrors.

"Lucid, you shouldn't just—" Art stopped as he came to stand before the mirrors just as the boy, but found only Lucid was reflected in them.

Confused, he noted the middle one was a normal reflection, showing the boy with his wild black hair, blue eyes and everything Art normally saw. The one to Lucid's right reflected the nightmare form, black, eyes completely white and long taloned hands. That in itself made some sense but the one to Art's left was a surprise. Before him was a large elaborate dreamcatcher, circular, with many threads, some of which held things woven and tied into it.

Before Art could ask what it meant the red eyes appeared in the black space above the mirrors.

"You have been seen, Lucid Dreamare. You may pass into the Consciatosium."

Lucid nodded and looked at Art giving him a reassuring face. He then turned back to the front facing mirror and walked through it as if nothing were there. Art gasped but when he tried to go after him he was greeted with solid dirty glass once more.

"What happened?" Ever and Orchid were suddenly next to Art.

"I don't know. The mirror or whatever that thing is up there, told Lucid he could go in and so he did! Now the door is gone!"

"Who next stands ready to be reflected in the Mirror of the Consciatosium?" The voice boomed at them.

"If we stand before you you'll let us in after Lucid?" Art asked to the strange eyes staring down at them. The voice did not respond, only the red glow glowered down at them.

"I feel that if Lucid thought it was safe then perhaps we can as well." Orchid said quietly.

"We know little about him, but you said he is something of a child of the Weaver and his reputation is that of great wisdom and knowledge," Ever noted.

"I wonder if you'll feel the same way once you meet the guy," Art mumbled recalling very vividly his short encounter with the Weaver and the many times he was certain he was going to physically die.

Ever was giving Art a deeply inquisitive look when the Weiriman sighed and said, "I suppose there is little for us to do but follow Lucid's example."

"I shall go next," Ever proclaimed.

Art nodded, not really sure what to think and took a step back. As soon as he was out of the way of all three mirrors Ever's form appeared along side Orchid. They were such a handsome pair, natural and fey beauty equally portrayed. It was easy to picture them as a couple, bound in love and devotion.

On the right hand side, Orchid appeared. But her form was different, more flower-like, more tree-like, hair of petals and vines, skin a graceful arching tree bark. At her core she was akin to a world separate from man: magical, nature and fragile beauty. That image was bathed in golden sunlight, shimmering in dew and rain. It was nature in a way Art had never taken the time to see: deep magic, pure.

The left side hosted Ever's image, stripped of his covering clothing and light armor he was more tree-like as well, washed in green hued moonlight looking strong and elemental. Hair far longer, the deep black-green of it shone in starlight as soft leathers and fabrics hugged lean, toned muscle. He was a stunning match to Orchid: virile, strong, natural and timeless. They both were creatures of another world and Art marveled at how they existed in the same state as he.

146

"You have been seen, Everther Nahrwel. You have been seen Orchid Sarathone. You may pass into the Consciatosium."

Again the middle mirror disappeared and giving Art a glance, the pair passed through. Art was left standing alone in the strange room. He felt nervous as the glowing eyes silently watched him from their dark cubby above the mirrors. A sudden whispering at the back of his mind reminded him the demon was trying to speak but he knew the effects of the Umbra Sweets were aiding him in suppressing it. Trying to focus his mind away from memories of the beast's voice, he took a step to the mirrors.

The middle reflection looked back at him, and he pulled his hood down to run his hand through the long dark blond strands. Nervous, the amber color around his green eyes brightened until finally he shifted his sight right. He was unprepared to see the two Weirimen from the vision at the Weaver's home, standing back to back. Behind them were two doors, two Haunting Weirs. In the woman's hand was, Weir Hewn. The man held the soul lantern he was now carrying. Art was frowning deeply, confused. But he was drawn to the other mirror and nearly jumped back as the Pith demon within him lunged forward in the mirror, smoke and black fire billowing around it, its huge and hideous form pulsing before him in dark, burning breaths.

Terror ripped through Art and he stepped back, feeling the demon would be reaching out for him with its taloned hands, ready to tear him apart and drink out his soul. Before he knew it he had backed into the right hand mirror.

Aghast and shaking, Art nearly yelped when the voice spoke, "You have been seen, Art Storygrove. You may pass into the Consciatosium."

Chapter Sixteen
The Consciatosium

Sweat had collected on Art's thin mustache and upper lip, his body still trembling post the rush of real fear. As he wiped his mouth with the back of his gloved hand, his eyes darted to the mirrors. They were clear again, reflecting nothing but the Weiriman. Collecting himself, he was glad Lucid, Ever, and Orchid had not witnessed his reaction to seeing the demon reflected within him. He had thought for that moment that it had been real, released from him and ready to consume. He had not drawn his knives, not guarded himself, or even thought about defense at all. He had displayed nothing but shrinking fear.

Flashes, feelings, and moments of the battle that had taken place in his mind with the demon between Wivenguilder and Catatoran blurred into his consciousness. Art closed his eyes, pulling his mask down, needing to breath more evenly. He had to shut it out. He had used one of his last few Scarlet Extinctions. There were only two left, and he could not afford to weaken now and call the demon up. He had not even entered the library yet. It would be such a waste to let the thing in due to his own fear.

He could feel it just under the surface of his consciousness, whispering, laughing at him but he could not make its words out. Turning his face, his eyes shut just as they turned amber. His abilities could keep the thing in check, the Umbra

Sweet was supposed to aid him in doing that. Still, he could feel it pressing on his Weir, threatening to force it open. Art grit his teeth, perspiration clouding on his brow. Though not part of his physical body, he could feel the pressure as acutely as if the demon was bending a joint in the wrong direction. He had to force the thing back.

A few moments more and Art could feel it withdrawing. He was grateful. He was certain if the struggle had gone on any longer he might have lost to the sheer pain it was causing. Breath wobbling out of him, Art pushed on the mirror he was leaning against and took a shaky step towards the center one. Composing himself, he looked up at the watchful red eyes. Though they said and did nothing, Art had the clear sensation they had watched and absorbed all he had just gone through and displayed. It made him uneasy but when the mirror before him vanished and a dark hole opened he took one lingering look at the watching eyes and passed through the empty frame.

Inside was chilled, smelling of dust and old earth. Walking blindly, Art had the thought of taking out his soul lantern again when a light drew ahead and he came upon a magnificent set of doors. A small single candle burned in a hanging lantern, casting only yellow light over the words scrolled above: "Consciatosium".

Art hoped to see the others, but he did not have to wait long before a smaller door in the great gate swung open and Lucid's head popped out.

"Lucid!" Art exclaimed, truly happy to see the youth.

Lucid gave a wave and beckoned him inside.

Once through, the gate closed on its own and Art was again happy being greeted by Ever and Orchid.

"We were beginning to worry," Orchid confessed, floating before him. "You were taking a while. Is everything all right?"

Art nodded, lying as he indicated everything was perfectly fine, though the images of the two Weirimen, the Haunting Weirs, blade and lantern all muddied in his mind. He had been so startled by the very real imagery of the demon that he had forgotten the other strange depictions.

"What do you think that mirror was?" Art asked.

"I believe the mirror was recording who we are. The images are likely renderings of our true selves, what we are inside. Lucid's showed both his forms, nightmare and as we see him now, as well as the dream catcher he was before he gained consciousness," Orchid answered before asking, "Why?"

"Just curious," Art lied again. He was even more puzzled by the images that were his portrayal.

"What did you see, Storygrove?" Ever's eyes were squarely on Art.

The Weiriman was beginning to be unnerved by the elf's ability to read him. Even guarded, Ever seemed to know when Art preferred not to talk about a subject. Before Art had to either create an answer or decide to recite the truth, the room lit up. It had been previously as dimly lit as the outer doors, the only thing visible, a huge empty front desk as high as their heads.

"Greetings and welcome to the Consciatosium. I am the Librarian. How might I assist you, seekers of knowledge?"

Art had to tilt his head back quite far to look up at the strange figure suddenly standing at the tall desk before them. Art was certain the Librarian had not been there before, nor had he seen it arrive. It was hard to make out the appearance but, before long, the figure was descending a set of spiral stairs leading from the desk to the floor.

Smaller than Art, the thing was about the size of Lucid, fully robed in rich, deep reds. The hood was so large that it hung well over the face, the only thing visible was a strange pointed beak-like mask that stuck out from the heavy hood.

"I'm uncertain of protocol," Art started, "but I seek the name of a demon."

"A demon you say?" The voice was odd, and when it spoke Art was uncertain if it were male or female.

"Yes, a Pith demon," Art confirmed.

"Ahhhhh," a smile could almost be heard in the tone, "the one you carry within you?"

"How do you know that?" Art's brow bent deeply.

"All who enter the Consciatosium add to its knowledge. You gave your consent before entering and the library has read and written your story. This way." Its scantily flesh covered hand, with nails long enough to be claws, beckoned to them. "I shall take you to the Hall of Demonic Tomes. There you may hunt for your name."

"I told you," Orchid whispered as they headed after the creature. "The mirrors likely looked inside us and learned all about who we are."

"Though I suspected this also, it makes me no less uneasy," Ever murmured back.

"It was likely some kind of payment for our use of the library," Orchid speculated, and Lucid who was walking alongside her, nodded his agreement. Art recalled the Weaver had told him Lucid could get them to the library. He wondered if that meant the boy had been before or was it just he would be able to actually lead them through the catacombs as he had done. The question would have to be posed another time.

"There is little we can do now," Art added, trying to swallow his own anger. He did not like the idea of anyone knowing his personal struggle with the demon and his very real fear and doubt about being able to save his own soul. The sadness and loss at the dismantling of his life and future seemed very far away now as the clear image of the demon in the reflecting mirror burned in his memory.

The group followed the librarian through a great stone archway along a rough red carpet so dark it was almost black. A hallway opened up to a wide stone staircase against a wall, a high cathedral ceiling stretching over head, braced by great arching supports, dangling a massive iron chandelier. As they approached the stairs, Art watched Lucid shuffle away from whatever he saw on the wall, causing the man to quicken his steps until he was next to the boy.

"What's wrong, Lucid?" He asked as his eyes fell on the strange carved masks that lined the entire wall leading up the stairs. They were ashen, like stone, but so lifelike. Just faces, suspended by no seen support, up to where the ears should have been. As odd as a line of facemasks was, the most disturbing attribute was from each of their closed eyes poured a continuous stream of blood tears. The line of tears was not just an illusion of paint, whatever the liquid was, it flowed down the masks' cheeks and disappeared back up under the edge of the thing so nothing spilled to the floor.

"Do not be alarmed," the Librarian spoke in its strange voice. "Those are some of our patrons that read things their minds could not processes. We did not let their condition go to waste and now their souls aid in the maintaining the Consciatosium."

"These people are alive?!" Orchid was horrified.

"In some sense, yes, but they are no longer fettered by a mortal shell. Their souls nourish the library."

"You speak as if this place were alive and evil," Ever's dark tone caused the Librarian to turn back, its strange mask poking out of the fabric, displaying no expression.

"We are just beyond the Veil here. To exist and allow both the physical and nonphysical to use the facilities requires...," the thing paused as if to think on just the precise word, "Energy. It requires energy. To call the Consciatosium evil is not accurate. It only feeds on what has met with unfortunate circumstances while in its walls, and only those that are drawn here."

"Like a carnivorous plant?" Orchid asked.

"Yes, lovely one," the Librarian's voice was smiling again. "That is correct. We ask our patrons to explore with caution, unless you would like to add yourself to the Consciatosium permanently."

"I have a hard time believing the souls you say power this place are here by their own choice." Art frowned.

"Oh, my young Weiriman, you would be shocked by the number of souls these walls harbor by choice or draw. The Library is always in use. So, be wary the resources you seek here often have a mind of their own. Caution, caution."

Art started to pull his mask back up when the Librarian, not even turning to see him, spoke again, "Do not bother with your filter, young Weiriman. Demonic miasma is filtered from the air and collected. Nothing is wasted within these walls."

Glances were exchanged as the Librarian continued to lead them up the stairs and into the grand expanse that was the central hub of the building.

The structure was tremendous with ceilings so high it was dark and hard to make out the actual shape. Great archways, slopping staircases and huge windows looking out into an unsettling blackness circled all round. Yet, as grand as the surroundings were, everything appeared in a state of semi-decay. The stonewalls were bruised and cracked with time, tapestries withered and worn. The furniture and shelves housings books in every wall, cranny, and alcove were tattered, old, and even seemed unstable.

"The place seems…a little…," Art wished he had not started the sentence having no polite way of finishing it. He had been too curious about the disarray.

"The library is ancient, but I assure you what you seek you will find here whether or not the appearance meets with your standards."

Art pursed his lips, wondering if the strange person could read his thoughts.

The Library only continued to unnerve the group as they ascended a flight of stairs passing many massive statues of people shrouded in fabrics, faces covered, bent in the strangest positions. Some had their arms outstretched as if trying to escape their stone prisons. Others were not facing them, bodies arched in painful ways, arms curled behind, faces towards the walls.

The higher they climbed into the structure, the more the décor took on strange disembodied body parts: sconces made of arms and hands folding together to mimic the shape, headless bodies were pillars, tables had actual legs, and arm chairs were made of a conglomerate of limbs all coming together in such a subtle way at first glance one would not have seen the arms nestled against one another. Everything appeared as wood or stone carvings, but Art was suspicious. A demonic library that fed on the souls of those who succumbed to its dangerous information, the experience left the possibilities of its activities wide open.

Finally, the Librarian took them off the stairs and to a set of double doors. Words tarnished and half faded on a plaque dimly shinning in lantern light read: Eternal Reading Room.

"What is this place?" Ever inquired, suspicion evident in the slight clip at which he spoke.

"A reading room of sorts. All information may be absorbed here, all information can be read here, but only by those willing to part themselves from their bodies. As most of you are physical, I plan to lead you to the actual book you seek. However, we must pass through this room to get to that wing. Won't you follow me, please?"

Not entirely sure what was being expressed, Ever and Art shared a dubious glance and followed the Librarian cautiously. With a wave of its boney hand, the doors flew open and a puff of old air rushed out as if a tomb had been suddenly exposed after decades. Art instinctively covered his nose and mouth, eyes squinting as he peered into the room. Light from the lanterns in the hallway poured in showing an empty reading room, book stacks at one end, tables and chairs in the center. A huge, unlit fireplace stood cold near the doors at the far end. Saying nothing, the group entered.

Two steps in, Art was certain he was hearing voices, whispers and flashes of ideas and mumbling. Frowning, he tried to quiet his abilities, uncertain the source until the doors slammed closed behind them and the room plunged into darkness. Alarmed, both Ever and Art started to speak when ghostly lights formed shapes in the space. Art placed his hand on Ever's forearm to quiet him as they watched the wisps of light come together and make figures of people. In a few moments it became clear that the room was teeming with ghosts, reading, lounging, some just standing and thinking, or perhaps just staring. Books were floating off shelves hovering around the transparent people, some being taken and leafed through, others just sliding onto stacks near readers and on tables.

"What in the world?!" Ever whispered.

"The eternal reading room," Art whispered back and pointed to bones strewn around on the floor. "It looks like people died in here just reading and reading." Some souls were actually sitting among their slumped over bones, having never noticed they had died.

Art steeled himself, the ghosts not noticing their presence. Carefully, he took out his soul lantern. Ghosts could be dangerous when angered but mostly they just needed to leave them alone. Art had no plans to try to move them on from their predicament. When the lantern came to life, every soul the light fell on disappeared. That was not normal and told Art these souls were forcefully trapped. It would take more than his skills to free them should he even want to try. They were part of the library now.

"Come," Ever urged. He was obviously uncomfortable.

As they neared the exit the elf started to feel strange. His normal confident step wavered and he stopped, placing a hand to his forehead, looking dizzy. Art did not notice, but Lucid grabbed his coat and the Weiriman turned, casting light on Ever's paling face.

"What's wrong?" Art started when he suddenly noticed Orchid was not right behind Ever as she had been.

Lifting the lantern, Art's eyes traced the tether linking them and found it stretched out much longer than he had seen it before. Frowning, he stepped behind the elf and followed its faint glowing line until he saw the woman floating towards the stacks of books. He called her name but she did not respond. Art's concern grew when Ever's breathing started to hasten and the Weiriman noticed the tether growing thinner.

"Orchid, wait!" he called again but she did not seem to hear him.

Something was very wrong and Art acted. He grabbed Ever by the arm and pulled the elf after him. Trying to protest, dazed and somewhat confused, Ever could do little more than allow himself to be pulled along, Lucid following.

"Lucid, if you can stop her, do it!" Art ordered and the boy broke into a run ahead of man and elf.

He came to a stop before Orchid, unable to touch, he stood in front of her. Art hoped that would slow her down but she seemed unable to see him and floated right through the boy even as he held up his hands to halt her. Art wasted no time and pulled Ever after him until they found her and Lucid in the book stacks. She was reaching for a book on the shelf when Art's eyes blossomed into amber-gold and he spoke in his Weiriman's voice.

"Stop, Orchid, I command you!"

That seemed to jar the dryad out of her trance, and she blinked rapidly, her transparent form flushing with the slightest hint of pinkish color. She looked around, seeming completely confused when her eyes fell on Art and Ever. The elf now slumped on the man just to stand.

"Ever! What happened? How did I get over here?" She rushed over, floating up to him, her dress and hair billowing around her as she moved. "What happened? What have I done?!"

"I don't think it was you," Art said eyeing the ghosts around seemingly completely unaware of their presence. "I think you being a ghost caused you to be drawn to whatever book in here you needed to read. It would be my guess, since you're linked to Ever, the library started feeding on both his and your life forces as it drew you into this room. It was trying to keep you, Orchid, and once it had you, it would have drained Ever and likely made both of you part of the Eternal Reading Room."

Orchid looked completely horrified, and Art watched as she agonized to touch Ever, to comfort him.

"I'm sorry!" she apologized but Ever was shaking his head.

"It is all right. I will be all right. I just need to recover myself."

"Wish we had some Umbra Sweets. They make those that can be consumed for demonic energy draining."

Ever shook his head again. "I will recover. Do not fret."

He lifted himself off of Art's supporting shoulder and teetered just a little, catching himself. Orchid wanted desperately to steady him but her hands moved right through his shoulder. Art felt for her as he watched her ball her fists up in concern and frustration. That in mind, he turned towards the bookshelf Orchid had been hovering in front of. Lucid was also there already inspecting the books.

"You find what she was looking for?" Art asked, lifting the lantern to read the titles.

Lucid nodded excitedly and pointed just as Art's eyes came to rest on a very interesting book.

"Abnormal Weirs: a Study in Experiment, Treatment and Ritual by Doctor Nicklaus Bancroft." Art reached for the book but his hand went right through it.

"All the books in here cannot be touched by physical hands," the Librarian suddenly spoke, appearing next to Ever and Orchid who both startled.

"Are we able to find this book in addition to the name of the demon I seek?" Art asked, coming out of the books, Lucid behind him.

"Oh yes. Please follow me now, follow me."

Both Art and the elf wanted to say something about the near death encounter to the Librarian but the whole party knew that was pointless. It had cautioned them, and as a servant of the Consciatosium, the suspicion was that the Librarian would rather see the party succumb to the place than aid them.

"It happened so fast," Ever spoke to Art in his mind.

Art was startled as they had never communicated telepathically before but answered, *"Far faster than I thought it would. We'll have to watch each other more closely."*

"Agreed."

Art could feel the whispers at the back of his neck, like hands caressing the hair at the base of his scalp with cold scaly fingers. The use of his powers had taxed him more than he wanted to admit. The voices could be his inability to keep the souls trapped in the library out or worse, it could be the demon trying to get through once more and speak to him. In such a dangerous place he was certain the thing wanted to take advantage and push him hard, hoping to break open his Haunting Weir and free itself.

Art shook his head. He had to banish thoughts of it, concentrate on navigating the Consciatosium, for it was as carnivorous as any demon, and its prowess was on display in its very walls. How much blood must be soaked into the bones of the building, Art had no desire to find out.

"Follow me, please, good people," the Librarian beckoned, its sloped back of deep red robes leading the way into the immense black of a hall that stretched out like a great throat opening just before the swallow.

Chapter Seventeen
Face of Hunger

The first experience in the Eternal Reading Room taught the party much. When the Librarian led them into a hallway even Art's lantern could not illuminate, he was already on edge and cautious.

"Where are we?" He asked, knowing the Librarian would answer, but that was where its aid would end.

"This is the Hallway of Endless Deep. Here you can find the collected works of anyone who has felt dramatic despair. Their stories have caused this deep blackness, devoid of hope." Its voice was almost too accommodating.

"This thing means to see us eaten by its master," Ever spoke to him telepathically as he pulled out a small glowing stone that could act as a light, only to have its illumination swallowed by the pitch as well.

"I had the same thought," Art answered in his mind. "Devoid of hope," he mumbled aloud thinking fast, not wanting to linger waiting for whatever danger the Library had in store for them to manifest.

"Art, what are we to--" Ever started but the man hushed him.

Art was running through what he knew of despair and its connection to demons. The darkness seemed to be making Lucid nervous and Art felt him move closer to both he and the elf. Art suspected that he had shifted into nightmare guise and still could not see through the black. Nothing they had could penetrate it. Suddenly, the man looked up and turned around. Orchid was behind the group, her glow not illuminating as a traditional light would, Yet Art could still see her.

"Orchid!" Art exclaimed and the ghost blinked at him surprised, her large eyes confused by his outburst.

"I can see her," Ever added. "Orchid, are you able to see in this darkness?"

She shook her head, floating hair shifting softly about her lovely face.

"She might not have to," Art went on. "She glows because she is a ghost, but she glows much brighter than most because she has hope that she will live again. Most ghosts do not have that and are locked in a constant state of despair. It's possible if Orchid wishes to leave this hall, her light will actually draw her out of the darkness."

"Will you try, my love?" Ever asked as the ghost closed her eyes smiling.

"Yes, of course. What do I do, Art?"

"Just think of what it would be like to live again, how this darkness is only temporary in your life. Concentrate on those feelings."

She obeyed, and though Art thought it would take a little time for her to focus, it was mere moments before her glow started to intensify. Art was actually quite astounded by her progress when her luminosity went from its ghostly hum to an almost shimmering blind, like a star. She started to float away from them and Art followed, telling the others to pursue. Before long they had walked quite a distance, guided by Orchid's light, until a door and the Librarian appeared right before her.

Art stopped them and Orchid returned to her natural state. They watched as the Librarian tapped its scaly hand on the door's latching handle and the room flooded with light. Art was about to follow the guide out when Lucid yelped, causing Art to turn and be greeted by a startling sight. The long hallway was much wider than he expected, a single rug running down its corridor. There was little in the space but aged wooden-lined walls. No furniture and few fixtures, but in the space between them and the long rug that they had followed to the exit door, was lined with row after row of lifeless standing bodies. They were all of mixed dress, race, and age, so many Art was not even sure how many were collected in the long room. They stood motionless with nothing in common but their state of being and the empty hole of black that occupied where their faces should have been.

Lucid looked pale, something about the rows and rows of empty people bothered him, but Art did not get the chance to ask.

"Depression and despair leaves you blackened and empty," Ever said quietly, his eyes full of pity. "I do not know if these things we look upon are people or if they are just the shadows of their pain, but these represent souls without hope, unable to dream. This is personal madness and broken life. We should leave this place."

His eyes lowered and he headed towards the door, Art following, taking Lucid by the arm and pulling him along. He was not sure if the boy was moved by the pain or if there was something more, but Art felt a tinge of real fear as well. It was not just demons and evil that reduced people to a state of emptiness. It was the loss of hope. Without hope, evil could get inside too easily and Art had to remember that. Once he learned the demon's name and he was able to cut it from him, he would be facing the exorcism of it from his soul. It would require strength, focus and above all hope. He would have to find a way to remember that the next time he faced the fiend.

More rooms, more stairs, and strange forms and figures: "patrons" victimized by the Consciatosium. After they passed a woman bent completely backwards so that both her knees and shins were on the floor but her from was so severely bent that her face too was laying flat against the carpet, Art was on his last nerve. She was not still alive, but she was also not quite dead. There was nothing he could do for her. The Weiriman grew angry.

"Are you going to lead us to the books we asked for or is this just a tour through hell before you try and devour us again?!"

"Good Sir," the Librarian stopped and waved his hand before a set of doors. "What you seek is just through here. I am sorry to keep you all waiting. The Consciatosium is a very large facility."

"That's been made very clear," Art grumbled and headed into the next room, expecting to be greeted with a huge monster or some other form of trap or trick. To his surprise, they walked into something that looked more familiar. Aged but warm colored wood pillars held up a second level, lined with books, reading desks and large comfortable chairs. Lamps lit the space well and nothing macabre or sinister haunted the room. Art was made even more suspicious.

"Here you will find what you have been looking for." The Librarian motioned to a table at the center where books lay on the polished wooden surface.

Art glanced at the hooded figure and hesitated, but Lucid and Ever proceeded to the table, Orchid beckoning to him. Giving a last glance at the Librarian, Art came to stand next to Ever and the elf pulled forward the first book.

"Demons of the Ever-Hunger," Art read aloud.

"The Ever-Hunger is a level of hell?" Orchid inquired as she admitted she had little knowledge of such places.

Art nodded saying, "Yes, there are many layers, more than we know about. No one is sure just how many. I don't know much about the Ever-Hunger other than it is a rare and deep layer full of the most dangerous and evil, though I suspect much of hell can be described as such."

Ever crossed his arms, tossing some of his long hair back saying, "It would appear your plight hails from that very place."

"So it would seem," Art muttered opening the book cautiously.

It was old, the pages a withered color, the leather binding worn and snug against its spine. The embossed emblem of some demonic symbol was pressed deeply into the cover brushed with gold and peeling at the edges. It felt heavier than it looked and Art slid a chair out to sit, setting the book before him.

The first page was blank but the next after depicted an illustration almost too horrible for Art to look at. Demons twisted together, writhing in flame and smoke, feeding on one another in violent tornado of agony and rage. Art did not want to turn the next page but knew he had to.

"I really don't want to see this." Orchid's voice was small and she folded her hands in front of her, floating away a little.

"Don't wander off," Art warned. "I could be here a while though. This thing is pretty large and I don't know how much I'll have to read to determine which demon I'm hunting."

"But how will you know?" Ever questioned, taking to a seat near where Orchid had floated. Lucid joined him, but sat on the table rather than a chair and smiled up at Orchid trying to get her to smile back. It distressed him that she was disturbed by the book's imagery as well as the whole Consciatosium experience itself.

"Normally, during an investigation of a possession, sessions with a demon would either reveal its name or force clues from it. It will use certain phrases, reveal details of the hell it comes from, or things it does during possession will hint at its origin. Our schooling taught us how to detect these things and usually gives us an idea of where to start the research. Also, every Weiriman has psychic abilities and at times interacting with the evil gives us a clear idea where to start. However, I'm the possessed this time. I'm not just engaging the demon, it's actually in my mind, taunting me, trying to break me down. It has given me little clue to who it is, and I'm sure it is doing this purposely."

"It does not want you to learn its name," Ever confirmed. "This is could be a positive development, though, Storygrove."

"I had the same thought," Art nodded, pulling his hood down and running a hand through his hair, feeling suddenly tired. His body had been sluggish and sore. Finally sitting after so long felt good, but also made him ache more as his muscles settled.

"You think it could mean it really is threatened by you?" Orchid asked understanding what man and elf were getting at.

"It's my hope," Art said, eyes scanning the warning at the front of the book that the demons contained therein were never to be summoned and never conversed with for they were of the most dangerous ilk. Art chewed on his inner cheek. "But everything I've seen so far would indicate I have little chance against this evil."

Lucid leaned forward and gave Art a pat on the shoulder. The man turned to look at him and the youth smiled. He gave him another reassuring pat and pointed to the book indicating Art should read.

"I agree with the boy. You should read the book before you waste a moment on despair." Ever was not looking at Art but reached out for the second book on the table. "Read, Orchid and I will see what can been discovered from this."

Art read the title upside down, Abnormal Weirs: a Study in Experiment, Treatment and Ritual by Doctor Nicklaus Bancroft. It was the book Orchid had been reaching for in the Eternal Reading Room. They hoped her draw to the book might indicate it would shed some light on her and Ever's predicament.

Before Art started to read, his eyes flashed towards the Librarian who stood unmoving, as if no longer alive, near the door of the room. The thing made Art nervous, and he hoped he was just on edge. Pushing other thoughts from his mind, his eyes returned to the tea colored pages of the book, to the first chapter: Lords of Hunger.

The title had a list scrolled under it of several different kinds of demons, some he had heard of and some that were unfamiliar. He stopped when he read Pith demons. Carefully, as not to damage the old pages, Art leafed through until he came to the title page. Anxiously he read:

Pith demon, also known as the demonic marrow or core demons, hail from a dense pit in the Ever-Hunger. Little is known about them as few have made their way out of the hell to the physical world. Once summoned and having crossed over to a physical form, they are nearly impossible to destroy. Imprisonment is the only tested and tried method of containment. The method of deporting them back to the Ever-Hunger is unknown as they get into the 'marrow' of the world and are very difficult to remove. They feed off of doubt, fear, and other core dark emotions. Known to be heavily intuitive. Also known to eat and prey on other demons.

Art rubbed his hand over his goatee and sighed long through his nose. There seemed to be no way to deport the thing back to hell. Even if he were able to exorcise the beast, what would he do with it? Learning its name might only give him the ability to exorcise it, but if even its name did not give him the power to expel it, he was at a loss. Knowing there was little to do other than to read on, Art turned the page.

A frightening image of a demon greeted him accompanied by a name. The picture was unfamiliar and there was little written about it. Art recognized nothing so he went on. He surveyed three more images of demons and three more names, nothing seemed right. They did not look anything like the demon he had seen.

Art found the depictions puzzling. There were always two figures pictured, though only one name was assigned. One bore an almost normal appearance with a face like that of man or other similar race. Though they still had horns, fanged teeth, clawed hands and other such demonic-like features, they were surprisingly mild. The other figure was grotesque, skeletal, frightening with all the imagery that invoked the word demon. Art suspected the demons had two faces, but not more than one consciousness unlike some nests of lesser demons. Demons with a singular consciousness were always more powerful. Nests of demons had to huddle together, because they needed each other just to survive, like smoky tendrils of wispy evil.

"Two faces," Art muttered when he flipped another page and his blood iced within him. There, in clear ink, was the demon from inside his Haunting Weir prison. The thing's horrific face grinned up at him from the paper, the empty eyes and the massive black twisted horns gleamed as it reached towards the reader from its illustration. "I found it," Art half whispered, feeling ill, a rush of sick washing over his throat, hitting his stomach.

The others were moving, coming to stand over him. Orchid made a small sound and covered her mouth with both hands as everyone's eyes came to rest on the horrifying depiction of the evil struggling to free itself from Art.

"This is your demon?" Ever asked, voice hushed, though he did not require an answer.

"Yes," Art mumbled, staring at the empty eyes of the thing.

"Art what is the meaning of this?" The elf asked, alarmed.

"What?"

Art frowned, starting to look at him but instead followed the point of Ever's finger as the Knight laid his hand over the illustration to the more normal looking face, smiling up at them, looking just as demonic, but handsome and familiar. Art griped the book and yanked it closer to him, eyes burning into the face.

"That….That's me!" he exclaimed his voice trembling, shock and awe shadowed by fear and confusion. "What?! What is the meaning of this?"

"The name…!" Orchid whispered, leaning over Art's shoulder.

Art's eyes fell on the name: Artcainecru, eater of kin, ilk of ink, seer into souls.

"Art…!" He uttered his own name in a shaky voice. His very name came from the demon's name. The floor felt like it had dropped out from under him and he was falling. He went on to read that the demon was one of the few to be recorded as entering the physical realm. It was mysteriously contained by a Weirimen hunting party but not before slaying many. Art read through the names listed but paused on two: Karvin Storygenner and Neth Grovebell.

"Storygenner….Grovebell…." Art was trembling.

"Storygrove." Ever breathed realizing the connection. "Are these the two you saw use the lantern and Weir Hewn to contain the demon in your vision when you were with the Weaver?"

Art had almost forgotten he had shared his experience with Orchid and Ever and he nodded slowly.

"I don't understand, what does this mean?" Orchid asked, looking at Art's ever-paling face.

"I don't know," the man confessed, confused and shocked, feeling almost desperate.

"You do not remember your past? Your parentage?" The elf pressed.

"No," Art felt the panic rising in him. "I have no memories of my parents. I was adopted by a Weiriman."

"But your name," Ever interjected. "Who gave you your name?"

"I don't know," Art shook his head, dropping the book down on the table as if it had given him some contagion. "I can't remember! It's just always been my name. My childhood is fuzzy. But this demon was sealed many, many years ago, long before my life began, before my guardian was even born. And what does this mean?! Why do I have this thing's face?! I…I don't know what this means!"

Art felt a rush of anxiety, his breathing hastening, the thump of his blood drumming in his ears. Fear coursed through, feeling like liquid fire between his ribs. Was he a demon? Was he something else entirely? What did this all mean!? He could feel the thing inside him, uncoiling like a great snake, smelling his terror, drinking his panic. It was going to come up from within him, it was going to consume him. His eyes glossed, air felt like it was burning his lungs.

Ever and Orchid were speaking but Art could not hear them. He wanted to be sick. He could feel it bubbling inside him. Why had Evendale never told him? Did she know?! How could she have kept something like this from him? Why had he felt the need to become a Weiriman if all he amounted to was some mirror of demonic filth? He wanted to die, wanted to be rid of the festering puzzle that was his life. He could feel the demon's hands at his throat, moving under the skin to grip the windpipe. It would melt into him and consume him.

"Brother!" Lucid's voice jarred Art back from whatever was happening inside him.

Blinking, Art slowly unclenched his hands; the bones clicking at the effort at which they had been squeezed. He sniffed, feeling blood trickle out of his nose and went to wipe as Ever handed him a handkerchief. His mouth tasted like old metal, and he let out a shaky breath, looking to the boy.

"Brother, you are you," he said quietly. "You are real and you have a soul."

Art stared at him a long moment, his amber brimming eyes slowly returning to their greenish color. The boy looked on him steadily as if to say he needed to let each word sink into his mind.

"You are not a demon."

Art let out another shuttering breath. "I am not a demon," his words were almost inaudible.

"You cannot be," Ever said drawing Art's eyes to him. "If you were this demon you would not have a soul it wanted to consume. Does it not covet your soul?"

"Yes, you mentioned something," Orchid reminded him. "It wants to eat your soul. A demon is incapable of having a soul, Art, it only consumes them. You have one."

"I'm not a demon," Art reaffirmed, his panic unraveling slowly. "I am real, I have a soul. Then…Then what am I?"

Ever and Orchid looked at one another and then back to Art.

"We do not have an answer. However, we know you to be Art Storygrove, a great Weiriman. You must keep this knowledge strong in your mind."

"Yes," Orchid floated down so that she was kneeling next to Art. "You cannot lose to fear. That will only allow the thing inside to destroy you. Now that you know its name you can force it from you. It does not matter where you came from."

"All that matters is the task before you, Storygrove," Ever spoke confidently, firmly, "and that has not changed. You now have the fiend's name. We can return to the Weaver and cleanse your soul of this filth."

Art's eyes were huge, staring at the demonic image before him. He sat, stone still, feeling the demon shift within his Weir. It whispered to him, recited his fears, but he would not listen.

"You are right," he muttered. "I'm going to cut this thing out of me. I won't let it consume me."

Lucid patted him on the arm, nodding and Art tried to smile, though it ended up looking more like a wince. He could do this, he told himself, getting to a shaking stand. He had to. He had not come such a long way, faced horrors and put his whole life on the knife's edge to be consumed by the very monsters he had been training all his life to defeat. It did not matter what he was before. He was a weapon now, and this knowledge would only seek to sharpen him against the demon against…Against Artcainecru.

The name rumbled through him and he felt the demon's deep chuckling.

"Knowing my name will only bring us closer together, boy."

"Good," Art bit the word out, hands balling into fists, "the closer you are, the deeper my blades go in."

Chapter Eighteen
Elven Aid

"What did you learn?" Art turned towards Ever, grimacing as he tried to ignore the laughter echoing between his ears.

The elf gave Art a strong look but said nothing more and slid the book he had been reading with Orchid over to the Weiriman.

"I am unfamiliar with the true name of the Weaver or his identity, but this book has extensive writing about the Weir Hewn blade you now carry. Do you think this could have been authored by him?"

Art leaned forward and looked at the book itself, frowning. "I'm really not sure. Lucid?"

The boy was already peeking around Art to see. He ran his hand over the open page before leaning in to take a sniff. Lucid let out a sound like he had sneezed and shook his head, rubbing his face.

"Not Father's." Lucid crinkled his nose. "This is man."

"The name sounds like a man," Ever noted, "Nicklaus Bancroft."

"Maybe a Mage," Art suggested. They were a rare lot, not always with the best reputations. "Perhaps, he had some experience with the blade before the Weaver hid it. What does he say about it?"

"Much," Ever explained. "Herein are many detailed rituals and procedures I am none too comfortable with."

"How so?" The dark expression clouding the Knight's brow had Art worried. Something in the book's content had truly bothered him.

"He writes in much detail about the removal of Weirs."

Art was alarmed. "Manual removal? For what purpose? That's barbaric."

"Indeed. He does not state the purpose, only that he succeeded in experimenting on them with that blade."

All eyes went to the knife at Art's hip.

"He says it is a blade that can be carried into the mind's eye, the psychic space in one's head, and can be used on the Haunting Weir therein," Orchid added.

"Used? How?"

"To cut into it for the removal or addition of something. Also he was able to sever the connection between Weir and host, even removing the Weir itself."

What she was telling him had Art's mind working feverishly. Without a Weir, a person would die but not before they were invaded by demons, ghosts, incorporeals, and all manner of darkness. It would be an agonizing and traumatizing death that would likely leave the soul in such a state of madness, that after death the person would almost certainly be left a ghost or hungry spirit, confused and vengeful. It was monstrous to even consider experimenting on a person in such a way.

"He does not go on to say how to reattach the Weir to the mind. It is my speculation that he did not experiment on this, only the removal and altering of Weirs. It is a sickening science." Ever's tone glistened with disdain.

"Did you read anything that might aid you and Orchid?" Art changed the subject, not wanting to think on the reality that they had to use the findings of such an unscrupulous person, but the need was dire.

"There is a detailed method of removing one Weir from another which, I believe, is our affliction. I would ask that you read it for yourself and give us your expert opinion, Weiriman."

Art almost flushed at the confidence the pair was putting in him. Hiding the pride, he nodded and took the book. Sitting to read, he covered the chapter on his blade as well as the procedure Ever had mentioned. When finished, he was actually quite surprised how easy it appeared. All that was required were the rare skills of a Weiriman to travel into another's psychic space, experience with manipulation of the Weir so that the cutting severance could be made safely and most rare of requirements, a blade such as Weir Hewn.

"I should be able to do this." Art grinned up at the pair, who had awaited his findings anxiously. "We will have to be near Orchid's body because once your Weirs are free of one another, she will have to go back to her own mind. But he does not write about how to reattach a Weir and I'm not sure how to get it back inside her and secure."

Lucid suddenly jumped up smiling and pointed to himself.

"What is it?" Orchid asked.

"I can carry her back!" the boy spoke, "I can carry her back, Art can attach."

"I don't know how to attach the Weir," Art protested.

"Yes," the boy nodded and poked at Art's bag.

Frowning, Art pulled out the lantern which Lucid's finger had jabbed into. "What? This?"

"It is a soul lantern!" Orchid exclaimed, "If used correctly, it can heal psychic wounds. Perhaps, with this you could heal my Weir within me."

Lucid nodded excitedly.

"And you can carry her Weir and her soul back?" Art asked again.

"Yes, I'm dreamcatcher, can dreamweave! I can carry that which dreams are made of and where dreams come from."

Art was not completely sure what he meant, but he trusted Lucid knew what he was talking about.

"I'm still not sure about the healing, but I'll have to try. That is, if you want to risk me trying?"

"We believe in you, Art." Orchid was smiling broadly, her lovely face looking more colorful than ghostly.

Art dropped his gaze at the blush of faith saying, "I suppose that's it then. We know how to help you both."

He was feeling lighter. The positive outcome that was very achievable was a much welcomed solution to their time in the demonic library. He had needed the news nearly as much as the two lovers did.

"But," Orchid placed a ghostly hand on Art's arm, and though he felt little more than a cold tingle, he looked at her. "Did you learn how you are to use the lantern and blade for your problem?"

Art had to smile at her concern for him. Even in the light at having discovered what she and Ever had been desperately searching for, she was still worried about him. She was a kind soul. It was far too easy to see why the stoic elf had fallen in love with her.

"I did realize something about the blade and I believe it will only be a matter of cutting its connection to my Weir to free me of our prison link. However, what that has to do with the lantern and how I'm going to actually exorcise it and deport it back to the Ever-Hunger hell, I'm not sure. I'm hoping the Weaver will have some answers for me. Once I have the name and the blade I am to return to him." Just as he said it, thoughts that the Weaver might not even remember him once he returned flared up in Art's mind. He was an odd one. Art had to hope the man knew more than he let on.

"We should return to him in haste then," Ever said, starting for the door.

"No, wait a moment," Art protested. "We have to go to your home where Orchid's body is before we return to the Weaver."

"You have but a few Umbra Sweets left and your control on the demon diminishes each passing night. Your situation is acute."

Art's face grew stern and he placed a gloved hand on the table saying, "I know how bad my situation is, and I want to believe it will work out. And while I want to believe that, stay strong and be confident, we can't ignore the fact that I might not survive this. I might have to die to send this thing back. If I die, I can't fulfill my promise to help you two."

"But Art...!" Orchid started.

"No." The man shook his head. "I gave my word. I said I would help you. Besides, from what I read this thing we're going to do would likely be considered a Dark Art. Cutting into fused Weirs, carrying souls back to bodies through dreams, having Lucid involved at all, this is all stuff the Weirimen would be uncomfortable with. It's highly unlikely you will find another to help you. For the most part, Weirimen are the only ones who can do this work. You can't just let any random psychic into your head. And really, how many other Weirimen do you trust to go inside your mind and carefully cut the woman you love from your Haunting Weir?"

Ever's face was icy, his eyes hooded and distrusting. "Your assessment is accurate and true. I do not trust the Weirimen."

"And we cannot have something happen to Lucid," Orchid said, floating next to the boy. "You believe the Weirimen would not like him?"

"The Weaver warned me to protect him from them. I'm guessing they would be tempted to imprison something made of nightmares. It would be hard for them to believe he is good and not evil, especially with a grown soul that was not actually born. After our last encounter with them, I'm also very leery. Face it Nahrwel, I'm your only hope. So we should just stop talking about it and get it done." Art lifted his hands into the air and gave a shrug, trying not to smile amused.

Ever said nothing for a long, judgmental moment, then only gave a short grunt and nod.

"Thank you, Art," Orchid smiled, leaning in to give him a ghostly kiss on the cheek.

Art felt his face bloom with heat, but he laughed. "All right, let's get out of this creepy place."

"Surely, good Sir, you would rather stay. You have not read the whole of your selections." The Librarian was suddenly standing near the table. No one, not even the most observant and aware of their surroundings, Ever had heard its approach.

"No, I think we're good here. We'd like to leave," Art said cautiously, wondering if he needed to be pulling out his blades.

"Perhaps there is another rare piece of information I can offer you? We have the most engrossing selection of information. Surely a young and unique Weiriman would love to research things your Guild has never been privy to. Knowledge is true power."

Ever was frowning deeply, Lucid and Orchid also growing concerned.

"I'm not seeking power," Art said frankly. "I've seen what indulging too much curiosity in this place does to someone. We would like to leave, now."

His insistent voice caused the Librarian to grow very still, folding its thin hands together and bowing deeply.

"Very well then, please follow me." The accommodating tone had left the thing's voice, and as it led them towards the door, Ever and Art exchanged a warning look.

The party followed the guide through the doorway but was surprised when the room on the other side was not the same one from which they had come through previously. It was a high staircase leading into a dark hallway.

"What is the meaning of this?" Art demanded angrily and reached out to take the Librarian by the arm.

The man gave a noise of shock when the thing seemed to melt in his hand, the arm turning weak, then wobbling and before him the Librarian's form collapsed. Spilling out of the robes and hood was nothing but old paper, stacks and stacks of tiny pieces of it all pressed together to look like a figure. The loose sheets slid out over the old carpet, the robe left hanging from Art's hand where he had gripped the arm. The pointed beak mask rolled onto the ground, an echoing cackle issuing from the emptiness of it. Art dropped the robe as it spoke.

"I hope to see you again, Weiriman. You are a most interesting subject. Come back to me when your knowledge comes against a wall. Should you survive the hell within you, I very much would love to read on the thing you will become. I will always be here."

Art felt a shiver ripple over his skin. The Librarian had been nothing but a construct. They had been speaking to the consciousness of the Consciatosium the whole time.

"We should leave," Ever said, taking to the stairs. The great and terrible idea of the library leading them around, observing them, "reading them" had the elf spooked.

"We have no idea where that goes," Art protested but he knew it did not matter. There were few options.

The party headed down the stairs and into the dark hallway. Lanterns lit up when they arrived. To everyone's surprise, they were at the front desk once more, coming into the room from a side door Art had not noticed the first time.

They wasted little time in heading out the huge double doors which opened at their approach. Before long, they were all back out in the catacombs returning to the surface. Art was grateful Lucid knew the way out, just as he knew the way in. Ghosts and spirits shadowed their footsteps, calling to them from dark cool parts of the tunnels. Art ignored them and hurried the group on, struggling to stay focused and unhindered by the demon. He would not waste one of his last two Scarlet Extinctions on a short trip through the haunted area.

Finally, when the entrance gate came into sight, Art sighed, relieved and very tired. They had completed yet another impossible leg of the journey Art was certain, just a few days ago, would have claimed his life long before. He had only a few more miracles to work.

The streets were lit by lantern light, but the unnatural darkness of a town plagued by strong Sin Breath ate up the light in ways still not well understood. Though the lanterns should have cast robust light on the cobblestones, they did little more than add dim illumination as the group hurried through the city.

"There will be Weirimen out patrolling the streets for us," Art cautioned.

"We have been gone many hours, would they not think we had moved on?"

Art shook his head. "I'm sure many of them have foreseeing and knowing psychic senses. They will just know I have not left the town. We should hurry before we're spotted."

"I thought people tried to stay off the streets at night." Orchid was flying next to Ever, as the group ran on.

"They do, but Weirimen aren't afraid of what is brought out by the darkness. If they think I'll unleash a demon into the physical realm because of my condition, they will brave whatever is brought out by the night to find me. If I were them, I'd do the same. This thing inside me cannot be unleashed into the world."

The image of the demon's two faces, the evil demonic blackness and the one much like Art's own, blurred through his mind. He wanted more answers, but knew there were none to be had. He just had to hope the Weaver would know something.

"Come, less chatter. I recall passing the Silver Whale Inn on our first passage here. It is likely where Finnafor's garrison spotted us," Ever directed.

"Yes, hurry," Lucid chimed in running a little ahead. "Men, close."

No one bothered to ask how Lucid knew, but it did push the group on into the night, weary of eyes watching them from windows and lost souls haunting the city.

"Here!" Ever announced when light over silver painted letters on a sign read: The Silver Whale Inn and Tavern.

It was almost completely dark but for a few glows in curtain drawn windows. Art was not certain how long they had been in the Consciatosium, or if time even traveled the same within the demonic space, but if he had to guess they were past midnight in the darkest part of the night's course.

"How are we going to get in? We can't just wait here on the street!" Art whispered, knowing they were in the heart of the town. With shops, inns, and homes all around he was certain they would be found at any moment.

"Everther Nahrwel!" A hushed voice came from a second-story window.

The group looked up to see an elf waving at them.

"That's not Finnafor," Art cautioned but Ever and Lucid were already taking to the climbing tree attached to the side of the Inn, using it as a ladder to head up to the window.

Art frowned.

"You can trust the whole garrison, Art," Orchid tried to soothe. "I trust Ever's judgment."

"Elves may not be Weirimen but it was his own garrison that did not want to help him and you, was it not?"

Orchid gave him a sad smile. "That is true…" There was a sudden pull on the tether between her and the elf. Remembering she could not linger while he wandered, she turned and floated up after Ever, leaving Art to stow his mistrust and follow the others up the tree.

Inside, Art was greeted by a dozen elves watching him climb semi-awkwardly in through the inn's small window. When he had finally gotten his long coat free of the sill and its trappings he stood, brushing himself off, trying to regain some of his dignity. Art had never been uncomfortable with elves or their Knights in general but, for some reason, he was feeling more self-conscious now that everyone in the room regarded him as a possible demonic possession threat.

He never liked to let others' opinions to pay any him bother. If he had, he would have done poorly at the Seminary where many thought he achieved attendance because of his guardian and shunned him for his superior talents. Yet, as he watched Captain Finnafor greet Ever and the adoration and willingness to risk open hostility with the Weirimen the whole garrison displayed, Art felt a slight tinge of regret. His guild had turned its back on him. All the allies he had in the world were likely in the room where he stood now and they had all been strangers not too long ago. The man felt suddenly hollowed.

Lucid was at Art's side and patted him on the arm, motioning he should follow the group into the main room. Art pushed down his dark thoughts, knowing the demon inside him was itching to break to the surface again. Dwelling on anything that might upset him was not advantageous.

Entering the dark room, one of the Knights lit a single candle, the light glistening off the intricate stitching and subtle beauty of the group's uniforms. Though slightly different from Ever's, each garrison having its own unique garb, it was still clear they were of one organization. All knew the Scarborough Knights. For much of the races of men and other town dwellers they were the only elves anyone ever came into contact with. Art himself had only met them on training assignments, and their interactions had been brief. He was not entirely sure how to behave now being in a room of them planning some clandestine escape from his guild patrolling the town.

"That is an unusual tale," Finnafor remarked once Ever had relayed a brief accounting of their adventure. Art would not have shared so many details had he been the one to tell it, but he allowed Ever what he thought was right. He trusted the Birchwood Garrison in ways one Weiriman would likely not trust another.

"Do you think you can help us?"

The Captain's eyes went to Orchid who was floating next to Ever, looking wide-eyed and nervous. She had rarely revealed herself to anyone after the Weirimen's ideas about exorcising her. Ever had been nervous she would be removed from him by force and now to have herself and situation explained to a group of Demon Touch elven hunters had set her on slight edge.

"Of course, we shall help you, Everther. There is a train leaving at dawn, only an hour from now. We shall all be on it. We should be able to ride the rails out towards your home and ride the last leg of the journey by horse back."

"They will be looking for me in every town," Art interjected, causing the whole group to look back at him and Lucid. They had not gathered about the center table but stayed to the outskirts of the room. Art was uncertain if the boy was also made nervous by the strangers or if he just wanted to sit next to Art.

"Yes, Weiriman," Finnafor nodded. "We will require you to wear one of our uniforms."

"Think a uniform will be enough to conceal me?"

"For movement from train to train we do hope so. But, there is an alternative idea should the Weirimen travel with us."

"And that is?" Art's eyebrow arched hard.

Two elves brought forward a large chest.

"This is one of our equipment crates," a female Knight explained.

"I don't like this," Art muttered noting the chest was large but only large enough to fit him inside should he lie down and curl up in the thing.

"It will only be a last resort. For now we will try to pass you as one of us."

Art looked over the group of perfect forms. Most of them were built very similar, toned but slender and tall, all fair and attractive. Art was not unattractive for a man, but he lacked elven beauty. He was also far more muscular then most of them.

"Think I'll fit a uniform?"

The group of elves exchanged glances.

"The fit will be tight, but I believe we shall manage," Finnafor said, looking to Ever.

"Come, Storygrove, get into a uniform."

"What about Lucid?" Art protested as the clothing was presented to him.

"He will have to wear one too."

"He'll never pass as a one of you! He's too small," Art protested but Lucid was already undressing, grinning as if the very idea of putting the new clothing on was amazing.

"He will manage," a female elf thrust the clothes into Art's hands. "On occasion we do employ fey kind."

Art scowled at her but she turned, ignoring him. Looking around, he expected them to clear and give him some privacy but, when they did not, Art glowered again. He forgot elves had lower modesty standards in their culture. Nudity was not a social taboo as it was among the races of men. Not wanting to make a fuss, and hoping his face was not burning with heat, he turned around and started to change.

The uniform was tight. It flexed hard over the muscles in his arms and snug in the chest, back and thighs, but he could not complain. He had gotten it on. Donning the new cloak, he fastened his own knife belts round his waist. It made him look different. The leather was not as delicately tooled with tree designs like the others, but he was not about to take his weapons off.

"There," Finnafor smiled. "You look the part."

"Only if he minds the hood," Ever pointed to Art, his finger drawing a line to indicate the look of Art's hair. "No elf would have such a haircut. It's long on top but shaved beneath. Someone would think you an oddity without our long hair. And then there are those round ears."

The group chuckled and blushing for no reason other than embarrassment at the attention, Art pulled the hood up curtly, saying nothing.

"Now, we should be off," Finnafor said, eyes going to the far window. "Dawn approaches."

Art knew there were differences between men and elves. Training with the Weirimen had taught him much about stealth and physical prowess, but he had not realized the enormous differences between himself and the elves until they were running through the city, hoping to remain undetected. They were so silent, so swift, and entirely too remarkable in their agility that Art felt his boots were booming echoes announcing each stride. He was certain his breathing from the sprint through the town could be heard all the way back in Wivenguilder. In comparison to the elves, he was just a loud, ungraceful, bag of rumbling, jingling, useless gear and muscles.

The elves said nothing but every time they came across something that could possibility be a Weiriman one or more elf made sure not only to alert him, but physically assure he was stopped, hidden, and quieted. He felt like a small child among many adults that thought he could not be left out on his own. Annoyed and ego-bruised as he was, Art struggled to say nothing even as they stopped yet again and a female elf pulled him by his arm into the shadows of a large building, well out of the dim street lantern's glow.

Art's ego was not so thin that it really should have burned him as it did. But before he could restrain himself, a voice rose up from within him. He turned to the Knight, eyes brimming Amber and green. "Do not touch me!"

It was low, graveled, and hushed, but it sounded less like Art and more like the demon within him. Art's face instantly portrayed his alarm and confusion at the utterance, but the elf withdrew her hand all the same.

"What happened?!" Finnafor demanded through telepathy.

Before Art could explain, Ever responded in an almost inaudible voice, "Do not use telepathy. Some of these Weirimen can sense the very transfer of thought."

It was too late though, and the whole garrison alerted as a pair of Weirimen approached. Art was feeling panic rise within him. They would certainly sense the demon, perhaps even his open Weir. They had seen some increased nightly activity already of shifting spirits, ghosts and lesser demons all brought out by Art's state.

The man wanted to curse aloud. They were so close to the railway station. The demon's ill mood might have ruined their chances of escape. Art's hands were in fists. He was hoping he would not end up hurting someone again. If he got into an altercation he was uncertain he would be able to control the demon's violence at this stage. He could not afford to use up even one of his Scarlet Extinctions on this wasteful scenario.

Chapter Nineteen
Woven Weirs

"Get him to the train. We will join you shortly." Finnafor was pointing to Ever and several other elves. "Go!"

With a near silent flurry of cloaks and boots, Art was hurried away, his ears catching the greeting remarks of Finnafor to the approaching Weirimen.

"Well met, Weirimen. I am Captain Finnafor of the Birchwood Garrison. How might we assist you this early morning?"

"Odd to see you out on the streets prior to dawn," one said but was cut off by his partner who spoke.

"Wait! Who are they, elf Captain? Some of your garrison is leaving."

"We must secure passage on the dawn train," Finnafor explained.

"How unusual. Don't passengers normally sleep on the train if leaving on the dawn trip? It's unsafe to travel the street at this time. We also hunt a very dangerous afflicted, a Weiriman."

"Yes," the elf concurred, "our departure was unexpected. I am aware of the current Crimson Dispatch. I apologize. We cannot be of any service to you. Dawn is breaking."

Art could hear no more as their small group entered the railroad station and headed up to the ticket counter.

"Art, what happened?" Ever's voice was serious as he slipped close to the man to speak in hushed tones.

"The demon spoke," Art answered, his brow folded hard. "I didn't even feel it trying to, and suddenly it was telling her not to touch me. I couldn't control it."

"You are getting weaker against it?" Orchid's voice issued from Ever's form. She had hidden herself before they had exited the inn.

Art did not want to admit it but spoke anyway, "I could be."

"You should take another Umbra Sweet." Ever advised.

"I can't," Art shook his head. "I need one for your ritual and the last one for my exorcism."

"If it over takes you before then saving them will do you little good."

Art did not meet Ever's eyes but gave him a quick nod just as the other Knights returned.

"We will wait for the Captain on the train," one said and Art, Ever, and Lucid followed them into the car.

Art was ushered towards a set of benches and some wall beds. The accommodations were nothing like the lavish cars he used to travel in with the Weirimen. He took to one of the benches, but Lucid pointed to the beds nearby, smiling. The man did not protest and followed him over, Lucid jumping lightly up onto the top bunk before hanging over and pointing to the lower, indicating Art should take that one. Shrugging, feeling tired all over again, he nodded and slid into the bed.

He had noted that all eyes, even Ever's, had been on his crossing of the car, but he pretended not to notice. Elven thoughts were much harder to hear, even for a psychic, and if he wanted to he could ignore them. He did not even want to know what they were thinking about him. He did not want to think anymore. How long had he been awake? He was not sure any longer. He was no longer even sure how long it had been since he awoke outside the catacomb town. Art felt like he had been running, thinking, surviving, avoiding for weeks without sleep. He wanted rest. He wanted to feel safe again.

A rumbling was trembling inside him. He shoved his pack between him and the wall, staring up at the ceiling of the bunk above him. Art felt the deep ache sigh over his whole body like one giant muscle unclenching. He was truly exhausted. Everything was tingling with tension. He felt the weight of his whole world had been strapped to his back. To his dismay, instead of feeling better now that he was lying down, it was as if that great burden was oozing over him like a blanket of sludge. There would be little rest between now and when he faced the demon. Each moment would be heavier than the next. That dark thought brought up the demon's inner laughter again.

"Even with this knowledge, you waste your precious time to aid this elf and his woman. Such a foolish man, Storygrove. You are even more pathetic than the cavern of buzzing insects you call a guild. Foolish, the lot of you."

"Quiet," Art muttered, "I don't want to hear you, demon."

"No use of my name?" Art could feel the thing's smile in the very arch of his shoulder blades as if the act was yanking at his bones inside.

"When I first address you with your name I want it to be at your own exorcism." Art crossed his arms over his chest, closing his eyes. Trying to silence the thing from his mind was giving him such a headache he could feel the pulse of his heart in his neck veins.

"You don't make friends easily, do you, 'Art'?"

Art could not have this conversation now. He hated that his very name was likely taken from the demon's. He could not face those implications at this time. Who and what he was led him to uncomfortable, dark corners of his mind he did not want to visit.

"Do you worry that you have always felt different from your peers because you were never really one of them? Do you want to know what you really are, 'Art Storygrove'?"

It used his name as an emotional club, reminding him, mocking him that all that he claimed to be could be wrong. He could be nothing at all.

"I command you, quiet." Art ground his teeth and shut his eyes, trying to find the kind of inner peace in mediation he never achieved very well in school.

The nightmares were far worse than before. Instead of faceless fears and dark rumblings, Art was desperately struggling, fighting for his life. Demons were tearing him apart. His screams fell into nothing but black and all the while the demon watched, its face just before his, hands embedded in his chest ripping the life out of him as it tore organs.

"Brother!" Lucid's voice shook Art out of his sleep. Eyes wide, body wet with cold sweat, Art tried to slow his breathing, his heart ramming itself against his ribcage as if to stay within him would mean its own bloody death.

He let out a long, shaky breath and wiped his mouth with the back of his hand. He had to take his gloves off when he changed into the elven uniform and he wished he was back in his old clothes. The tight, unfamiliar feel of the garments only made him feel even more out of his own skin.

"I could not eat your nightmares," Lucid's usually carefree demeanor was worried and concerned.

"I'm fine," Art lied, his voice off. He felt cold, nauseous and sluggish. The demon likely was waging some kind of psychic warfare on him, attacking him in dreams, weakening his spirit. Images of similar nightmares floated through his thought stream like oil on water. His battle with the thing when they left Wivenguilder had been made of up several similar dream experiences he did not want to recall. He pushed them down again and sat up. "I'm fine, Lucid. Don't worry."

The boy did not look convinced but nodded and left Art's side, allowing the man a moment to himself. He had not taken the candy as Ever had suggested but Art knew he could not delay too much longer. Even his body was weakening against the thing's internal assault.

The respect and trust the Scarborough Knights afforded from the races of men and the Weirimen was clear in the next two towns they stopped. As long as Art stayed within the group of elves, patrolling Weirimen over looked him. In the third and final town, a Weiriman had approached them, saying she had heard interesting thoughts emanating from the group. Finnafor produced Lucid and claimed he was an unusual fey member. Curious, but not entirely certain she should question an elven Captain, she allowed them through.

Art was grateful. Had they not been Knights, the Weiriman likely would have noticed Lucid's similarity to the descriptions of Art's companions from the dispatch. But they were not really looking for Lucid. No one would ever expect the Knights to harbor Art. Ever's alliance had served the man in ways he could never have anticipated.

By the time they were retrieving horses from an outpost on the outskirts of elven territory, Art was past the point where he could maintain a civil composure. He was snapping at anyone who spoke to him, angering at the smallest of inconveniences and refusing to eat anything but meat. Water tasted like metal, and he had a strong craving for hard liquor. He knew he was losing his battle.

"You must take one," Ever urged as they headed into the woods that would take them to the elf's home. "If you do not, I fear the demon will consume you at any moment."

"No," Art growled.

Lucid had originally started riding with the Weiriman, as he did not seem to want to ride a horse alone, but had moved to Ever's horse when Art had barked at him for little reason and nearly spooked the animal into tossing both of them.

"Storygrove, you will not last much longer." Ever was grave.

"I said no!" Art barked, causing several of the Knights to turn back, expressions displaying their growing concern for the afflicted man.

They would allow Ever to handle Art only to a certain point. The Weiriman knew their trust would not hold if he actually physically lashed out at someone. He knew he was slipping but his anger would not let him think beyond the point until suddenly Lucid was leaning over from the back of Ever's horse, the candy in his fingers. Art had not felt the boy fish the thing out of his pack. Both elf and youth were stern faced but it was Orchid's large eyes and look of fear that made Art realize the danger he was invoking. Before he could think much more or let the demon influence him to refuse the sweet, he took the Scarlet Extinction and popped it in his mouth. He could not think on the consequences. It was his only option left.

Art knew the majesty of the woods was being lost on him. There was such a dramatic difference in the forests inhabited by elves from the haunted and tainted woods he had been experiencing on his journey. The trees were massive, thick, and rose so high above them, arching his head into a nearly vertical tilt was the only way to look into their heights. Light filtered through the leaves, casting all in the golden and green glows, blessing everything with a silent rolling lushness Art had almost forgotten existed in the world.

Weirimen lived in a hard, dark world. The haunted grounds, demons reaching across the land, and the fight for souls from the devouring of evil often obscured the remembrance of natural beauty and a world that had once been peaceful. It was clear why the Scarborough Knights fought to protect their lands and free animals from the taint of demons. Woods like Ever's home were worth defending.

Art could sense the revulsion the demon had for his elven companions, for Ever's love for Orchid, and for the lengths the ancient race would go through to protect the animals and peoples of their native wood. It brought the man a measure of peace. Whatever the demon reviled could only be pure and real. He let their very presence give him some resolve. Perhaps, being surrounded by the goodness of a natural world would help steel him against the evil he carried inside.

After an extensive trek, Art's mind had wandered into pointless thought. Whispers of the demon kept him floating about with negativity. The pending tasks ahead and the darker outcome should he not survive, balanced with the uncertain outcome of what would come next should he actually win. Would the Weirimen even take him back? If not, what would he do with such a life? His gut swam with the haunting lack of possibilities. He was nothing without the Guild.

Just as he was slipping into bleak worry, Lucid was tugging on his jacket arm.

"What?" Art started to snap but cut his irritability short when his eyes lay on the glow and magnificence of the elven city.

It seemed grown out of the very forest itself, the architecture a graceful, stunning blend of trees, buildings, and function. It was unclear what had been built and what was just tree and forest itself. Though completely entwined with its natural surroundings, it was in no way primitive. Pure grander and elegance was in every window frame, each archway, and every rooftop of the city that rose into the wood as seamlessly as the branches, leaves and other foliage themselves grew. The city hummed with warm golden light, cradled by the deep blues and greens of the forest's evening. Art could do little more than gape as he followed the elven garrison into the enchanted environment.

"Your city is a work of beauty," Art mumbled to Ever once they dismounted and left the horses to their proper lodgings and care.

"I have been long from my home." Ever smiled, his handsome face portraying his positive feelings; his regular coldness melted.

"Should we accompany you, Nahrwel?" Finnafor asked once his garrison had gathered around them, their presence as normal to the beautiful elven inhabitance as the trees growing alongside their roadways and out of every shop building.

"I thank you, my friend," Ever extended his hand. "I do invite your garrison to my home, but the ritual I am scheduled for is best done without an audience."

"Understood," Finnafor nodded and spoke softly with his lieutenants before following Art, Lucid, and Orchid as Ever led the way.

Art had not expected the Birchwood Garrison to follow them, but when they arrived at Ever's home, more near the edge of the city than the center, he could see privacy was not an issue. The home was large, bigger than Art had expected with at least three stories, and a staircase larger than the whole of Art's cell at the Seminary. Once shedding traveling gear and outer wear in a front entry big enough to accommodate the whole group comfortably, the garrison disappeared into the dining area and kitchen when Ever suggested they should seek rest and nourishment.

"Come." Ever motioned to Lucid and Art saying nothing of his grand home, only taking the little group to the back.

A garden path led out of the back space. Art was uncertain if it was natural forest or immaculately designed gardening. The place was magical, teeming with flowering trees, shrubbery, and full-growth bushes perfectly lined up to make an enchanted stone-lined walkway. Art had not imagined a place could be more beautiful. He started to question why men lived in cities when places such as Ever's home existed.

"What do you call your city?" Art questioned as they followed the elf through a bend in the path towards a more open area and a single, stand alone tree.

"This is the central elven city in the Farahgall Woods, this is Scarborough."

"Oh," Art nodded, knowing less about elven cities than most other geography. "So your garrison hales from the main body of Knights."

"My former garrison did, yes." Ever nodded, not looking back at Art.

"Perhaps that will all change once this is over," Art said quietly.

"My priority is the safe return of Orchid's soul and Weir to her body, everything else is secondary and of little importance."

They stopped before a stunning tree. Art was not certain of what kind as he had never seen anything so beautiful before, long limbed, adorned with delicate leaves and flowers. Yet as stunning as it was, there seemed to be something wrong, as if the wood was darker than it should have been, the leaves a strange off color, almost translucent.

"This is Orchid's tree," Art exclaimed understanding that the tree was as much a part of a dryad's existence as her own body.

"A dryad is tied to the life of her tree," Orchid explained. "Should my tree die, I die. Should I die, so shall the tree. It is me."

Art nodded, watching the ghostly woman float towards the trunk and first place her hands on the ripples of the bark, then her forehead as if gaining some spiritual connection at the reunion.

"Had I not been a Tree Elf, Orchid would not have survived even as ghost."

"Yes," Orchid turned a bright smile on the elf and floated back towards him, their tether, circling them like a ghostly string. "Ever has been my savior for many reasons."

Art was suddenly feeling uncomfortable at the deeply loving stare the two were exchanging. He wished he had Lucid's lack of shyness, as the boy only watched, interested, a smile across his lips.

"We should do this now," Art muttered, knowing the candy's effect had expiration.

"You did not need to rest first?" Ever asked, sounding slightly nervous.

"Can't chance that. I have only one Umbra Sweet left, let's make it count. Where is her body?"

"Here," Orchid indicated, floating back to the tree.

To Art's amazement the trunk opened up, as it if were made of flower petals. Inside, nestled among the heartwood was the dryad's body. Her skin was ashy white, her eyes closed and no breath rose and fell from her breast, but she was not dead. Her flesh still felt and smelled of life.

"My tree has kept my body alive just as Ever has kept my soul. I am linked to both of them now. I have two trees."

Another loving glance, and Art was trying not to flush at the pure affection and whispered hope of anticipation. The two lovers wanted so much to be together in the same plane. Their love had come after the violent accident and they had existed in this limbo of physical and incorporeal companionship since the blossoming of the powerful devotion between them. Art could only marvel at the strength and depth of their love.

"All right. I will enter Ever's mind now. Lucid, you are able to follow me?"

Ever motioned for them to take sitting positions on the grass before Orchid's tree: Lucid sitting next to Art, the Weiriman across from Ever.

"You lead, I follow," Lucid confirmed sitting cross-legged, wiggling down until he was comfortable.

"I lead, you follow," Art muttered, hoping he was up to the task. From his pack, he pulled his soul lantern then drew Weir Hewn out of its sheath to lay the blade across his lap. "I don't know how to bring these things in with me."

"Just bring. Think it, bring it," Lucid answered, giving Art a look to assure it was just as simple as his few words.

"Right," the man mumbled again. "Think it, bring it."

"What shall I do?" Ever asked, Orchid floating behind him.

"Close your eyes. If you can, enter a state of meditation. If you can't, I can always pull you into your mind's eye after I enter your psychic space. We usually have to do that with the possessed anyway. Most people can't enter a state of psychic meditation."

"All elves can," Ever interrupted Art's instruction. "What else must we do?"

"Of course you can." Art chewed on the elf's natural arrogance which both annoyed and amused him. "That's all. Orchid is already in your mind's eye. She should just go to your Weir. I'll see you both on the inside."

Art calmed his mind, shut out the whispers of the demon as best he could and reminded himself this was likely one of the riskiest things he had ever attempted. He cared about these people, more than all of his Seminary classmates put together. He was not sure when that had happened, but his desire to do right by them was overwhelming enough to risk his very soul for. He had to be the best he could muster, be the Weiriman his guardian had always believed he would be. He could do this. He had faith, and he carried that feeling with him as he dropped out of his body and entered Ever's mind's eye.

Most possession psychic space battles took place after the afflicted was already in a dark place. The environment where the Weirimen did battle was almost always dark, formless and empty. Art had done little mind's eye exploring other than that and he stood struck by the ambiance of Ever's psychic space. He had known it would be forest-like, a wood of some type. Ever was a Tree Elf, and seeing the inner glimpse of the elf in the enchanted mirror at the Consciatosium had given Art a unique look into Ever's true person. Yet, the sheer beauty of the elf's mind was still awe-striking.

Unlike Art's inner mind, there were no crumbling buildings. There were no structures at all. The whole of the elf's mind was an old growth forest, lush with tall trees, green with even more foliage than the magnificent garden they had just strolled through. The very leaves glinted with inner light, hinting at the strength and luminance of Ever's being.

Eyes scanning, Art was starting to wonder where he would find the Knight's Haunting Weir when Lucid appeared by his side. The boy smiled and pointed, bringing Art's attention to the blade and lantern in his hands. Art had almost forgotten he was uncertain if he would be able to bring the items in with him. In exorcism he often used his blades to battle the demon in the person's mind but in reality those blades were not real. They were just a manifestation of Art's power. This case was different. He actually needed the real Weir Hewn and the soul lantern for the unique properties they possessed. He had no real idea why he was able to take these items into a non-physical place with him and would have to find the answer to that question later. He was just grateful he had carried the much needed tools in.

Lucid was beckoning him, and he followed the boy through the wood and around several of the trees until they came to a sizable gate built into the forest itself, not unlike the glorious city they had just went through.

One look told Art's trained eye this was not the elf's Weir. On further inspection, he found it was the only way in through a collection of closely knitted trees, shrubbery, and general forest growth. There was no way to get through it or scale the forest construction; it was a wall of nature. Lifting one eyebrow, Art and Lucid returned to the gate and found the thing locked but harboring a window allowing the pair to peer in.

Ever was pacing, his form almost blurred. Confused, Art watched as the elf's movements became strange, then normal, then blurring again as if he was watching a dream in which time and movement did not have the same properties as the physical world. Art called out to Ever, but the elf seemed unable to hear him, his form blurring and shifting.

"Something's wrong," Art chewed on his words, thinking somewhere in his memories of training this felt familiar. "Ah!" he proclaimed remembering, startling Lucid who had been chewing on a branch trying to find a way into the space beyond the forest wall. "His mind is fighting us," Art explained. "We're out of sync with Ever because he doesn't actually want us here. I read about this. Weirimen don't usually make a habit of going into the minds of people who aren't possessed. If we do end up inside someone's mind, it's during an exorcism and the demon has already broken down the afflicted's walls. We need to make contact with Ever, remind his mind he invited us."

Lucid ticked his head to the side, clearly uncertain how to do that since when Art called to Ever he had not seemed able to perceive him.

"It's simple." Art smiled at the boy. "Come here." He motioned as he slid Weir Hewn back into the sheath at his hip and placed his hand on the handle of the locked gate. "Close your eyes and imagine your life force actually touching the handle. I think that should be enough to get Ever to acknowledge us. Think you can do that?"

Lucid nodded enthusiastically and grabbed the handle of the gate. Art had hardly taken a breath when the gate door swung open for the youth and Lucid marched through. Shocked, Art blinked when the gate closed again, leaving the man to do the task Lucid had so easily maneuvered. Taking a deep breath, Art cleared his mind again. There was an itching at the back of his brain, a slight burning and fear bubbled up in him that the demon was starting to make its way back through the treatment of the Scarlet Extinction. It was too soon. He could not have that thing interfering in what he was doing here.

Swallowing the swell of fear in his throat, he forced himself to focus, concentrating on the task, on the people he was to help, and the very strong fact that for the first time since he left the Seminary, he felt he was truly performing the tasks of a Weiriman. On that fact and sheer desire alone, he felt he could force the demon back and complete his function.

With a light clicking, the gate opened again and Art passed under its arched frame of wood and branches. Lucid and Ever greeted him inside what looked like a long forgotten forest garden, lit by source-less shimmering light. Ever was not dressed in his regular tunic, that was mostly Scarborough Knight uniform without the insignias. His mind's eye self wore something more comfortable, similar to the styles Art had seen the inhabitants of the city clothed in. His hair was loose from its ties and hung around him in very long waves of black green.

"Do you know where your Haunting Weir is?" Art asked, looking around the dense greenery.

"Here." Ever motioned and led the way around a massive tree.

Art's lips parted when he finally saw the visual manifestation of Ever and Orchid's shared problem. Tall and solid, Ever's Weir was less like the slabs of heavy wood and iron that the Weirs of men usually took the shape of. The elf's was in an elaborate form of twisted wood and branches. Yet, among the branches, interwoven like a vine in a garden wall, another tree was looped and growing out of the Weir. On closer inspection, Art found it was not only a tree, but in the woven wood was a woman's face. This tree was Orchid's Weir, maybe even part of her soul, wound into the elf's Haunting Weir.

"You...can still help her?" Ever's voice was full of apprehension as he watched Art's expression.

The Weiriman was not entirely certain. Going over again, in his mind, what he had read in the book at the Consciatosium, he nodded as he handed Lucid the soul lantern.

"Don't worry." Art let out a slow breath. "I won't harm her." He had to keep the confidence, stay focused and above all be careful. Unsheathing Weir Hewn he approached the fused Weirs.

Chapter Twenty
The Walking Weir

Cutting Orchid free of Ever's Haunting Weir read as a straight forward procedure. Art was nervous, but also fairly confident that he could achieve what he had read in the strange tomb. When he made the first slice into the fused Weirs, Orchid's soul burst out of the female tree form, screaming as if Art had actually cut her deeply. The man knew then why he had felt so hesitant to follow any process laid down in a book authored by a monster that would actually experiment in cutting Weirs out of people in the first place.

She was as ghostly in Ever's psychic space as she was in the physical world but that did not stop the elf from kneeling by her, showing his agony at being unable to physically touch and comfort her. Translucent tears floated out of her eyes like clear pearls, rather than stream down her face. Her arms were wrapped about her, showing the pain had wracked her whole form.

"What happened?!" Ever turned rage filled eyes to Art.

"I don't know! The book didn't say anything about the procedure being painful."

"Look at her!" Ever stormed, pointing at Orchid who was trying to stop her sobbing, shaking her head.

"It's all right," she stammered. "G-go on. I can endure it."

Art hesitated as Ever's face paled, his expression a clear hatred at even the idea of causing her pain.

"Please," Orchid spoke, her voice shaking. "Please go on. I will endure it."

Art looked to the elf for permission, knowing that even if Orchid gave her consent, should Ever object, he could be facing the same angry elf that had nearly killed him to take Weir Hewn. Orchid was clearly the most important thing to Ever in his whole life. His quest to free the woman from his Weir might have started out as a humanitarian act, but it had become something else entirely for the elf. It had become a labor of pure love. When elves fell in love it was almost always for life. Should Art harm or kill her, Ever's wrath would be unpredictable.

The two males exchanged a long, tense moment. Art was uncertain what was going through Ever's mind when Orchid spoke again, pleading for Art to continue. Her voice was small but persistent. Ever's jaw tightened almost painfully, but he closed his eyes and nodded shortly at the Weiriman. Art was not certain he was glad he had told him to proceed.

Turning back to the Weirs, he chewed on his tongue for half a moment then sliced another of Orchid's tree limbs from Ever's gate. The woman tried but could not stifle the cry of agony. Art's psychic abilities, as un-tuned as he was trying to make them, could hear clearly the momentous amount of pain the cut had caused her. This pain was far more than that of the body. The cutting and bleeding as deep as the soul, was like the mixing of physical and emotional pain, amplified by the raw cut of something meant to be hidden within you. It was an intrusion on a severely violent level. Art felt sick.

"I can't do this." Art turned to the couple.

Ever was next to Orchid, his hands around her, unable to touch her. Their faces were masks of fear and heartache. Art felt even more sick, seeing them in such a state.

"But if you don't cut it, I'll be stuck inside Everther!" Orchid protested though heavy breathing and stifled sobs.

"But look what it's doing to you!" Art's face was twisted up. "I can't hurt you like this. I can feel what it feels like for you. It's a violation to do this to you."

Ever's eyes were large, his face stony. Art turned away from them. There had to be something he could do. He had been confident he could help her. There had to be another way other than this ugly thing. He wanted to help them, even needed to help them. His intuition was saying that he could in a way that did not cause such deep seeded agony. He looked at Weir Hewn.

"Yes, Art Storygrove, there is much more to our function together than blade and Weiriman."

Art almost dropped his blade. It had spoken to him. He frowned at it, confused, alarmed. Perhaps it was the demon. Could the demon trick him into thinking the blade had a voice? Yet the voice carried no malice, no malevolent feeling. The weight of its words were light, like the shine on the Crimson ripple running through its handle.

"You…You spoke to me. Are you Weir Hewn?" Art answered it in his mind.

"Yes, I am the blade. The other half of Meliveraze, the soul lantern. We existed before you, but you are our perfect master. No soul before could use us in such ways than those that shall be open to you."

Art was stunned. *"I don't know what you mean."*

"You, Art Storygrove, are a walking Haunting Weir. You are the soul born out of two sacrificed Weirs."

Art's mind flashed to the two Weirimen he had seen in the ritual with the demon and again in the mirror at the demonic library.

"Karvin Storygenner and Neth Grovebell?!"

"Yes," the blade's voice continued to speak into his mind. *"They sacrificed themselves, their Haunting Weirs, to imprison the Pith demon within you. I was taken by the Weaver, locked away for my dangerous violent abilities that could be used by anyone strong enough to wield me. While the lantern, Meliveraze, was passed down through the generations to your guardian, Evendale Trenaveeve."*

"But, what does that make me!? What am I?"

"Your body was born of the power and energy of every Weirimen that used Meliveraze, through their pure intention and their battle with the darkness. Over time it was enough to take the power of the two Weirs and give you soul and form. You became the walking prison for the demon, more powerful than the lantern ever could be, with a Haunting Weir and soul all your own, life born of sacrifice."

Art suddenly understood and his eyes fell on Lucid. This was why the boy had called him brother, why the Weaver had alluded to them being the same. Art was like Lucid. He was a soul born out of something that fought the darkness, a balance to the evil. While Lucid was a dreamcatcher, Art was a Weir. Stunned, he swayed on his feet, his knees shaky.

"What have you learned?" Ever was suddenly standing next to Art.

"The blade spoke to me," he said in a faraway voice and proceeded to explain.

"Your resemblance to the demon's humanoid form is purely environmental. You were born to house the thing, so in a sense your body just took on the characteristics of its face." Ever was astounded.

"It would seem so," Art affirmed, still feeling dazed.

Lucid suddenly clapped him on the back, nodding, as if he had already known.

"The Weaver suspected this, didn't he?" Art turned his eyes on the youth, who nodded again.

"What does this mean?" Ever pressed. "Does this aid you against the demon or in your task with Orchid and myself?"

Art stared down at the blade and turned the shinning metal over in his gloved hand.

"Yes," he said, ideas forming in his head as he ran through everything he had learned about soul lanterns, the use of his own life's energy in the battle against darkness, and what he had learned about the power of a Weiriman's soul. "Yes, I think I know what to do to help Orchid and you."

Art removed his gloves, handing them to Lucid. He gripped the blade in both hands, knowing his eyes were changing to their amber-gold. He was no longer limited by the thought that he was just a man, lacking history, lacking a future. At this moment he was a Weiriman in a truer sense than any of his brethren had ever been. He could sheath this blade and protect Orchid from the pain, he could absorb that pain and set her and Ever free.

With his eyes fully amber, Art was opening himself up to feeling and sensing all he could. He knew this made him more vulnerable to the Pith demon, but he had to take the risk. He could sense and feel the life forces of both the dryad and the elf through their Weirs. He could even now see it as lights, flowing through the branches, each at its own pace, its own color.

Blade in hand, Art touched the lantern as it floated free of Lucid's hands. For the first time he could sense it, a quiet consciousness like the blade. They were alive in some fashion, perhaps even more so now that Art was connecting with them. He was sharing his life force with the things. He could feel the blade encircle in energy: his own amplified by the healing light of the lantern. Through this, Art somehow knew the knife would behave differently than before.

Carefully, he brought Weir Hewn to another of the branches of Orchid's tree Weir. Eyes wide he felt her Weir pull back, like a flower folding up for the night, rather than the blade actually cutting her. Shifting his gaze slightly, Art caught a sideways glance of the woman and elf. She no longer acted like she was in pain but seemed more like she was slipping into a quiet unconsciousness. Art could hear her thoughts, feel her emotions, and knew the blade was no longer harming her.

Gaining confidence and getting a feel of the energies moving through him, Art repeated the task slowly, carefully with each part of her Weir twisted in Ever's. Each time a branch curled back, Art felt more of the woman return to herself, her form taking on more color, becoming more solid. However, with each "cut" Art could feel his own energy waning. It was taking quite a toll on him to manipulate the powers of his own soul, the lantern and the blade.

As he neared the end of the procedure, only a few more branches left to separate, Art felt the demon at the back of his mind, clawing at him, its voice muffled but carrying weight. He could not allow the thing to break through and stop him in his task. He was not finished. Powering through, Art's head grew hazy, pain hummed through his ears and down into the depth of his brain, but he ignored it until Orchid was finally cut free.

The woman, nearly completely solid and teetering on the edge of unconsciousness, floated over until she started to fall. Ever reached out to catch her, but Lucid stopped him. He left Art's gloves with the Weiriman and caught Orchid's slow fall. Lifting her, he nodded at Ever.

"I have her. She is safe." Lucid headed towards the protective gate they had passed through.

"You did it," Ever breathed, hardly believing it. "How can I ever thank you?"

"This is only step one," Art's voice was ragged. "I have to reattach her Weir. We need to head out of your mind's eye now."

The elf nodded and closed his eyes, disappearing from his own mind, Art following.

Back in his own body Art let out a shuttering breath. His body hurt all over, aching, trembling and tight with pain. The ritual had taken much out of him and he felt as if he could not catch his breath. A stream of blood had started from his nose, dripping down his lips and chin, but Art brushed it off hastily with his gloved hand and moved towards Orchid's body still nestled in her tree.

"Art, you are bleeding," Ever said but the Weiriman ignored him.

Lantern in hand, blade sheathed once more, Art held the thing up to the woman. He closed his eyes. Lucid was within her mind, he could hear him though Art had not entered her psychic space. He did not need to. The lantern whispered to him, in a softer voice than Weir Hewn, almost wordless just feelings. Art knew what he needed to do.

His life would help her, the lantern would aid him, he could do it. He could almost see her Haunting Weir in his mind, a beautiful circular gate of vines, flowers, and gracefully arching branches. He could see it in her own garden, placing it back where it belonged, natural hinges slipping into place, attaching. Art was trembling but he knew he had to hold on, heal her, put her right. Finally, it was done and the Haunting Weir opened, allowing Lucid carrying the unconscious Orchid, through into her mind again.

Art felt faint and stumbled as Ever leaned in to support him.

"It's done," the man breathed, his mouth tasting like blood.

With his words, the woman in the tree opened her eyes and took a sudden deep breath. Lucid was suddenly by Art's side, shouldering the man's weight as Orchid's tree released the woman floating out and into Ever's arms. Tears filled both their eyes and the coupled embraced for the first time, arms around one another, crying and laughing, hands touching faces until their lips met.

Lucid had helped Art to the ground, where he lay breathing shallowly but still smiling. It had worked. He had done what no other Weiriman could have. The happiness he witnessed gave him all the vindication that had been robbed of him since his expulsion from the Weirimen Guild. He felt whole for a moment, content and happy that he had aided people truly in need of his gifts. He had righted a wrong done by evil, and it felt euphoric despite his pain.

"How can we ever repay what you have done for us?" Ever was leaning over the man.

"I wouldn't have made it this far without your help." Art smiled through tired eyes. "But I'm afraid I have another problem."

"The demon," Lucid said, very seriously. "We have to get him back to Father!"

"I'm afraid I need that last candy if I'm to make the journey back to the Weaver and I don't have another to take before my exorcism. It might be no good. I…I might need you to end me!"

Art could hardly believe what he was saying, but the demon baying in the back of his mind was very real. He knew he would not have the strength to battle the thing now.

"Can you not take the Umbra Sweet and then exorcise the thing here?" Ever said, horror in his expression.

"I haven't the strength," Art protested. "And even with the blade, cutting it free of my Weir would only free it. I still have no idea how to actually deport it back to the Ever-Hunger hell. I need the Weaver to help me. I don't know what to do with the thing."

"You need rest?" Orchid asked, her face solid and full of color for the first time since Art had seen her.

"Yes, but more than that, I need the demon to be stilled long enough to get back to the Weaver."

"I can do this!" Orchid exclaimed, her excitement enhanced by the flow of her long sleeves when she brought her hands up and grabbed Ever by the arm.

"What? What do you mean?"

"I can suspend him with the pollen of my tree. It will put him into a deathless sleep for a short period. His mind and body will still. My healing abilities will keep him alive while he slumbers."

"Will we be able to return to the Other Side Woods in time?" Art asked, not daring to hope yet.

The elf's eyes grew large. "We shall, with the help of the Birchwood Garrison. They will accompany us in our passage. Orchid, perform your slumbering, I shall speak with Captain Finnafor."

Ever rose and departed the garden, and the woman moved to place Art's head on her lap. Her face was still pale, the color in her cheeks not as pink as Art suspected she looked. Still, she was the loveliest woman he had ever laid eyes on. As she leaned over him, her cool hands on his temples, he noted how light and ethereal she seemed. Her movements were still so floaty and she gave off a slightly ghostly light.

"I didn't know you were a healer," Art mumbled, hating the taste of blood in his teeth, and tried to wipe the blood trickling down his cheek from his nose.

"I was before the accident," Orchid confirmed as warm light emanating from her hands washed Art with a pleasant tingle and started to numb the thundering pain in his head and the screams of the demon within him. "They believed it was part of the reason I was not instantly killed and able to fuse with Ever's Weir."

"Explains a lot," Art chuckled as petals started to fall round him from her tree above. The air filled with a rich perfume scent, making Art tired and so comfortable a sloppy smile spread across his face.

"Thank you, Art," was the last thing he heard of her lyrical voice before his eyes rolled into the back of his head and he slipped into a soundless unconsciousness, the demon's wails of frustration falling away.

Chapter Twenty-One
Blade and Lantern

Art was groggy and disoriented, but he felt instantly something was wrong. Though his lids felt like steel wool, he forced them open to blink several times. He was hot and uncomfortable, a thin sheen of sweat glistened over his face and down his neck. Where was he? Trying to move he found himself pinned. Nothing was responding. Glancing around, Art was met with darkness, his heart started to thump rapidly.

He opened his mouth but found he had no voice. Crying out was only swallowed by his own throat. He felt like he could not breathe. Art wriggled his shoulders, trying to free his arms, when something caught his eye and lifted his gaze to a growing light like the glow in a faraway tunnel. It neared him slowly, floating and shifting, a flame suspended by nothing, giving off a sticky amount of light until it came to settle above him on a solitary candle stick.

Confused, trying to slow his panicked breathing, Art craned his neck until he understood the strange scene he was a part of. Art was not strapped down to a bed, but found he was somehow suspended on the ceiling of a room. Nothing seemed to be holding him in place but he still could not move. The sudden realization of the disorienting position caused his stomach to drop followed by a wave of dizziness.

The floor had first looked like dirty carpet but now seemed to be gray, ash covered floor. The walls were only partially there, large pieces of paneling missing. The room was half built and half exposed to an eerie sort of misty night, where a red moon hung streaming filtered light in through gray clouds. What had happened? The last thing Art recalled was Orchid's face, Lucid nearby, both watching as he slipped into an unconsciousness that she had induced in him.

Unable to free himself, he tried calling out with his mind to whoever he thought he could contact, but instantly regretted it when a familiar laughter smoldered up from the filthy floor below him. The ground twisted and swelled, forming a face, as if the thing was pressing itself against a sheet of fabric until the floor gave way and the demon's skulled grin greeted him. Panicked and terrified, Art tried to will his body free, but it would not respond as the demon rose out of the floor, the ground falling away around him like sand slipping off a beach shell.

The thing uncrossed its long black arms, flexing its clawed hands. Its veins rippled with crimson fire as if it was ablaze on the inside. It slowly tilted its head back, the long horns protruding from its onyx skull heavy and loosely curved. Art tried not to look, but its black, empty eye sockets drew his gaze to it, lit by just a prick of light and burning intelligence. Even without real skin on its face, it still seemed to smile up at Art.

"That dryad thought she could keep us apart with her pollen and her sweet healing hands, but our connection runs far deeper than that, doesn't it, 'Art'." He spat the name like an insult.

"Leave me be, demon," Art's voice finally came out as he tried to sound even through his fear and inability to move.

"Now, how can I do that?" The thing's insipid tone mocked Art's play at strength.

To his horror, the ceiling started to move. It was bringing Art down towards the demon until the pair were face to face, only inches apart. Art could feel its hot breath on his eyes.

"We are one, Art Storygrove. You have learned your whole life is because of me. You exist because of me. You are no man, no Weiriman. You are nothing but a fleshy prison to house my great self."

"That's not true," Art stammered, terror threading through him like thread and needle sewing away his confidence.

The demon laughed a noise so deep Art felt it rumble in his own ribs.

"Even your face is proof of all I speak!"

Reaching up with his long clawed fingers, the demon gripped its own face, digging its nails into shiny black bone until it broke off in a crackling sound. Art tried to turn away but was drawn back to what appeared when the demon pulled its torn face away. Inside the head was another face, grinning back up at him with blacked out eyes, shinny and wide. It was his face, demonic but horrifically familiar.

"You're nothing but another tool, boy! A tool with my face! You are my mirror! My prison! You are but a shell I will break out of to burn my malice across the world. You cannot hold me! The Haunting Weir is open! It's only a matter of time now. You, yourself released me! I'll consume you and everyone around you! You've failed this life, failed at all you desired, all you wanted, even at being a tool of my imprisonment! You are nothing but food."

Art was shaking his head violently, tying to shut his eyes. The demon's laughter gave way to an even more terrifying experience as dozens of hands came out of the ceiling Art was pinned to and started tearing at his face and body. He was screaming; sound issuing out of him as he tried desperately to get free, desperate to make them stop. He was in pain suddenly, something had struck him.

"Stop it! Don't!" He heard a female voice plead.

"If I don't wake him now, he could die in there!"

Art was confused and pulled out of panic for a moment, but the hands were tearing his flesh again. Thinking there could be a way out, he struggled to figure out where the other voices were coming from, when he was suddenly struck by the invisible force again. It was not the hands, it was not the demon. He was bewildered.

"Wake up, you idiot!"

Art knew the voice, the Weaver!

"Come on, you stupid Weiriman! Wake up now or I'll kill you myself!"

Once more he was struck. It was becoming clear. He had to be in his own mind, unconscious. This was all taking place inside him, and he had to wake up before the demon consumed him. The thing started to growl and reached towards Art, claws grasping, when like an eye blinking, Art was suddenly awake. The Weaver's hand was coming down towards his face again but Art caught it before the man could strike him once more.

"Art!" Orchid cried, relieved. "You're awake! Ever, he's awake!"

"I can see that." The elf was smiling.

"There you are!" The Weaver grinned, his silver mustache curling at the corner of his mouth. "Thought the demon had gotten you for a moment."

Art released the man's hand, his frown accenting the smarting of his face where the Weaver had struck him several times.

"What happened? Where am I?" Art brought a hand to his hair and dragged the glove through it, wincing at the thunder of his headache.

"You are in my home, boy. A true surprise. I was not sure I would ever really see you again. Not alive anyway." Art dropped a dubious glance on the Weaver but he only chuckled, watching Lucid aid the Weiriman in getting up off the bed he had been laid out on. "Lucid, and your new companions with the help of a whole group of Scarborough Knights smuggled you cross country from the elven city to drop you all here at my door step."

"The Birchwood Garrison had to move on, but they were most gracious to us," Ever explained.

"Yes," The Weaver nodded. "Hoodwinked more than one patrol of Weirimen, I might say, but don't be surprised if they will be on your scent before long.

Weirimen may not be as relentless as a Blackenmancer hunter but they are formidable and have a great deal of skills at their disposal to find you."

"You don't have to tell me that." Art made no attempt to hide his poor mood. He ached all over again, the taste of rust and blood thick over his teeth.

"They will end you, *Storygrove*, should they catch you. But I will devour you long before their leather clad forms darken the doorway."

The demon's voice was sharply pronounced and Art struggled to keep its oppressive presence from overwhelming him.

"You're losing the battle with the Pith demon, aren't you?" The Weaver was suddenly stone faced and serious.

"I don't have much time," Art confirmed. "I hope you have something to help me…"

The Weaver crossed his arms over his smallish frame and tilted his head to one side.

"Now that you know what you are, I suppose I do have an idea, but you won't like it."

Art turned dark rimmed eyes on the Weaver and said quietly, "There has been little I've liked in many days now. Tell me what you know."

The Weaver explained he always thought it was highly possible Art was a soul grown out of the Haunting Weirs of Karvin Storygenner and Neth Grovebell, given birth by the energies of the Weirimen that had used the soul lantern, Meliveraze, over many long generations. He surmised that Art's guardian, Evendale Trenaveeve, had been the latest wielder of the lantern. Her talents had been legendary, unusually gifted. He thought it was likely a touch with this last rare person that gave Art's growing soul a body to be born into.

"So she was not truly your mother, Storygrove, but she was very near to that," the Weaver explained, making Art feel strange.

He had always revered Evendale, but knew she was not his mother. To find now that she was as close to one as someone like him could have, made him sad he had spent any time wishing he knew a family that had not existed. She had, in fact been his family, blood related or not. She had known he was some strange creation from the lantern and yet it had not caused her to turn him over to the Weirimen as a possible oddity or danger. The Weaver feared they would react this way to Lucid, so it would have been natural for Evendale to fear Art as well. Instead, she had taken him as her own and raised him. She had given him a good life, teaching him the noble pursuits of a Weiriman, and above all, keeping his secret. Evendale had wanted a life of purpose for him, playing to his natural gifts and strengths as any good mother would.

"Did she know about the demon inside my Weirs?"

"I'm not sure," the Weaver admitted. "I want to say no she didn't. I don't know if she knew what the lantern truly was, or of its function in the sealing of the Pith demon and its dark past."

"They had it locked in the Wine Vault when Cindervail retrieved it."

"Likely, they put it back there when she died. You were not a Weiriman yet and such a powerful soul lantern could not have been left in a civilian's hands." Art nodded, following the sense of it. "Likely, your professor could sense at the edges of her mind that you would have need of it. Weirimen are all at least a little bit precognitive. It's why your intuitions are usually so accurate."

"How do you know all this about me?" Art said suddenly realizing the Weaver had more information on him than he should have. Art had explained very little of himself on his last visit. Truly, he had not expected the man to even remember him at all.

"I had a visit from said professor days after your departure."

"Cindervail came here?" Art was astounded.

"She was concerned for you," the Weaver said as he made his way to the door, motioning the others should follow. "From what I learned, you were not liked much by your peers, but she always knew you were special, that your potential was boundless. She foresaw you becoming one of the greats, like your Evendale. And above all else, she found you to be a good man dealt an unfair fate. I suppose not all Weirimen are bad. She was nice enough."

Art had to smile at that as he and the others followed the Weaver through his tree themed house and to a room Art recalled.

"This is the Veil room," Art started before giving Ever and Orchid a quick explanation that it existed between the worlds.

"Yes," the Weaver mused. "Here you will cut the demon from your Haunting Weir and then exorcise it, though your method of exorcism will be complicated."

"I don't understand." Art placed a hand on the hilt of Weir Hewn, marveling at the ache of just lifting his arm to do so.

The Weaver clapped his hands together, an excited smile spreading over his face. "Boy, you are unique, much like your brother Lucid, born of an object created to battle evil. Your soul's growth is in response to this threat. Therefore, it is logical that you are uniquely able to deal with this demon. You have been its prison for all this time, but I believe you are more than just a prison. Soul, life, consciousness, all this does not need to exist just to be a prison. The lantern and the two Weirs, given by your fallen comrades of so many years ago, should have been enough."

"The question is, what purpose was Storygrove created for?" Ever interjected.

"Yes, elf!" The Weaver grinned. "And I believe this is a complicated question with an equally complicated answer. Something about this demon could not be simply contained in a prison. What that is, I don't know, but Art had to be created to balance its evil."

"But what's that reason?" Art asked, frustrated.

"I don't know," the Weaver exclaimed, looking more amused than worried. "What I do know is you will require Weir Hewn and Meliveraze to do whatever it is you need to do, along with the strength of your own mind and soul. Facing this thing, facing who and what you are, you will find the knowledge of how to defeat it, or you will fail in the very purpose for what you were born for."

Art stared, mouth open, eyes huge for a long moment before exclaiming, "What?! Th-that's it? I returned to you for you to tell me I have to figure it out?!"

"No!" the Weaver snapped, an expression clearly depicting how stupid he thought the young races could be, blurred across his face as he said, "You finding out what you are has told me you are meant to figure it out. Before, I was concerned you might have just been one of Bancroft's experiments gone wrong and there was no real hope for you, since the demon was a Pith demon. Yet, I hoped that the other possibility of your being a walking Haunting Weir was true. But you had to find out. You had to take this quest and learn the demon's name and your origins. Now knowing what you are, who you are, and how you came to be, you have all the pieces to put together with all your gifts and figure out how to defeat this thing."

"I...I don't understand," Art's voice sounded more defeated than angry, though he really wished he was feeling the latter.

"You will," the Weaver insisted and motioned for Art to sit across from him on the cushion. "You have learned much more than you realize. The journey has given you all you require to win. Dig for it, boy, use your gifts."

Lucid had already sat down and was looking over at Art, who was hesitating, his expression horrified.

"I believe he is right, Art." Orchid was by the man's side and almost startled him out of his racing thoughts. She was still floating but her form was solid, radiant, and alive.

"You, you're floating...!" Art said quietly, knowing very little about dryads but did know they were not capable of flight.

"A side effect of her experience," Ever said, coming up from behind her and slipping his hand into hers. Art could hear the whispering of joy and the effect the simple touch gave the pair as now they were no longer held apart by her ghostly condition.

"Though you separated us a little part of me is still part of Ever," Orchid explained. "The Weaver told us this has made my soul just a little lighter and therefor I retained some of my ghostly attributes." She rose up and over Art's head, giving him a great smile before returning to hover just over the floor. "We are changed from what befell us, but the outcome was not bad. We are better for it and that is thanks to you and your abilities. I believe you can do the same with your condition. You can defeat this evil. You were born for it."

"Believe in yourself, Weiriman," Ever added. "There was much doubt you would achieve even this length and survive harrowing tasks at such impossible odds. All this you have achieved."

Art blinked several times. Never since his guardian had someone showed such pronounced faith in him. He had always made his own confidence, leveled his own odds. When he had times of doubt, there was nothing but his own voice to carry him through. Now that voice was dark, silenced by fear and the screams of the demon within him. Yet, as he felt Lucid tug on his jacket and hold up the bottle rattling with the last Scarlet Extinction, he could feel the support and belief of everyone in the room. These people had aided him, relied on him, and believed he could accomplish what the people he had spent the last six years with had been ready to condemn him for, without any thought or help to his affliction. His strength had inspired the strength in others. He would have to take their belief within him and go on faith to honor that trust. He could do this. He had to.

Hesitating slightly, Art took the bottle and sat on the cushion next to Lucid. He popped the lid and took the candy out.

"I can't go with you, brother, but you don't need me. You are strong."

Art stared at the youth, who smiled back at him, wild black hair and pure blue eyes seeming so confident in his words. He wanted to take that confidence with him, he hoped it would suspend his fear.

"A little fear is good, boy; you face a great evil, but you are stronger. You are brimming with life. Although a soul can nourish a demon and give it unimaginable power, it can also resist that demon, even defeat it. Your soul can do this. Take the lantern and the blade, but remember, you are the real weapon." The Weaver pointed at him, eyes stern.

Once more, Art nodded and pushed the candy into his mouth, almost resisting the sweet flavor on his tongue. It would give him clarity, help with the pain, allow for focus, but his battle would be won in the strength of his soul, candy or not.

Art dropped down into his mind even before he meant to. He suspected the demon might have helped with the fall. It wanted him there. Both of them were itching to destroy the other. It was not threatened by the faith Art's comrades had in him. It did not believe in trust, inner strength, or the power of self worth. Those things were illusions to the soulless. Art had to remember that when he faced it.

He appeared outside of the temple in his psychic space. The world around him was in pieces, trees were uprooted, suspended in the air. Rocks, boulders even, floating up and into the darkness of his mind. The ground was broken in open shifts of earth and Art had to climb up and over many cracks and openings of the changing environment. He was not sure why it looked the way it did. He suspected the demon was destroying his mind's eye, but he did not linger on the ideas and headed straight for the temple.

It was no longer dilapidated. Everything was as it had been in the vision of the demon's sealing. He now understood why it looked like a chapel and why it always felt so creepy to him. His mind's eye was just a stage of the demon's last stand. It was no more a reflection of who he was any more than a random building would be.

"Oh that is not entirely true," the demon sounded behind Art and he turned, drawing his blade. The thing laughed, no longer inside the Weirs. It stood, towering over Art, free of the barrier. The color drained from the Weiriman's face. "This place is a reflection of you. All of this is the real you. These other thoughts, these ideas that you are a man unto yourself, that is the illusion. A soul born of a lantern, a blade, and two cut Weirs. The idea is absurd. You are nothing, you are not even a man."

Art's mind was flying. The demon was free. Its last act would be to consume Art's soul and take over his body. With those two things the demon would be unthinkably powerful. The devastation it would cause...

"How dare you think of anything but what I say to you now," the thing bellowed, the sound so loud Art's ears rattled down to the bones of his neck. "Your concern cannot be for the lives I will drain once I'm free. All your attention, all your concern, all your focus must be on the very fact that I am going to devour your soul as one would drink a fine wine. I will savor its flavor, relish its agony. Your fear will blossom in my mouth like heat in winter."

Art steeled himself as the thing made a lunge for him, claws out, long thin frame agile and swift. He knew a battle between them would likely come to combat, he just hoped he was strong enough. He had to be. Lantern in hand, Art could only use his single blade. His first swipe at the demon missed and it rose over his head knocking the lantern from his other hand. Alarmed, Art watched as it sailed through the air only to stop and hover above them.

He had little time to think for the demon was upon him attacking, swiping, bearing an open mouth, and long black tongue. Art was barely holding his own, dodging, moving, using his blade to parry the nails that could disembowel him with just one slash. Driven back, his footing stumbled and he slipped making just enough of an opening for the demon to gash his arm, cutting through his leather and into the flesh. Art cried out and pain rushed through him. He may have been only in his mind's eye, but everything felt real. If he perished in his mind, his body would die. Pulling back, Art went for his other blade. Now armed with two long knives he tried to advance on the demon again, ignoring the pain of his deep wounds.

"You are well trained." The demon grinned, too easily deflecting Art's blows, out maneuvering his footwork, and slashing again this time into Art's thigh. The man hobbled back, blood and pain rippling out of him in burning. "It really is a shame just to end you. Given more time, you could have been one of the greatest Weirimen, that is, if you were actually a real person." It laughed as Art advanced on it again.

The fight was furious. Art had never been so agile, so determined. He out performed every combat situation he could remember but it still was not enough. Before long, the demon cut him again and then again. Bleeding, breath labored and ragged, Art was not sure how he was to defeat a thing so clearly more skilled than he. Towering over Art, it was stronger and faster than any he had encountered. As if reading his moves, it anticipated his blades, maneuvered out of his strikes too skillfully. The thing was likely too deep in his mind for him to break it down in this way.

Wiping a line of blood from his split lip, Art turned his eyes squarely on the thing, going from amber-rimmed green to fully gold.

"Oh," the demon mused, tilting its head to the side. "We have changed tactics, have we? Shall you try a battle of wills now?"

Art ignored the thing's mocking, drawing up his soul's strength as he had been taught and using his Weirimen's voice. In the low, deepened rasp he spoke with all the force he could muster, "I know your name demon of the Ever-Hunger, Artcainecru! By my will alone you will never enter the world of the living."

The world around them expanded as if the whole place had drawn breath. The sheer magnitude of Art's will surprised even the Weiriman. Golden-eyed and standing strong through his injuries, he watched as the demon drank in the scent of his power. Before bearing teeth, the thing looked angry rather than amused for the first time since they had started their showdown. It gave Art hope, but also warned him of an important lesson. Demons were always most dangerous when truly threatened. Facing the possibility of being sent back to hell after all their agony and effort to claw their way from their dark world, was enough to frenzy the evil in to real madness and extreme violence.

Art readied himself when the demon's massive presence filled the room as heavy and visual as a blackening storm.

"You are centuries too young to even think of challenging me, child. I am a demon of the Ever-Hunger, hell of wanting and need. I am the drinker of souls, master of wills. I consume evil and light in the same mouthful, a dark star of suffering. You cannot hope to subdue me with your manufactured might and false soul."

It rose up before Art, gaining in size and weight as its very presence pressed down on the man so much that Art's knees buckled and he was forced to the floor of the chapel. His wounds screamed, bleeding anew as he fought to press his own soul's purity against the growing darkness. The thing swelled until it was twice the size, a pillar of billowing smoke and oil slick muscle as it extended its arms to toss its head back and laugh.

"You are a insect in my fire, a moth's wings burning as I smolder and rage, my flame so hot you need not even plunge into the depths of its heat to burn."

Art did feel like he was burning, his soul small against the great evil that had overwhelmed so many Weirimen before him. How could he even dream that his single soul could turn back such an evil? He did not even know what sacrifice and unforgivable acts had allowed this beast so nearly into their world to begin with. Sheer force alone would not defeat the monster.

Sacrifice. The thought slipped inside his mind as his body wailed at the pain the demon was inflicting on him. It raged once more, the evil threatening to tear his soul apart. The two Weirimen before him had sacrificed themselves to imprison the thing within their Weirs and those within Meliveraze. As the demon worked its way out of its prison, the lantern had collected energy of every Weiriman who used it. Each sacrifice they made to battle evil seeped into its healing light and Art was the result. A gift of life could stop evil, a sacrifice could hold the monster back.

The idea cooking in Art's mind was insane. There was little precedence for it other than the loose idea of evil verses sacrifice. He was losing the battle of wills against it. Even knowing its name could not give him enough of an edge to deport it back to hell. He would have to trust his instincts.

Clawing his way to his feet, he moved through the blowing darkness, his bloodied hand going out and feeling in the dark for the lantern. To his surprise

Meliveraze came to him, floating unaffected by the demon's storm tearing up the temple around them. He grasped the thing and headed towards the Haunting Weirs. With it lighting his way, he managed to stumble to the heavy panel, standing open where the demon had exited the prison.

Fear threatened to stop him, but he knew of no other way then to give up his life to end the monster. It was tearing his mind apart and soon it would consume him. He could feel the demon dreaming it now, ready to taste. It would destroy his mind's eye and leave his soul bare for consumption giving all the power it needed to enter the physical world seeking more destruction, more blood, more souls. It would never stop, ever hungry. Art could not bear it. No Weiriman could allow this abomination.

Blade and lantern in hand, the man entered the dark void beyond the Weir. As soon a he crossed the threshold the storm ceased. All became silent, more quiet than Art thought possible. Even his breath seemed without sound. His wounds, though still present numbed quickly until they ached no longer and his head started to clear. For a moment Art feared he had died in that strange darkness. But, as the moments ticked by, the soul lantern started to blossom with light and the man knew he was still alive.

Artcainecru had not followed him into the prison and for a moment Art thought it odd that all this time he had not thought of the demon as really having a name. It had always just been "the demon", a great formless evil to be conquered and destroyed. It was not like a person. Its desires and reasons, Art knew, he could never understand. They were never taught to see demons as anything but aimless primary evil. The reasons such things existed were without explanation.

But standing in the soulless, timeless prison, Art started to see the thing as at least a beast with a name. Artcainecru: ancient, evil, and with a thirst for destruction and consumption. It said it had eaten light and evil in the same breath. Art had never thought about demons eating one another before. If that was true, could light eat darkness? Could he consume evil as the evil consumed life and still remain untainted? It was possible. When a demon ate a soul it did not gain some measure of purity, it just turned that goodness to its own darkness.

Art's eyes widened as thoughts whipped into a tornado of possibility just as his eyes fell on the other Haunting Weir, the one that blocked the demon from escaping back into any world: demonic, Veil, or physical. His idea was evolving and he knew he had to act quickly. Releasing the lantern so it floated free of him again, he dashed to the far Weir. It was of a different design than the one he passed to get in. He suspected they differed because these were actually the Weirs of Storygenner and Grovebell. They had not changed at all, even after being cut out of the Weirimen.

The one that stood before him was round, suspended in the dark void, but did have black iron hinges just as the entrance Weir. Weir Hewn in hand, working as quickly as he could, Art leveled the blade above the hinges and sliced down. It was like cutting through glass. It felt strange, almost as if it would not give, perhaps shatter, but the blade moved through the hinge and separated the Weir from its invisible anchor. It bobbed a moment as if it were suspended in jelly or liquid, then stopped and gently floated.

Finding it fascinating but also eerie, Art's eyes were wide. He was not sure his insane plan would work. Time was spent, the hourglass of his life was nearly out. Rushing back to the entrance Weir he did the same thing with the hinges there. With both free floating, Art doubted for a moment what he was attempting.

Moving back to what felt like the middle point between the two hovering Weirs, Art drew the soul lantern to him. Its light was brilliant but did not make him squint. He paused, looking down at Weir Hewn, the years of his life rushing through his mind. Did he regret any of it? Parts, he admitted, but he found he did not find any real reason to be sad. Life given in defeat of darkness was what he had always sought. This act alone would make him a true Weiriman, regardless of title, license or graduation. Evendale would have been proud. He could be proud.

 The final thought had just glossed over his mind when suddenly he felt the presence and turned to see Artcainecru standing behind him. The demon was near his height, its magnificent display of smoke and rage gone. It was just a tall, black figure, empty eyes, soulless and evil. They stared at each other a moment, Art unmoving; the demon seeming curious at the man's sudden calm.

As the moment expanded out into more time that Art thought the thing would stand motionless, the demon's clawed hand came up and plugged into the Weiriman's chest. Art gasped in shock and pain, eyes wide as the gold color ebbed until they returned to their amber-rimmed green. He gave a great shuttering breath, one hand trembling as it reached up and gripped the demon's wrist.

Artcainecru grinned, its black skeletal face never before looking more satisfied. But the joy turned to confusion when Art, sputtering blood from his mouth, lifted Weir Hewn in his other hand and proceed to plunge the blade into the demon's hand, piercing it before embedding it into his own chest. Art's whole body jerked against the savage self stabbing but had successfully pinned the demon's hand to his body.

He lifted his head, his eyes glowing gold once more, and Art willed the entrance Weir towards him. After a moment of agony and trying, the thing started to move. Fueled by confidence, Art turned his head and did the same with the other Weir. The demon screamed, panicked and confused by what the man was doing. It was unable to remove its hand from Art, the enchanted blade keeping the pair pinned together. Art closed his eyes and waited for the Weirs to collide, the outcome all rested on his instincts. He let go and the two Weirs crushed him and the demon together, light exploding from the lantern at the impact.

Chapter Twenty-Two
Guild

Art never expected to have another thought again. Sensation, future, life, he had sacrificed all. Whatever awaited him in the afterlife was a mystery, but he was not expecting to open his eyes to soft even light and the smell of greenery. Sitting up with a shock, Art whipped his head around. He had not imagined death to leave him so many memories of what had just transpired. The fight with the demon, the last harrowing moments before the Weirs crushed he and the thing together were a blur, but clearly present in his memory.

Looking down at his body, his wounds were gone, his clothing intact. Next to him was Weir Hewn, bloodless and clean, sitting in soft grass. Picking up the blade, he turned slightly when Meliveraze floated near him. Cocking his head gently, Art removed his glove to reach for the lantern but recoiled when he found his hand was changed. Though his own, the skin was onyx black, the fingers bearing a talon-like shape. Turning it over revealed faint but glistening orange red veins beneath the dark flesh. It looked very much like the demon's hands.

Confused, Art rose to his feet, the lantern shadowing his movements. He flexed his hand. Everything felt normal, the skin was cool to the touch. He had no explanation. Sheathing Weir Hewn, he looked around. Nothing was the same as he had left it. The world was bathed in warm moonlight, a forest clearing. Before him stood a cottage, covered in ivy a structure reminiscent of the home he grew up in but much more beautiful. Amber light lit frosted glass windows casting color on the greenery around the cottage.

Art was walking towards it before he could access it. The door opened for him and he passed through to find a large house within it. There seemed to be no roof, though Art could not have discerned that from the outside. The moon was overheard but near the east corner he could also see the sun. The mixture of both cast glorious light into the space.

Though furnished with things that Art would have loved, great arm chairs, a large bed, a fire place to read by, and more books than he could dream of, the man was drawn to a singular thing in an attached sun room off to the left of the main house. Walking through the doorway, Art stood in awe of a huge structure, wood and curving metal. The black iron looped and circled bent and flourished in beautiful elaborate designs, fluid and natural in its elegance. The frame was carved just as intricately as the metal was forged, but all of that was unnoticeable to the thing in the center of huge wooden barrier.

There was no mistaking that the great thing was a Haunting Weir. Art had never seen one with a sculpture mounted in the center like a figurehead on a boat. It was buried waist deep in the Weir, its arms shackled by the iron flourishes. The horns protruding from its head were also chained in the same way. The hair was long, hanging about its shoulders, smooth and braided elaborately, the color like Art's dark blond. It was the face that scared the man the most, as it was as much his as it was the demon's.

Cautiously, Art approached it. The figure was unmoving and he was uncertain if it was carved out of the wood of the Weir. As he inched closer, the thing's eyes burst open and it turned its head towards him, the metal of its shackles giving to allow its gesture. The eyes were black and Art recognized the smile that spread over his twinned face.

"Artcainecru," Art breathed, completely bewildered.

"The same," the demon spoke, his voice more like Art's than ever before, though smoother and a touch deeper. It lacked the heavy demonic pressure sending only an uncertain feeling through the man, rather than an evil shutter. "Yet, changed. You have bested me, Art Storygrove."

The man wished he knew what that meant. Even though he had somehow orchestrated whatever he was experiencing, he was clueless to what had come of it all. The thing took a rooted breath, its skin deeply black but also bearing the slight texture of the dark wood it was now a part of. Bare chested and wearing Art's handsome face, it looked more like a forest god than the sinister creature that had plunged its hand into Art's chest.

"I have bested you?" Art asked, suspicious.

Artcainecru tossed its head back and laughed, the Weir rattling but it did not seem to give at all. The demon was a part of the thing now.

"Oh I should be swelled with rage that you have changed me so. Yet you have no clue as to the feat you achieved. Yes, child, you bested me. The Weir prison could not hold me. You could not defeat me, so instead you consumed me. You took me into yourself, absorbed both your parent Weirs and with your own life and blood bound me to you. You, a life born of a Haunting Weir, now have the most powerful Weir ever created with a demon as your mantelpiece. You have filled me with life and robbed me of my demonic hunger."

Art knew his face mirrored his dumbstruck awe. He had intended to crush he and the demon with the two Weirs, hoping that force would destroy them both. What had happened was more than a surprise.

"It is now apparent that you were born to keep me from entering the physical world. Your soul grew to consume me, as I could have done to you. Clever and infuriating. It will take equal cleverness on my part to discover the key to the shackles of your soul. But for the time being it looks as if we are chained to one another, I as part of you and, it would seem, you as part of me." His dark eyes fell on Art's blackened arm. "An interesting future awaits you, Weiriman, should your Guild allow you to live it."

The thing was laughing again, amused, but it lacked all the heavy madness Art had sensed before. He truly had found a way to contain the evil, and it no longer perforated his soul. Its cold evil was not inking its way through him. His mind was his own, his thoughts pure again. Somehow, he had been exorcised through he was still gazing at the demon on his newly formed Haunting Weir.

Suddenly Art was moving. His soul was flying and in a blink of an eye the man was awake, heart hammering his blood through the veins in his neck. He was alive!

"Art! Art, are you alright?" Orchid was in front of him, her hand on his forearms. He could feel her warming, healing magic pulsing through him. The ache of his body was pronounced but not the pain he had expected.

Eyes wild, Art lifted his hands and gripped the woman by her shoulders before crushing her in an embrace. She was real. He truly was alive. She was startled but he released her as Ever put his hand on Art's shoulder.

"Storygrove! What happened?!"

Art muttered an apology and released the dryad, taking a few shaky breaths before grinning widely. Lucid was next to him, a smile equally as wide over his face. Overjoyed, Art embraced the boy, slapping him on the back before getting to his feet. In rushed explanation, he told all that had transpired. The small group was stunned but happy, the Weaver nodding all the while.

"Well done, boy. Well done. You are all my guests tonight. Come!"

The Weaver turned out to be a better host than Art had expected. Dinner was an odd mixture of foods Art had never tasted before, but flavors were more vibrant, smells more appealing, and the wine sweeter than he ever could remember. He was truly happy to be alive. The storm of the incident had dispelled and he slept well for the first time in what felt like years.

Art half expected to be plagued by nightmares or even to have to visit the demon chained within his mind's eye. When morning came and he was blissfully without memory of dreams, he allowed himself to truly breath easily again. Rising just as the sun started its climb, he found Lucid and the Weaver in the living room Art had first spoken with the Weaver in. The fairies were gathered about again, listening intently to the conversation unfolding.

"But he's well now, you can stay here," the Weaver protested. "His demon arm is just a side effect. It might even give him new abilities, time will tell. But he is out of mortal danger, at least from the demon inside him. But he's a Weiriman; his life will always be on the hunt for evil. Why do you want to go with him?"

"It is time, Father." Lucid smiled, his eyes curving into little half moons with the gesture. "We are brothers."

The Weaver pouted for a moment then noticed Art in the doorway.

"You did this! You made him interested in that dark world out there! Now he wants to travel with you, turning back evil and putting his life in danger. He could stay here with me, where it is safe. The world is touched by so much pain, so much ugliness."

"It is," Art said gently, "but as a Weiriman, I try to alleviate some of that. Surely you can see Lucid has a gift for it as well. A dreamcatcher purges nightmares, just as a Weir keeps the demons out of a soul. We have to do what we're meant to do. Isn't that what you meant when you told me to do what I was born for? The boy's right, Weaver, we're brothers."

Lucid nodded, rounding his cheeks up at Art's words. The Weaver did not look happy but patted Lucid on the shoulder before rising.

"I see I won't change your mind. But you promise to protect him out there, Storygrove. I'll hunt you down myself should you let harm come to him."

"He's my little brother, I'll protect him. Don't worry."

The Weaver stared for a long, hard and uncomfortable moment before rolling his eyes and sighing heavily. He took one last glance at Lucid, then walked by Art and patted him on the shoulder.

"You should depart today. You still have unfinished business, Weiriman."

Art nodded and watched the Weaver go. Lucid walked up to him but not before waving to several fairies, who flew down to play in his hair, kiss his cheek, and weep a little before returning to their perches and little houses circling the room.

"You sure you want to go with me?" Art asked when the youth came to stand next to him.

Lucid nodded.

"I don't know what's going to happen with the Weirimen. I don't know what they will do."

"We are brothers," Lucid said, his blue eyes clear. "But you are wrong about one thing."

"Oh?" Art cocked his head to the side, smiling at Lucid's sudden seriousness.

"You are younger, Brother. I am older. I am eighty-four." Lucid gave him a wide, full smile before passing him and heading into the kitchen after the Weaver.

Art's mouth popped opened, stunned.

The Weaver gave the group fresh supplies and after a few more threats about keeping Lucid safe, Art, Lucid, Orchid, and Ever departed the Weaver's house heading for the path between the two woods.

"Storygrove, I want to inquire about the condition of your arm," Ever started when Orchid floated up next to him, giving a quiet shushing noise.

Art turned and the dryad smiled at him apologetically, which made Art smile back.

"It's fine, Orchid." Art shook his head. "I would want to know too. I'm not really sure to be honest, Ever. The Weaver thought it might be a new source of abilities but what those are yet, I'm still wondering myself. The only thing I really know is I no longer qualify as possessed, but the arm and the demon in my Haunting Weir, that's all going to have to be explored."

Before Ever could comment any further, a figure appeared on the road ahead of them. At first Art did not recognize them, but as they drew closer he realized he knew them.

"Senny?" He called and the woman removed her hood. Though still wearing her Sin Breath mask, Art could easily tell it was his schoolmate.

"Stop there, Art," she commanded, her voice wavering a little before she lifted a crossbow and pointed it at him.

Ever's bow was out and drawn before Art could stop him. Before any arrows were exchanged Art's hands came up.

"Wait!" he ordered.

The elf did not relax. "She is not alone," he growled, stepping in front of Orchid who dropped down behind him. Her current clothing was more practical for travel than the dress she had worn as a ghost. It did not billow as she moved, and she fit snugly behind the Knight, only peeking over his shoulder.

Art stepped between Senny and Ever just as a party of Weirimen descended upon them. They had to have been laying in wait for Art, weapons drawn, and masks up. Art scanned the group, recognizing only a few but knew clearly the man who rode up on horseback behind Senny.

"Storygrove." Professor Minevur squinted his eyes. "Glad to see we are not too late and you have not released the Pith demon on the world."

"He is no longer possessed," Orchid said, popping her head up before Ever shifted his eyes to her.

"Who is that?" Minevur demanded but Art ignored the question.

Lifting his chin Art spoke clearly, "She is correct, Professor. I am no longer possessed. There is no need to execute me. I have remedied the problem."

Agitated, the man dismounted. Squaring his shoulders, he marched up to Art, his hand on the blade fasted at his hip. The group of Weirimen did not move, their crossbows still trained on Art. Minevur walked right up to the man, much shorter than Art's tall form, and looked up into his face. His brow crease hung so low over the professor's eyes that they looked even more like two shiny beetles embedded in his face.

Art held his breath as Minevur's eyes rimmed silver then flashed into a shimmering gunmetal as he looked inside Art with his Weiriman's abilities. If Art had desired it, he could have fought Minevur's intrusion into his mind. He was far more talented than the stumpy professor, but he needed him to see Art's condition for himself to verify what Art was saying to be truth. He allowed the man to feel with his mind for the signs of possession, the inking darkness, the heat of a burrowing demon working its way into someone's soul, or in this case, out of Art's Haunting Weir.

Finally, after an unnecessarily lengthy and thorough investigation, the professor scowled saying gruffly, "You are no longer possessed, but you still harbor the demon within you! It is attached to your Haunting Weir! Permanently!"

Art felt the flurry of thoughts, feelings, and confusion rise and exchange in the minds of his fellow Weirimen.

"You have made a pact with this demon for your soul, haven't you?!" Minevur accused, stepping back as the others looked to one another for clues if they should attack Art.

"No!" Art shook his head. "I haven't. I've made no such pact!"

"I don't believe you. There should be no way to have stopped a Pith demon with your abilities alone, not without blackening yourself."

Art knew the term blackening was applied to those who had made pacts, deals, or contacts with demons for power, abilities or other such rewards. Particularly mighty demons could bestow lavish might upon those willing to do unspeakable acts to nourish the beasts. Once the person died, their soul was usually forfeited to the demon as well. The Blackened were hunted by the Blackenmancers and hated by Weirimen, but not regularly dealt with by them.

"I have done no such thing," Art insisted removing his gloves. "See! I have no Scorch Scars!"

The Blackened always carried a mark of their covenant with the demon, known as Scorch Scars. Over time they became hidden, only detected by Blackenmancers, but a fresh bargain would still be visible on him. He instantly regretted his action when his strange black demon hand was revealed.

"What is this?!" Minevur shrieked, pointing to the arm.

"It's a side effect of my battle and imprisoning of the demon to my Weir. It's not a Scorch Scar! There's no rune, see!" Art thrust his arm towards the man who jerked back but did not take his eyes off of the obsidian colored flesh.

"How do I know you have not taken the mark somewhere else? It is usually on the hand, but you are a clever one, Storygrove. And this! I've never heard of someone suffering something like this. It could be a sign of an even more evil pact with an unfathomable demon!"

"I have made no pact!" Art protested. "Would you have me strip down right here in the road to prove myself?! There is nothing written anywhere that a Scorch

Scar would look like my arm! Isn't it enough you no longer sense the evil perforating my soul?!"

"No!" Minevur grimaced. "I say you are a Blackened or some form thereof. Your fate is clear." He brought his hand up to signal a man on his right, who took aim.

"You will not kill him before I kill both of you, Weiriman," Ever warned.

"You cannot kill all of us, Scarborough Knight. Be gone. This is no business of yours!"

Lucid had started to step forward but Art, brought his hand up.

"You can't kill me here in cold blood. I demand you take me back to the Seminary and have the Grandmaster and the others examine me. I am no threat to you."

"He's right, Professor," Senny spoke from behind and the two men turned to her. "You said yourself on our graduation day that our gifts and skills are a rarity. In a world threatened by such tangible evil, we are a treasure and needed necessity. If he is not afflicted nor tainted by evil, would it not spit in the face of all you said to waste someone as gifted as Art Storygrove?"

Art was stunned she spoke for him. He could hear the whispers of the thoughts of those around him. They were all concurring with Senny's wisdom. Minevur was visibly angered. He was not keeping his personal feelings towards Art very quiet, or perhaps Art could just hear thoughts more clearly now. He had always disliked Art: his natural gifts, his ability to carry on even without the aid or acceptance of others. His confidence, his good looks, even the silent admiration the others, especially the professors, harbored for Art despite his lack of peer acceptance, enraged his jealousy. He hated that now Art had befallen a misfortune, it would be Minevur who would be escorting Art back to the Seminary, unharmed.

Taken back by the fact that this man would rather see him dead than help him, Art was at least grateful he was Weiriman enough to bend to the logic Senny presented. He knew that slim fact would get he and the others to the Seminary. Art had always thought the Guild protected their own like a family would, jealously and rivalry aside, when it came to a life. Art's glimpse into how much Minevur hated him further jaded his feelings towards the Guild, making him wonder how his trial would actually end. Should the other professors entertain dark feelings towards him, he might end up beheaded just for having the demon within him, even though it seemed contained.

As the group gathered around Minevur, discussing their path back to the Seminary, some eyeing Art suspiciously, Ever moved to Art's side.

"You don't have to come with me," Art spoke lowly to the elf. "I...I don't know how this is going to end."

Orchid popped up over Ever's shoulder, her eyes wide.

"You think they could condemn you after all you have been through, after what you have accomplished?!"

Art dipped his head, his hair spilling over one eye. The past events since his Weir test had taken a dramatic toll on him. Though still handsome, his eyes were darkly rimmed, face pale. He was thinner, his skin a touch gray, lips slightly dry. He gave a long sigh.

"I don't know. But I wanted to be a Weiriman and I'll stand before their justice now to end this trial one way or another. It's what I want. But, it could end badly and I don't want you to have to be there if it does. You should take Lucid and—"

"Brother, we will go with you." Lucid looked up into the man's face and patted him on the arm. "We will all go with you to whatever end."

Both elf and dryad did not say anything but the looks on their faces and the quiet way they smiled at him, told Art all he needed to know.

The trip back to the Seminary had been quiet. Not even Senny spoke with him or anyone in his party. From the thought whispers alone, he could tell everyone was curious as to why Art was traveling with such an unusual collection of folk, as much as they wanted to know about his journey and truth of his condition. All that curiosity was overshadowed by his impending fate when he was finally led into the observation hall at the Weirimen's Seminary. It had been Art's home for many years, but now it felt cold and foreign.

Art had never expected to be in the observation hall under the threat of a trial for his life. The Weir test felt like months ago, even years, after everything that had befallen him. He was a different person standing before the judges and the audience that had gathered in the seats around him. The audience had been empty when he had done his final Weir trial. No one had cared enough to see if he could graduate and join their ranks, but so many were present now to see if he would keep the life he had fought so hard to render back from the invading demon.

Cindervail was at the middle of the judge's panel just as she always had been. Art took a slight comfort in knowing she had at least gone looking for him when he did not return from the Weaver's. However, should he be a threat, she, like the others, would choose the world's greater good over his life. It might even be her to end him. Art held his fears in check.

"This branch of aging crows could not invoke more terror in you than I did, Art."

Art almost startled out loud when he heard the demon's voice in his head. Without its demonic presence and aura it was almost like his own dark inner voice speaking to him. He did not entirely like the fact that it almost brought him a hint of comfort.

"They hold my fate in their hands."

"Surely not," Artcainecru mused to him. "If you were to use my strength, your abilities, and the aid of your odd allies who stand with you now, surely you could escape these walls of mere stone."

"To what end? And by what means?" Art asked in his mind. "I won't be hunted by my own kind again."

"None that judge you now are your kind, Art Storygrove. You are unique and should not stand judged by these lesser than you."

"You're wrong. These people hold a line between the minds of the innocent afflicted and the darkness that birthed you. If I am a threat, I might not even know it. I'm not so arrogant that I would say in my battle with you, that I know now the ebb and flow of that line. I'll stand judged and accept what they pass over me."

"Even though one that sits on this panel is so jealous of you that he would rather have murdered you on the road than bring you here?"

Art flinched at that. He had always known Minevur did not like him but he had not expected to hear the depth of those dark thoughts. After a long moment Art nodded.

"Yes, even knowing that, I would rather trust this system than fight against it. I must be on a side, light or dark, and you, demon are the darkness. Though I hold you in check inside myself, I will trust the world I was brought up in now. I still believe there is real goodness in this. I still stand as that goodness, even though I harbor you now within me."

Art felt the demon within him smile.

"Art Storygrove," Cindervail's voice was louder than he expected and Art jumped. "We have looked inside your mind and seen your trial. We have heard your thoughts and know of your experience."

Art blinked in shock. He had not even known the trial had begun.

"With the help of a Sootsayer Seer, we have looked deep within you, seen all that has befallen you since your Haunting Weir was cracked open. Your suffering has been great, your danger far more dramatic than we had originally thought. In hindsight, it was wrong for us to have let you leave the Seminary and break out on your own. Many times, the demon could have broken free of you, devoured your soul, and been set loose on an unsuspecting world."

Art's blood was running cold, his hands and feet numbing. He could see none of the other faces, only Cindervail's and her expression conveyed little comfort.

"Yet, here you stand before us, alive, intact, and in command of an evil not even all of the skills of this judgment council could turn back. You have achieved the impossible, not only by being who and what you are, Storygrove, but by taming an evil long fought by this institution, claiming many precious lives. Even in the light of what you have accomplished we cannot accept you. We cannot have one embedded with such an evil force among the ranks of our guild. Your origins are strange to us and your life could be unpredictable, even for that of a Weiriman. Should you be granted life you would be without a Guild, alone. There are none here who would partner such a bearer of darkness. If we are wrong, let him or her speak now."

Art's shoulders were tensing up. If no one spoke for him would he be banished from the Guild? What would become of his life, should he even be allowed to keep it? Gingerly his eyes went to Senny, who sat in the front row of the observers. When their eyes met he ignited a tiny hope she might speak for him but when her gaze shifted and dropped, his heart did the same. Even the one closest to him in school would not risk working with a Weiriman carrying the very thing they were sent to destroy.

"Art is not in need of a guild." Ever and the others were standing behind him, near the great doors of the observation hall. He strode to Art's side now, Orchid and Lucid following. "He has previously been accepted by a company. We stand before you now willing and committed to assisting him in whatever capacity he should require to pursue his calling."

"You, elven Knight, we have learned of your story and what Art Storygrove did for you and Orchid Sarathone. Are you not free to return to your garrison, now liberated of your previous affliction?"

Art's eyes were wide. He had fully expected Ever to return to his life once Art was cleared or condemned. Scarborough Knights had a calling to keep their world safe from Demon Touched.

"I am," Ever confirmed. "My former garrison would have me back. In addition, I have an invitation to join the Birchwood Garrison under Captain Finnafor as second in command, an honor and privilege. However, knowing this man, his life, his quality, and his dedication to the defense of our world, I would gladly serve that purpose at his side as the greatest honor I could be afforded."

"I too feel this way," Orchid spoke. "Though my life has always been about nature, beauty and harmony, I have been inspired by the heart of this man, his sacrifices and courage, to take up arms and also defend our world as aide to him."

"He is my brother," Lucid crossed his arms over his chest and smiled broadly, feeling all that he needed to say, he said.

Art was stunned and for a long moment there was much psychic talking happening between the judges, locked away from Art's mind. Finally, after the longest moments of his life, the discussion ended and Cindervail's attention returned to Art.

"Art Storygrove, it is this council's judgment that you will be ejected from the Weirimen Guild, as one who carries a demon cannot be among its official ranks."

Art's heart sank into his stomach.

"However," Cindervail added, causing his heart to leapt back into his chest and climb into his throat. "Since you have been declared one of the most gifted among us, even since a time before the Weaver graced us with wisdom, it is our judgement that you will be licensed and labeled the first independent Weiriman. To each Guild House, it will be up to their Grandmaster should you be allowed to use their facility, but you will have all the authority and prestige afforded one that has earned the right to call himself one of us. You have come through a darkness that would have defeated all who sit before you now. Though we cannot have you among us as a peer, we salute your skill and moral core, Art Storygrove. Welcome to the Weirimen."

The Haunted Weir Workings
will continue in Book Two:

Shadow Confectionary Preview

Prologue
Knife

Shadow Confectionary; a profession of opposites, spinning sugar and candy from evil and darkness. The very idea of taking Sin Breath and dark energy, polluted into the world by demons and their ilk, and purifying it into something that could actually aid a person in staving off their invasive force was revolutionary. It began with hunters. There had always been hunters. Since the time evil started to invade the physical world, hunters of many different kinds had risen up to defend and drive back the monsters that sought to devour souls.

From these hunters, developed the Haunted Weir Working professions. Weirimen exorcised and protected the Haunting Weirs: the door to the mind's eye and the gateway demons had to breech to break inside a person. Scarborough Knights of the fey and elven races hunted packs of demon infested and touched animals that turned more beast and monster than earthly creatures. Blackenmancers specialized in hunting down the Blackened: those who made covenants with powerful demons, devils, and lords of evil. Pitch Threaders created toys and novelties to protect and ward against demonic stalking, haunting, and nightmares. There were many others. So many professions had developed to stand against the darkness and protect the weirs of the world.

The Shadow Confectioners had risen out of this lot. Like the Pitch Threaders, they found a way to take the evil miasma, leaking into the world that turned people's thoughts and hearts dark, into an anti-version of darkness. Like some of the other professions, many families had talent that ran through the generations as strong as blood. Great families rose to stand as institutions to their chosen calling. One of the first and best had always been the Bohurst bloodline.

Many long years ago when the first Bohurst came to the city of Riftenshire, even then a place tormented by nearby haunted ground, there was a man who had made a pact with demons, becoming one of the Blackened. He was said to be the first master of the Shadow Men demons. Then, the Bohursts were Blackenmancers. The city had been fraught with negativity from Shadow Men and their master. These lesser demons could only become stronger by feeding on the negative emotions of people. The stronger the emotion, the more powerful the Shadow Man would become. Shadows themselves could hold nothing and the life force they collected could only last for a short while within the demon. Their master siphoned most of the energy. This created the ever-hungry drive of these creatures. Shadow Men only lived to consume and bring misery to those they fed on, an unbreakable demonic cycle.

Riftenshire had been at its worst back then, covered in a black haze of dark feelings. It trapped the people inside, feeding off them for a dark purpose and no clear end. Into this bleak situation, Knife Bohurst, a relentless Blackenmancer, had come. He brought a unique and unusual solution. Finding and thwarting the Blackened and his Shadow Men was only the first step. There was the matter of cleaning up the environment corrupted by the evil. Where the Blackened had made his home, was now even more potent haunted ground and would always spawn evil. If the town was to be saved, there had to be a continuing solution.

Though brilliant hunters, the Bohursts had a love of making candy. Through this interest, a strange and palatable solution was forged. It was said that Knife could slice away the evil that plagued the town straight out of the air. He could draw the Sin Breath in with his abilities and purge it like a Weiriman would exorcise a soul. The left over substance became known as Umbra Sugar. Through these unique techniques and ingredients, the profession of crafting Umbra Sweets birthed the Shadow Confectioners.

Knife Bohurst saved Riftenshire with his Umbra candy and drove the Shadow Men infestation out. A new industry in warding off evils had been created and the great name of the Bohurst Shadow Confectionary would stand as a pillar and example to all the Shadow Confectionaries that would spring up in every major city and place that could be bothered by the demonic.

Chapter One
Shiv and Bow

Bow Bohurst had grown up hearing the legendary story of Knife Bohurst. His family still lived on the very same land where Knife had built the first Shadow Confectionary. Over the years, they had added to and rebuilt some of the old building, making the Bohurst Confectionary a beautiful blend of traditional and innovative. Time had not diminished the family name of Bohurst. It continued to be the finest place to get Umbra Sweets. His family even specialized in the rarest sweets available, since their bloodline harbored some of the most talented Confectioners in history.

That was the first thing Bow thought of when he heard a knock at the front of the shop after they had already closed up. The Bohurst Confectionary was on the outskirts of Riftenshire, on a little hill beyond a short stretch of dense woods. The city was not safe after dark, but the area about the Confectionary was even more dangerous, so whatever soul was calling at the touch of twilight had to be a seeker of something quite dire and most rare.

Going to his window, Bow had an awkward view of the man at the front. Tall as his brother, dressed in a long dark coat, Bow's interest peaked as he caught a flash of metal and red. Hearing his brother hesitantly open the front door, Bow tiptoed to the stairs that separated the shop and the house. Peering down at the stranger below, he had been right. The visitor was a young Weiriman. Rare, gifted and almost like anonymous celebrities, the heavily trained exorcists were well respected and revered. Everyone had a Haunting Weir that kept demons out of their minds and souls but the Weirimen were the only ones who could manipulate, clear and close a Weir that had been invaded. Umbra Sweets were often used in those tasks.

Even knowing that, Bow could tell just by the serious conversation and late hour of the Weiriman's visit, that this was far more serious than most needs of the Weirimen. The Bohursts saw much business from the multiple Haunted Weir Workings professions. Weirimen, Blackenmancers, Pitch Threaders, and many more, in addition to regular folk, traded in Umbra Sweets. But the Bohursts were one of the few that people would travel for miles to find. Their quality and selection was unmatched.

Bow listened as his older brother, Shiv-Blu, gave the stranger a rare sweet and another he recognized and dealt with daily. He wanted to know what ailed the Weiriman, and wanted to be part of what was happening but he stayed quiet and hidden. He knew Shiv would dismiss him and send him back to bed. Bow was to have no real dealings with the delicate parts of the business yet, and it had nothing to do with his age.

It was normal for a Confectioner to exhibit abilities as early as eleven years old. Twelve was the most common. In rare cases it might not show until early thirteen. Shiv had been a prodigy, one of the youngest to manifest the talents at age nine. Bow had just begun his sixteenth year and his eyes remained brown. All Confectioners had either purple or orange eyes when their abilities bloomed. Every morning had become a painful ritual of Shiv checking his little brother's eyes for change and everyday it passed with silent disappointment that Bow's talent would likely never manifest.

Hate did not accurately describe how Bow loathed it. He wanted nothing more than to be a great Confectioner like Shiv, like their mother before them. Even their father had some talent, though it was their mother who was of the Bohurst line. With Saber Bohurst missing and presumed dead for the last six years, and their father buried since Bow was three, it had been up to a young Shiv to take care of and raise Bow, as well as run the Confectionary. Bow hated that he turned out to be just another dark disappointment in their family's history.

The Weiriman was leaving and Bow rushed back to his window to watch him go. Those talented in the ways against demons always fascinated the talentless teenager. He wanted so much to be a part of those who stood against the evil, but he was little more than a glorified errand boy and assistant to Shiv's grand business. He ground his teeth as the Weiriman's form disappeared into the dense forest between them and town.

Bow's hands gripped the windowsill, unnamed anger swelled within him. He knew morning would come and his eyes would still be brown, his powers unsurfaced if they were there at all. He wished he could be more than the useless thing he was. Eyes boring into the falling night, he stared at the trees just beyond the clearing of their home and suddenly something moved. Bow leaned back a little, startled. Squinting his eyes, he looked out again wondering if it had been an animal.

Just beyond the light of the shop, a tall genderless shadow stretched out long next to the shadows of the trees. As Bow gazed at it, he became alarmed. The shadow did not appear to be stemming from anything. At that angle he should have been able to see the figure the shadow was attached to. Almost as if it knew Bow had seen it, the thing moved, melting into the darkness of the trees around it.

Confused and afraid, the boy looked again, hoping he had been wrong and there had been a person out there somehow casting the shadow. But the night was quiet and dark. The only other person that had been at the Bohurst Confectionary that evening was gone. Bow hated being afraid. Without abilities he could do nothing against the darkness in the world. He was not like their ancestors, nothing like his brother. He was just a boy, gazing out at shadows, feeling a fear he could neither suppress nor conquer. If a Shadow Man came for him, he would have nothing but his brother's candy to protect him. They could easily claim a Bohurst life, regardless of the fact that Knife's blood flowed thickly through Bow's veins. He wondered if he would always be afraid of the bedtime story of Knife Bohurst and the Shadow Men cult.

Please Review, we need your help!

We sincerely thank you for reading Haunting Weir.
For indie authors and publishers, reviews are the life blood of our business and creating.
They feed, inspire, motivate and help others to find us.
If you liked, hated, or had any feelings at all about
Haunting Weir, please review and share.

We appreciate your support!
~Three Muses Ink
www.3MusesInk.com

Exclusive Content Available!

Are you of fan of Haunting Weir Workings? Want new release notices, reviewer circles, fun and exciting news about latest works and even a free and/or exclusive content and artwork?
Then join Three Muses Ink's mailing list!

All who join will receive the Haunted Weir Workings novella, **Blood Lantern**, a fully illustrated story that takes place between book one and the second book, Shadow Confectionary, of the Haunted Weir Workings series.
It is available **exclusively** to those who sign up for the free mailing list!

Sign up is free, easy and will take less than one minute.
www.3MusesInk.com

We will never sale, give away, or share your information.

About the Authors

Kari L. Ronning

Now a life-long Alaskan, Kari was transplanted at a young age out of Texas. Her passion for folklore, legend, myths and especially all things elf-related, has inspired her to be a prolific writer. A University of Alaska graduate with a Bachelor's in Art, Kari surprised her instructors with her organized and systematic approach to creating and storytelling, both narrative and visual. Since grade school, Kari Ronning and A.M. Gagnon have been forming stories. With the establishment of Three Muses Ink, they found the vehicle by which they could share their creations with others. When not writing and drawing, Kari can usually be found with her cats and dog, ever creating a wide host of craft disciplines from crochet to painting, beading, sculpting and putting together whatever comes to her imagination.

A.M. Gagnon

Born and raised in Alaska, A.M. Gagnon has had a passion for the written word since an early age; her great loves range from Edgar Allan Poe to Shakespeare and many forms of poetry. She is a graduate of University of Alaska and has worked for Southcentral Foundation for over 10 years. Always partners in crime, A.M. Gagnon and Kari L. Ronning have been dreaming up stories, characters and world-building since the inception of their friendship in grade school. A video game fan and movie buff, especially of super natural horror, A.M. can be found hanging out with her huge cat, Mjolnir, seeking inspiration in many media forms, visual and written, or crocheting and crafting.

Three Muses Ink

Three Muses Ink is a trio of authors and artists from the great northern state of Alaska. Always fans of fantasy and story telling the love affair with the idea of creating our own world started early. We are inseparable friends who have turned our passion into an independent publishing company, Three Muses Ink, producing novels, storybooks, artwork, and all manner of artistic creations. To find out more about Three Muses Ink projects check out our website:
www.3MusesInk.com

Character Names and Locations Pronunciation Guide

Characters:

- Art Storygrove (ärt Stôrē-grōv)
- Evendale Trenaveeve (ˈevən-deh-l Trē-nah- ēv)
- Grandmaster Belnahla Cindervail (Beh-nah-lah Sinder-vahl)
- Professor Minevur (Mīn-vur)
- Professor Shimtil (Shi-m, til)
- Professor Vestor (Veh-st-er)
- Senny Greiventine (Sehn-ee Grēvn-tie-n)
- Lucid Dreamare (Loō-sid Drēm-mare)
- Neth Grovebell (Neh-th Grōv-bel)
- Karvin Storygenner (Kar-vihn Stôrē-Geh-nr)
- The Weaver (Wēvər)
- Everther "Ever" Nahrwel (Evər-thur Nah-r-well)
- Orchid Sarathone (ôrkəd Sair-ah-thoh-n)
- Captain Dahnaren Finnafor (Dah-nah-rehn Fin-nah-four)
- Korfa Heavykel (Core-fah Hevē Keh-l)
- Grandmaster Felvase (Feh-l-vās)
- Joss Lirecolden (Jah-s Lērə-cold-ehn)
- Artcainecru (ärt-cane-eh-kroō)
- Weir Hewn (Wir Hyoōn)
- Meliveraze (Meh-ee-vur-rah-zeh)
- Consciatosium Librarian (Kan-sī-uh-toe-see-um)
- Doctor Nicklaus Bancroft (Nik-lah-oo-s Band-krôft)
- Vishfahl (Vish-fahl)
- Knifecaren (Nīf-kah-rehn)

Locations:

- Solenweir (Sōl-ehn- wir)
- Nothmire (Nah-th-my-er)
- Riftenshire (Rift-en- SHī(ə)r)
- The Wyld Lands (wild lands)
- Woods of Reaching
- The Other Side
- Crestbelth (krest-behl-th)
- Wivenguilder: (Wiv-ehn-gild-er)
- Catatoran: (Kat-ah-tor-ann)
- Farahgall Woods (Fair-ah-gahl)

www.ingramcontent.com/pod-product-compliance
Lightning Source LLC
Chambersburg PA
CBHW081145170626
46809CB00011B/3153